"You're A Fool, Maddie."

★

He turned her toward him and before she realized what he was doing, he covered her mouth with his own. She tried to pull away, but he moved his arms around her, imprisoning her within them, and suddenly all the heat of the day concentrated itself in his mouth, the liquid fire pouring into her from him and heating her insides unbearably. Her arms went up around his neck and her fingers met the thick hair at the nape and twined into it.

"No—" she protested, not because she wanted him to stop but because she had to tear her mouth away from the source of heat before it melted her. But he would not let her go, and then it was too late, and when he released his grip to pull her down on the grass, she moaned only to protest that he had stopped.

"There isn't a cold or unloving bone in your body," Devin said. "You just haven't been loved as you should be—as I can love you," and he kissed her again, less violently, and again.

Sweet Secrets

Sweet Secrets

Elisabeth Kidd

WARNER BOOKS

A Warner Communications Company

WARNER BOOKS EDITION

Cover illustration by Gregg Gulbronson

Warner Books, Inc.
666 Fifth Avenue
New York, N.Y. 10103

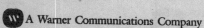 A Warner Communications Company

Printed in the United States of America

First Printing: March, 1988

10 9 8 7 6 5 4 3 2 1

This book is dedicated to Robin and Anita.
Long may they prosper!

Historical Note: The itinerary given to the Prince of Wales in this work of fiction is not the one he followed in 1899, but it might have been. An assassination attempt did take place—but not that year, and not in Baden. It happened in Brussels the following year—the year before the prince became King Edward VII.

—Elisabeth Kidd

Chapter One

DEVIN Grant was playing for time. He had always prided himself on his ability to read character, and it disturbed him that he couldn't make this woman out, couldn't penetrate her disguise—for disguise it was. Of that much he was certain.

She had seemed straightforward enough at first, but he soon recognized that he had made the conventional male assumption about beautiful American women—that they were spoiled but naive, outspoken to a fault, and incapable of deception. She had probably intended him to think that when she made her entrance, looking like a Worth manne-quin and pausing in the doorway to his office so that he could get a good look at her. She was tall, and her luscious curves were covered but not concealed by a dark red skirt and matching, tight-fitting bodice jacket buttoned up to the chin. She had waited a moment before pulling back the veil fastened with a long cloisonné pin to her hat and

1

letting him see her face. She looked directly at him from a pair of long-lashed, deep brown eyes.

"Mr. Grant? Mr. Devin Grant?"

He nodded.

"I am Mrs. Edward Malcolm. I want you to help me find my husband."

He stared at her for a moment, hoping his face did not betray his surprise. For the first time since he opened the detective agency as a cover for his real work in the service of the Prince of Wales, it occurred to Grant that he was getting more than he had bargained for.

The original idea had been to provide a plausible excuse for his having access to police files and consular memorandums—as well as a location convenient to Marlborough House and accessible to the Foreign Office by means of a secret underground passage. The agency did actually take on—and often solve—cases of theft, blackmail, and even murder, but, as the head of the agency, Grant had been involved in them solely in an advisory capacity.

Up until six months ago, at least. The prince had invited him to join a shooting party, and although Grant had gone to Sandringham suitably equipped to mingle with the other guests, he was still aware that he was there as an employee— a glorified bodyguard, in fact. Although the Princess of Wales had welcomed him with special warmth for just that reason, Grant did not expect he would be allowed to relax and enjoy himself. He was certain of it only two days later, when the earl of Southington's valet, who had been standing off to the side to watch the hunt, was killed by a stray shot and Devin was asked to assist the local police in their investigation of the incident.

It was a simple enough request, and it should have been a simple matter, easily resolved. But the shot that killed the valet had come from the end of the woods opposite to where the shooting party stood; the valet turned out to have forged the references that had persuaded the unsuspecting earl to hire him only weeks before; and the sighting of a stranger in a village pub had led Grant on a further investigation that was proving far from simple or easily resolved. Six months later, he was no nearer identifying the murderer than before, and the case had developed complications within complications to the extent that Grant was now suspicious of any new turn of events or chance acquaintance. He knew he was becoming obsessed with the case, but he was also convinced that any unlikely event—even the appearance of an American beauty with an apparently unrelated, apparently easy to solve, case—could have a connection.

So he asked Madeleine Malcolm to tell her story from the beginning, and he used the time to gather his thoughts. At least he tried to pull himself together, but every time he looked at her, her beauty struck him as disturbingly as it had the first time he looked at her, making it increasingly difficult to concentrate on her story.

She told it in a low, slightly husky voice, with no digressions into domestic asides or emotional irrelevancies. It was this lack of detail that finally began to clear Grant's senses and free his mind to suspect some major gap in the information she laid so candidly before him. He probed for the missing truth, gently at first, but with mounting impatience. Grant—well-born, good-looking, a bachelor by inclination rather than financial necessity—hadn't reached the age of thirty-four without learning a good deal about women. Or so he had thought. Here was one who didn't reveal herself instantly and completely to him, and he was a little surprised to find that the mystery irritated him as much as it attracted him.

"When did you last see your husband?" he began.

"On the night of April twenty-eighth of last year, at our home in St. Louis, Missouri. I reported him missing to the police three weeks later."

"Why did you wait so long?"

"Teddy—my husband—had mentioned to me earlier in the week that he intended to go to Kentucky for the derby, which as you may not be aware takes place on the first Saturday in May, unlike your English *darby*, which I believe is run on some date in June chosen by astrological means."

"It always falls on a Friday, within a fortnight before or after Whitsun," he felt obliged to respond. "You can't get much more specific than that."

He thought he detected the beginning of a smile on her ripe mouth, but it died unborn. He found himself suddenly becoming possessed with the idea of forcing her to reveal herself, to drop that beautiful but rigid mask, and he wondered if laughter might be a means of catching her unawares. He could try to seduce her, of course, but somehow he was certain she would know how to deal with that. Other men had doubtless tried to penetrate her de-

4

fenses that way, and Grant was not so burdened with past conquests as to suppose that he could succeed with Madeleine Malcolm where others, presumably, had failed. He wished the idea hadn't occurred to him, however; it was going to be difficult to get rid of now.

He stood up again, coming around to the front of the mahogany desk that stood between them and perching himself on the edge, close enough to catch the echo of her perfume—patchouli, mostly, but he couldn't identify the blend. No doubt she had it made specially for her. She had the money; now that he was closer to the workmanship of her *peau-de-soie* dress and to the diamonds in her ears and the brooch on her collar, he could almost smell the expense behind them.

She did not change her position to maintain the space between them; her spine was still straight against the back of her chair, and she held one leather-gloved hand firmly over the other in her lap. But she did lower her head slightly, so that her wide hat obscured her face. Disappointed, he asked the first question that came to mind, just to get her to look up again.

"Wouldn't you have gone with him—to Kentucky, that is?"

"No," she said, raising her head but looking at the window behind him rather than at him. "I am not enamoured of horse races. I try to inform myself about them, for my husband's sake, but he and I agreed at the start that he would be free to go to any he wished without me."

"He is a gambling man?" What he really wanted to

know was what sort of a marriage the Malcolms had that required such things to be spelled out.

"He's not addicted to it. But, yes, he does bet on the horses. Happily, he seems to win as often as he loses, and he does enjoy it."

"Whose money does he gamble with?"

"I beg your pardon?" She did look at him then, with the kind of expression a duchess might level at a dustman who had just addressed her by her Christian name. Grant did not back down.

"Is your husband a man of means, or do you have a larger stake in the marriage than he does?"

She hesitated briefly; he wondered how much longer she would tolerate his impertinences.

"We have simpler laws in America than you do here regarding inheritance and the property rights of women, Mr. Grant," she explained, as if to a child. "When my father died, he lelt a considerable fortune to me, his only child. As my husband, Teddy naturally enjoys the use of a good deal of it. He had very little . . . he had *no* money of his own when I married him."

Very good, Mrs. Malcolm, very candid. But you made your first slip just then. I shall put it in my pocket to mull over later.

"And when he did not return home when he said he would, you became concerned?"

"He didn't say precisely when he would return. I met one of his racing friends by chance, and he mentioned how sorry he was that Teddy had been unable to attend the derby that year. I led him to think my husband had been

called to Chicago on family business, and the same day
went to the police."

"Who were unable to be of assistance."

"You put it kindly, Mr. Grant. They as much as told me
that boys will be boys and I should not waste their time
until I received a ransom note from the Black Hand. So I
went to Pinkerton's National Detective Agency."

"Who believed you?"

"Perhaps not at first. But you can only attempt to bribe
the police. The Pinkertons work on a daily retainer and
were more than willing to take on what looked to be a
time-consuming case. I had no clue as to where my
husband had gone, but I had plenty of money to spend on
finding out."

Grant wondered idly how often she had had to bail her
wayward husband out of jails and whorehouses before this
last escapade. There was a faintly caustic note in her voice
that suggested he had been in more than one such scrape.

"What makes you so certain your husband is not dead?"
he said, using the harsh word to see if she would flinch at
it. She didn't.

"The body that was fished out of the Seine could not be
positively identified," she replied, equally blunt. "Most
of the clothing had been removed by the current, and the
corpse itself was no longer in a whole state. Indeed, I
understand that the police did not even attempt an identification, assuming the body to be that of one of the vagrants
who make their homes under the bridges of Paris. It was
buried in a pauper's grave, along with a dozen others, so
that it cannot even be exhumed."

7

She paused then, and her full lower lip trembled slightly as she added, "I can't, of course, *prove* that it was not Teddy's body. I just *feel* it was not."

She was overacting now. Grant was disappointed; it had been such a good performance up to then, but that speech wouldn't convince anyone. He snatched unchivalrously at it, even as he hated himself for doing so. Placing his hands on the edge of the desk and leaning slightly toward her, he said softly, "Are you certain, Mrs. Malcolm, that you are not deceiving yourself? That you do not feel in some way responsible for your husband's death and so refuse to accept its certainty?"

She raised her lovely face to him. Any further sign of weakness he might have found in it vanished—if it had ever existed—and she looked at him with those bottomless brown eyes.

"Mr. Grant, I love my husband. That is why I know that if he were dead, I would feel it. I do not. That is why I'm certain he is alive. I came to you on the strongest recommendation of the Pinkerton office in St. Louis, and I am prepared to pay any sum necessary for your services. But if you do not wish to help me—and you can't if you don't accept what I tell you—then I will make do with the *second* best detective agency in London."

He said nothing, rising and turning his back on her to look out the window, as if considering her proposition. A tram rattled past in Whitehall, two stories below, and a gaggle of schoolgirls in white straw hats shrieked with delight as it bumped to a halt at the corner of Downing Street. *Damn and blast, he couldn't let her get away. He knew now that she was on a fool's errand and wanted to drag him along with her, but he couldn't let anyone else go. He would have to get involved himself.*

"Very well, Mrs. Malcolm," he said at last, reseating himself where he could face her. "I accept your case. I shall, moreover, accept everything you tell me on the understanding that you keep nothing back. You have been very frank, but often the family of a missing person is too closely involved always to be able to differentiate between what may be relevant to the case and what may be beside the point. You must agree to let me make that decision."

She nodded, looking up at him expectantly, as if to say she was prepared to submit to his inquisition there and then. *Curse her, she was acting again, and again he was almost convinced by the performance.*

"I will, of course, have to review the Pinkerton report before I can proceed," he said in the pompous tone he used to intimidate undersecretaries of embassies. "How much time, by the way, did the Pinkertons consume in their fruitless search?"

"It wasn't precisely fruitless," she conceded, "as you will see from their report. I had suggested to them myself that Teddy might have joined the army, as we had only just heard the news of the declaration of war against Spain, and it is just the sort of quixotic gesture Teddy would make. They spent several weeks vainly attempting to find his name in the army lists before it occurred to Oli—to an agent there to trace Teddy from the drafts on his bank account in St. Louis. That was how they discovered that he had gone to Pittsburgh, then to New York."

He didn't miss her hesitation and waited a moment before he spoke again.

Finally she said, "I should tell you, Mr. Grant, that the Pinkerton agent who originally took my case is still in my employ and will be glad to . . . will report to you after you have had an opportunity to study his agency's findings."

Why was she so prickly about that, of all things? Grant didn't know, but he did know when questioning would not only be useless, but would probably set him back. He said only that he would look forward to comparing notes and asked instead, "Why would your husband have gone to New York?"

"I don't know. He has no friends or family there. I can only assume he met someone who invited him, for what purpose I cannot imagine."

"He never wrote to you, to set your mind at ease?"

"He would not have expected me to be concerned."

"Why not?"

"I don't have my husband on a leash, Mr. Grant. I don't question his movements, and I make him feel welcome when he does come home."

"Had he gone away for such a length of time before?"

"No."

"Yet still he did not write."

"I didn't say that. He did write, twice. You'll find it noted in the Pinkerton report. Once from Pittsburgh and once from New York."

"Did he mention any names in those letters?" Grant found that he was having some difficulty pronouncing

Edward Malcolm's name. "Perhaps of people he met in his travels?"

"No, he spoke only of 'a fellow he met on the train' or 'a gent who recommended a hotel' . . . people of that sort."

"Do you still have the letters?"

"No. I burned them. They were mainly of a—of an intimate nature. I told the detectives the facts they contained, but I didn't consider the rest to be anyone's business but my own."

"Did he ever ask for more money?"

"He didn't have to. The St. Louis account was his own, so I could not stop his drawing on it, even if I had wanted to take such harsh measures. In any case, he stopped making withdrawals, and it was some time before it was discovered that he had sailed for London. Here he apparently fell in with a group of radical anarchists."

"Had he expressed any strong political convictions before?"

She hesitated again but said at last, as if by way of compromise, "He hadn't expressed any such convictions to me—that is, he always seemed more interested in people than in politics, and whatever opinions his friends had he made his own. That is why he got on so well with everyone."

And that is why, my beauty, you will eventually shed that mask of yours. There are already three tiny cracks in it, and the more you talk, the more you are going to reveal of yourself.

As if she were conscious of his mental processes, she moved her gaze from him to the wall behind his desk. A vein had begun to pulse in her temple, but it would take a good deal more pounding to break down her defenses. And Grant was reluctant to be any cruder than he had been already.

"What are your plans now, Mrs. Malcolm?" he asked, more gently.

"I'll be in London for two weeks—I'm staying at the Savoy, by the way—and then I'll go on to Paris." She looked at him again and explained, "It seems to me that if I make myself conspicuous in places where Teddy has been or is likely to turn up, he may try to contact me."

"What are you telling people about him? I imagine there have already been questions about your traveling alone."

"Yes." She frowned, and he guessed that natural curiosity on the part of chance acquaintances irritated her even more than having to lie to satisfy it. "I've let it be known that my husband has been in India on business and that we will be meeting in Naples when his ship docks there in late summer."

He gave her a skeptical look, but she smiled slightly and said, "I—that is, my agent and I—have worked out all the details, Mr. Grant, even down to learning the steamship schedules through the Suez Canal."

"I trust you have written all this down for me. I should not wish inadvertently to contradict you."

She indicated the thick envelope she had left beside him on the desk. "You'll find it—"

"In the report. Yes, somehow I thought I might."

He tried to think of something else to ask that was *not* in the report, but his mind went blank suddenly. Or perhaps it had been wandering for some time, diverted by the two or three soft brown strands of hair that escaped from her coiffure and blew gently about the back of her long, lovely neck. He had tried not looking at her face, but the moment his eyes drifted downward, his imagination began drawing vivid pictures of the shape of her legs under her satin-smooth skirts.

"Perhaps I'd better leave you to it, then," she said.

Good God, how long had he been staring at her?

She smiled, as if to make it clear that she was aware of having regained the advantage. "To read the report, that is."

She rose gracefully and held one slim hand out to him. He took it automatically and was conscious of being slightly surprised at how firm her handshake was. For a woman pining away for a lost lover, she was remarkably in control of herself.

In fact, she held onto his hand just a fraction too long, until he raised one eyebrow questioningly at her. She was smiling, once again in the way his imagined duchess had smiled at the dustman. She said, "We haven't discussed your fee, Mr. Grant."

"I beg your pardon. I thought my assistant—"

"He did. He also explained that a minimum toward expenses was required, and I gave him a large check toward any you may incur—within or without reason. In return, I don't expect you to *like* me—"

"Mrs. Malcolm—"

"—nor to explain this strange antagonism you seem to

have conceived toward me. My motives, Mr. Grant, are none of your concern. Your only business, for which you are being so well paid, is to find my husband. Whether or not we like each other should not enter into our transaction, but I trust we may at least be civil in our dealings. That is, if you can refrain from cross-examining me every time we meet?''

At a loss to respond to this unexpected attack, Grant could only nod. And only then did she release her grip on his hand.

He escorted her downstairs, where her maid waited for her at the door, which opened onto a quiet back street, rather than directly onto crowded Whitehall. She pulled her veil back over her face and stepped into a waiting hansom cab, letting the maid climb in and close the door before she looked back at him.

''Good-bye, Mr. Grant. I trust you'll have something to report to me shortly.''

He started to lift one hand to wave it after her and was absurdly disappointed when she made no corresponding gesture. She did not even smile, and she looked away so quickly that she would not have seen him raise that superfluous hand in any case. He lowered it again and thrust it angrily into his pocket.

Chapter Two

MADDIE held her breath until the cab turned a corner, until she could no longer feel the keen eyes in that stony face boring into her. Then, very slowly, she let out a long breath and closed her eyes.

She had not expected this to be such a physical strain. Every muscle in her back and shoulders was as stiff as if she had been tied to that chair in Devin Grant's office for days. Tentatively, she opened her eyes and moved her head to look at the watch pinned to her bodice. Less than an hour!

"Is everything all right, ma'am?" her companion asked. Maddie smiled and tried to sound more confident than she felt.

"Yes, thank you, Louise. Everything went nicely."

Louise's small "humph" and the look in her myopic pale eyes suggested that she saw through Maddie's bravado.

Anyway, Maddie insisted to herself, the morning had

seemed to go well until her foolish outburst at the end. What had possessed her to become so belligerent, particularly when she had up to then succeeded in answering the man's impertinent, and increasingly personal, questions truthfully, if not with complete dignity? She did not think she had revealed any more than he genuinely needed to know, but obviously he had probed more deeply than she realized when he was doing it. And he had left her feeling stripped to the soul.

Even if she could explain it to herself, she could not even hint at her uneasiness to her devoted maid, who was a worrier at the best of times. Maddie had long ago learned that news, good or bad, must simply be announced to Louise, and matters of opinion, especially where there was any cause at all for pessimism, should not be broached at all at the risk of causing Louise to lose what little sleep she enjoyed at night.

At bottom, Maddie had a considerably more hopeful disposition than did Louise Drummond, but her view of the world was not obscured by rose-colored glasses either, and despite her carefully laid plans for the campaign she was embarked on now, she was still uncomfortable with any kind of subterfuge. Furthermore, despite the experience that told her most men responded like uncritical lapdogs to her smiles and melting looks, it was all too obvious that Devin Grant was not like most men.

She was not precisely certain wherein the difference lay. He was certainly better looking than the average man, although not, Maddie supposed, in a style that would have appealed to her when she was a girl. He was nothing like

Teddy, who was handome in a clean-cut, very American way, and who possessed charm in abundance. Devin Grant was a good deal taller than Maddie, which was admittedly a treat for a change, and he could not be much older than thirty, although his face already showed faint lines around the mouth and eyes. His hands, though strong and capable looking, were rougher than one would expect from someone who worked in an office all day, and his dark blond hair and mustache looked as if they were infrequently trimmed. And those eyes . . . Maddie shivered just to remember how they had bored into her as he threw those unexpectedly penetrating questions at her.

Why did he want to know such things? Why did it seem that he already knew a good deal too much? Her mind kept going back to his strangely hostile questions—and to her defensive answers. Their encounter had resembled the cautious circlings of wild animals around each other before a battle for supremacy. More often than not, Maddie had not known how to respond to his unanticipated questions and so had reverted to her habit of saying the first thing that came to her mind, which may have been exactly the wrong thing to persuade him to take her case. The fact remained, of course, that he *had* taken it. She would have to hope that it was because he really believed he could find Teddy.

To help me find Teddy, Maddie corrected herself. She was uncertain, too, of why she had hesitated to tell him everything. She could hardly expect him to help if she kept such obvious things as Oliver Drummond's work on the case a secret from him. *I don't trust Devin Grant,* she admitted to herself. *Why should I? He doesn't trust me either. And it's his job to prove himself trustworthy, not mine.*

She sighed, not entirely satisfied with her reasoning but feeling a little more in control of herself now that she was away from Devin Grant's disturbing presence. She raised her veil again and looked out the window of the hansom cab—one of those blessedly anonymous little black carriages available for hire all over London—as it turned into Trafalgar Square. The driver, apparently a born Londoner, maneuvered smoothly in the congested traffic, among the narrow horse-buses and wayward bicyclists and snobbish private broughams, in the direction of the Strand. Maddie had once thought St. Louis a good-sized city, but it was nothing compared to the hurly-burly of commercially prospering London in the last year of Victoria's century.

This was Maddie's first trip abroad, and she often forgot the worldly pose she had adopted for the purpose of her journey when gazing as wide-eyed as any other tourist at the marvels she found around every corner. She was not entirely unsophisticated as a traveler, her father having taken her often on his business trips to San Francisco and Seattle and the wilder parts of the American West, where his fur business had its roots. And she had honeymooned in New Orleans. But even that elegant old city on the river was a babe compared to London. When they were there, Teddy had promised to take her to Mexico and Europe and India—anywhere she wanted to go. Maddie smiled at the memory of all the reckless promises Teddy had made her during that blissful honeymoon. That was the only one she would have held him to, but she had taken too long to make up her mind where to start, and there had always seemed to be so much to do at home, separately and together, that somehow nothing ever came of that promise.

Their horse was clopping along at a steadier rate now, as the cab climbed the slight slope of the Strand. Maddie looked out to see men in the almost universal uniform of long frock coats and top hats and women in the neat pastel caps and white aprons of housemaids, or the straw hats and shirtwaists of office typists, hurrying along the pavement, carefully avoiding the curb where they might be splashed with mud from passing horses' hooves. A trio of young bloods were finding it a lark to test which of them could escape with the fewest spatters while coming closest to the source of the mud, and Maddie jumped when one of them inadvertently stepped into the street, narrowly missing the passing cab and collecting a fine sprinkling of coffee-colored mud on his immaculate white spats.

"Oh, look there, ma'am," Louise said, pointing up the street on Maddie's side.

On the pavement in front of Charing Cross Station, a young man with an old-fashioned folding-bellows camera on a tripod was attempting to take a photograph of a child with a dog, neither of whom seemed either eager or able to sit still for the operation. The young man's task was further complicated by a growing collection of friends of both the child—a girl, judging by its pinafore—and the dog. The other children scampered about, trying to examine the camera at closer range; the dog barked, setting up a chorus of doggy commentary; and the camera began to wobble on its tripod. The dog, which was a mangy specimen but of a formidable size, then leaped up on the young man's waistcoat. The camera toppled over, caught just in time by an urchin in a ragged jacket, and the cameraman fell onto the pavement.

Maddie laughed aloud, and although the young man could not have heard her above the bustle, his eyes caught hers as he picked himself up, and his bemused gaze followed her as long as he could see her face framed in the cab window.

For some reason Maddie could not define, the incident raised her spirits. She supposed it was simply the merriment inherent in the little comedy, but she was sufficiently self-aware to know that the innocently adoring look given her by the young man had something to do with it. For whatever her gentlemen admirers might think, she had never been able to take male adoration for granted.

When she arrived five minutes later at the entrance to the Savoy, the smile lingered, dazzling the young footman who opened the door for her as she entered the hotel lobby with her graceful long-legged stride and a confident swish of her skirts.

Her smile widened a moment later when a voice called out, "*There* you are, my deah! Ah've been lookin' *every*-where for you!"

The voice belonged, unmistakably, to Florence Wingate, who swooped down on Maddie from the other side of the lobby and enfolded her in a jasmine-scented embrace. The white lace all down the front of Florence's white bodice and the velvet trim on her pale suit-jacket whispered against Maddie's cheek and hands as she attempted to subdue Florence without seeming to reject her very public welcome.

Mrs. Geoffrey Wingate was a fellow American, although she never ceased to lament that the British simply would *not* comprehend the difference between Missouri and South Carolina. She had taken "poor, *deah* Mrs. Malcolm" under her wing when, on Maddie's first night in London, Florence had spotted her over the lobster bisque with only Louise for company and had declared that such an absurd situation must be rectified at once. Maddie had attempted to explain that she was perfectly content with her own company, being accustomed to it as an only child brought up in a sheltered environment, but to persist in her protestations, she soon realized, would be churlish. Besides, Florence would dismiss them out of hand.

Maddie had then become concerned that Florence would take it into her lovely blond head that it was masculine companionship Mrs. Malcolm needed and would dredge up an endless parade of gentlemen with dubious titles and antecedents for her to choose from. Florence was three or four years older than Maddie's twenty-six, and her husband, Geoffrey, was nearly twenty more than that, but theirs seemed to be a match of affection, if not deep passion. They were not constantly in each other's company, as an infatuated young couple might be; yet they displayed an easy familiarity, as well as discreet indications of physical attraction, when they were together. Florence lost no time—as she had lost none in making herself intimate with Maddie—in extolling the virtues of such a union, not the least among them being each partner's privilege of enjoying the attentions of any other lady or gentleman without having to justify it to the other or to anyone else. In this, Maddie reflected, the Wingates were much more "European" than she ever expected to become.

Fortunately, Florence had accepted unquestioningly Maddie's explanation about Teddy's "business trip" and sighed over the romance of the Malcolms' forced separation. She assumed that Maddie looked forward longingly to a loving reunion in Naples, and she had not attempted to alleviate Maddie's period of loneliness with any other than her own and Geoffrey's company. Maddie, who began to find Florence a comfortable sort of companion despite her frivolous interests and her volubility, went along with her assumptions. It was nice, now and then, to be just Maddie and not "the rich Mrs. Malcolm," who felt far too often like the star turn in a gaudy circus. Florence, who was "home folk," as she herself put it, was just the kind of companion who would allow her to be herself.

"Darlin' child!" Florence gushed as she led Maddie to an overstuffed armchair in the tearoom, "you will never guess! My clever Geoffrey has snagged a box for us at Newmarket on Tuesday—right next to the Prince of Wales's! Or at least, close enough so that we can ogle to our hearts' content. You will come, my dear, won't you?"

"Of course I will, Florence."

Maddie did not know how to refuse—any more than she could refuse the lavish tea Florence proceeded to order—and so she accepted both. Florence chose the creamiest cakes and the fattest little sandwiches on the cart, saying that since Geoffrey had never taken to tea and liked cream cakes even less, she depended on Maddie to approve her indulgence in them.

"What all have you been doin' since this morning?" Florence asked, and Maddie, having had time to think of something, replied that she had been to the City to draw on her letter of credit with Coutts's Bank.

"Oh, good!" Florence exclaimed artlessly. "Then you'll have plenty of cash to bet on the races."

Maddie smiled at Florence's utter lack of subtlety. She was like that about most things, but especially about money; she so openly enjoyed being lavishly provided for by her indulgent—and apparently lavishly endowed—Geoffrey.

Maddie, too, had always taken money for granted. She knew that her father had struggled as a young man to build his fur business in St. Louis, but by the time his only daughter was born, relatively late in John Jerome Osborne's life, it was thriving, and Madeleine Osborne had come into the world in the well-appointed master bedroom of a mansion in the fashionable part of town.

She had grown up much cosseted, particularly by her father, for whom nothing was too good for his beautiful little girl. Her birthdays were extravaganzas of hand-carved rocking horses, dollhouses the size of the piano in the parlor, organdy dresses with real pearls sewn on them. She was saved from being spoiled only by the fact, obvious to everyone but her father, that she was not really a very attractive child. She was too thin, her nose was too long for her small face, and her feet were far too large for her stick legs. Secure in her father's love, Maddie would not have been troubled by her plainness, except that her mother's beauty made her only too aware of her own lack.

Maddie adored her ethereally lovely mother and wanted nothing more of life than to be just like Constance Osborne. She sat beside her mother's dressing table in the morning, watching the maid arrange her pale blond hair, then begged to be taken along when Constance went off on her missions in behalf of the charities, which, as a leading matron of the town and chairwoman of a half-dozen committees, was how she passed the time.

Most of all, little Maddie loved to watch her mother dress for evening occasions, when she wore exquisitely lacy pastel gowns and delicately set jewels, usually the sapphires her husband had given her on their first anniversary. When she was ready at last to go out and stun the world, she first did a little parade around the room for Maddie's benefit, pretending to dance or to speak to the mayor or to do whatever that night's occasion might call for, and which Maddie was not yet allowed to stay up to witness.

Constance was pleased that her daughter adored her. She had not particularly wanted to have a child, fearful that the birth would spoil her figure and that the growing child would be a continual reminder of the passing years. She was happy to discover that the first fear was groundless—despite the pain, which she did not forget as she was assured she would in the joy of holding her baby—for when the doctor told her that she would have no more children, her recovery was remarkably swift. And because her sole issue grew into so unprepossessing a child, Constance's own beauty could only grow by contrast.

But then Maddie turned thirteen, and almost overnight, it seemed, she shot up six inches to tower over Constance, a disaster that affected Maddie even more than her mother. She felt clumsier and uglier than ever. But worse was to come—for Constance—when Maddie's body almost immediately caught up with her height. Her face filled out, her hands and feet assumed a grace they had hitherto lacked, and her hair turned darker, from a nondescript red-brown into a magnificent chestnut. Her hips became gently rounded, instead of having to be hidden beneath layers of petticoats, and her breasts were so perfectly shaped that she had no need of any padding in her bodices.

John Jerome was delighted, which was just as well, because it now fell to him to show Maddie off to the world. Constance refused to be seen with a daughter who threatened to outshine her, even if the pastel gowns and sapphires Constance lent her were so unlike Maddie that they did nothing to speed the process. Maddie's father bought her silks and rubies instead and praised his ''little girl''—he chuckled when he said it—more than ever. Still, Maddie was sixteen before she began to believe that she really was, at long last, beautiful.

This came about when one of her mother's many admirers—who were usually young men delighted to be invited to take tea with the lovely Connie Osborne so that they could boast about it at their clubs afterward—almost literally ran into Maddie on his way out of her mother's parlor. Constance had never invited her daughter to her little teas, and Maddie had no interest in being present, for she would have had to share her mother's attention with other people. So she made a point of being out of the house between three and five o'clock on Thursday afternoons. This Thursday, however, she had twisted her ankle while at the skating rink with her friend Julia and had come home early, only to find young Richard Brokmeyer gazing raptly at her in her own front hall and forgetting to remove the hand he had used to steady her when he so clumsily knocked her down.

Maddie had assumed all the clumsiness to be on her side until she saw the look in Mr. Brokmeyer's eyes, and somehow, drawing the knowledge from some ancient feminine source, she had smiled at him in a way that made him her devoted slave from that day forward . . . or at least until he met Julia two months later. But by then, Maddie had discovered the joys of being a belle. Richard was only the first in a long string of beaux who picked up what her father had begun and plied her with flowers, lace handkerchiefs, chocolates, and professions of love. Even her father had not succeeded in making Maddie feel desirable as well as loved, and now the power that went with desire seemed to her to be even headier than the gentler power of love.

The real source of her power Maddie only discovered at seventeen. Despite her mother's somewhat impatient explanation that the handsome young men paying her such extravagant court cared less about her "bottomless velvet eyes'' than her father's bottomless purse, Maddie had been too much in love with love to believe it. One of these sweet young men would prove to be *the* one. She was certain of that and had no objection to enjoying the others until he came along.

But then, the one she thought—that week—might prove to be *the* one, proved to be something much less delightful. Having spotted him across the street when she was out shopping, she thought she might tease him by sneaking up unseen behind him. But when she did, she discovered that he was talking to one of the other candidates of the week and, like most eavesdroppers, Maddie did not like what she heard. The young men were laying a wager over which of them could get the heiress to say yes first, the winner to stake the loser, after the wedding, to a trip to Hot Springs in pursuit of a substitute heiress.

Neither suitor got past Maddie's front door again, and she never found out if they got to Hot Springs, singly or together. After that she began to more carefully scrutinize her beaux, whose very number was becoming suspect by her eighteenth birthday. By the time she was twenty, she had become such a cynic about male sincerity that Teddy Malcolm's careless assurance that he adored her money almost as much as Maddie herself sounded so refreshingly honest to her jaded ears that she encouraged him despite her mother's warning that he was no better than any of those other, less charming fortune hunters. But her father understood, and when Maddie fell in love with Teddy in earnest, he indulged her yet again by not only accepting but welcoming Teddy Malcolm as a son-in-law.

*   *   *

It was not until Devin Grant pointed out something Maddie was well aware of but had never before felt any embarrassment about, that the matter of money forced itself back into Maddie's consciousness—so forcefully, indeed, that she had not hesitated to use it as a weapon against Grant. Yes, it was true that she controlled the purse-strings at home, but what did that matter? It had never mattered to Teddy. She had never used her control against him.

Do you have a larger stake in this marriage than he does? Grant had wanted to know. Maddie was still not sure what he had meant by that. Indeed, she was struck now by the uncomfortable suspicion that she had not fully understood anything Devin Grant had said to her. He seemed to have been in possession of some secret about her that even she was unaware of. The only thing she was sure of was that it was not safe to trust anyone just now—least of all the disturbingly attractive Devin Grant.

Chapter Three

"THERE is a young man making eyes at you," Florence said, intruding herself suddenly into Maddie's train of thought. "He looks rather a lamb, too. Wherever did you find him?"

Maddie looked around to see the young photographer from Charing Cross Station standing in the doorway with his hat in his hands. His dark curls and the supplicatory expression on his pale face—very much a lamb, indeed, Maddie thought with a smile—made him look even younger than she had at first glance supposed him to be.

"He seems to have found me instead," Maddie said and, curious to hear what he wanted from her, smiled at the young man in an encouraging way that he wasted no time in misinterpreting.

"Mrs. Malcolm?" he said, approaching her and handing her his card. "My name is Laurence Fox." This was confirmed by the engraved calling card that also stated

"Photographer of Famous Faces." Her curiosity now thoroughly aroused, Maddie motioned Mr. Fox to sit down. He did so without taking his eyes away from Maddie's face, charmingly unaware that his sleeve had brushed the jam pot and his bowler hat had missed the table and fallen on the floor.

Florence caught Maddie's eye and winked, then scrawled her signature across the chit for their tea and stood up, declaring that she would keep Geoffrey waiting for his dinner if she did not go up at once and begin the ceremony of changing her clothes. Mr. Fox jumped up again to shake her hand and be overwhelmed by her professed delight at meeting him, then sank slowly back into his chair as Florence drifted away in a cloud of jasmine and lace.

"Some tea, Mr. Fox?" Maddie said, her eyes warm with amusement at his expression. He was a curious cross between an awkward schoolboy—and a very good school it must have been, judging from his accent and manners—and a man confident of his professional abilities.

"I beg your pardon?" he said before he noticed the clean teacup Maddie was holding invitingly up to him. "Oh, . . . yes, thank you."

Maddie poured the tea and maintained her silence long enough for Mr. Fox to regain his equilibrium before she inquired after the fate of his camera.

"I left it with the hall porter," he said.

"I'm glad it came to no harm as a result of your little misadventure in the street earlier."

"Oh, no, ma'am. It's a sturdy old machine. Anyway, I paid a shilling to the boy who rescued it, which seemed ample to ensure its safety between Charing Cross and the hotel.''

''And did you also discover my name from the hall porter?''

''Yes, I did.'' Mr. Fox put down his cup and assumed a more straight-backed posture, as if in preparation for a speech. ''I trust you will forgive my boldness, ma'am, but the fact is . . . I would like to take your photograph. With your permission, that is to say.''

''Why my photograph, particularly?'' Madeleine asked. ''You have seen Mrs. Wingate, who is more beautiful than I am and, I expect, a more suitable subject. Why don't you ask her to pose for you?''

''I intend to,'' Mr. Fox admitted. ''But I saw you first, and—begging your pardon again, ma'am—you have a kind of beauty that is rare here. Mrs. Wingate's is almost English, you see, while you are unmistakeably American. Or at least, most English people's idea of American.''

''Oh, dear,'' Maddie said. ''I'm not at all certain that I care to represent my country in such a way.''

''Oh, but the English are mad for the Gibson girl look,'' Mr. Fox assured her, ''and you are that look brought to life! Why, I could have your photograph in every illustrated magazine in the country within a month. . . . You would be the most celebrated professional beauty since Lillie Langtry!''

Maddie had to laugh at the young man's eagerness. ''But why should I want that?''

''Why?'' This put the first damper on Mr. Fox's enthusiasm. "Well, I mean, wouldn't you *like* to be so widely admired?"

This was obviously the first time he had encountered a woman whose first desire was not to be praised for her beauty, but Maddie was reluctant to refuse poor Mr. Fox outright. It occurred to her suddenly that if, as she had told Devin Grant, she wished to make her presence in England known, this was a quick, painless—and, if Mr. Fox's influence was as wide as he intimated it to be—foolproof way of going about it.

"I should add that I do not photograph only ladies," Mr. Fox said, interpreting her hesitation as a sign of modesty, or even suspicion of his motives, as if such an open, ingenuous face could conceal even the slightest improper intention. "I have photographed many of the most important ladies *and* gentlemen in England. I am reluctant to name all of them, but I carry with me some of the studies I have supplied to the illustrateds and the newspapers."

So saying, Mr. Fox drew a slim leather case, divided into compartments to hold photographs, from his jacket pocket and displayed the contents. Maddie recognized the faces of several members of the nobility—Florence would doubtless have known them all—as well as the musical hall luminary Lottie Collins and the actor George Alexander.

This gave Maddie another idea, and she interrupted Mr. Fox's persuasions before he reached the undignified stage of pleading with her.

"Do these gentlemen subjects of yours by any chance include Mr. Peter Kropotkin?"

"Indeed, yes!" Mr. Fox exclaimed happily. "The famous anarchist theorist, a surprisingly kind and modest gentleman. Are you acquainted with him, Mrs. Malcolm?"

"No, but I should like to be," Maddie said, "perhaps . . . as a fair exchange for my sitting for you?"

Mr. Fox considered this proposal and found it satisfactory, if unorthodox. "I should be pleased to perform the introduction for you, ma'am," he said. "When would be a convenient time for you to come to my studio?"

"Shall we say, the day after I meet Mr. Kropotkin?"

Mr. Fox grinned appreciatively. "So it shall be, ma'am. If you will excuse me, then, I shall go away immediately to make the arrangements."

He held out his hand to shake hers in a businesslike fashion, and Maddie heard herself saying for the second time that day, "Good-bye. I look forward to hearing from you again shortly."

"Be assured of it, ma'am," Mr. Fox said, retrieving his hat and tipping it to her. "Good-bye."

Maddie watched him go, giving him a little wave when he turned at the door for one more look at her and blushed to find her observing him. She smiled, sighed, and rose to go up to her suite, very soon putting even the winsome Mr. Fox out of her mind in anticipation of a long, hot bath.

But she found it difficult to soothe away entirely the events of the day, even in a luxuriously fragrant tubfull of steaming water, with Louise within earshot and a glass of champagne within reach. Teddy had taught her that trick, saying a warm bath was always more invigorating when accompanied by chilled champagne. It was nonsense, of course, but Maddie had fallen into the habit, and now Louise brought the wine even when she hadn't asked for it.

She took a thoughtful sip of it. Teddy was full of ideas that sounded like nonsense but were not always far from wisdom. He believed life was to be enjoyed, and since Maddie had never had any reason to believe otherwise, she had joined in his games.

Teddy had been so eager to initiate her into every pleasure life offered, and Maddie was a willing student from the first heady days of his courtship. He had stood out at once from the rest of her beaux, if only because he really seemed to enjoy coming to see her and doing nothing more when he got there than sitting in the parlor gazing at her. Of course that didn't satisfy Teddy for long. After he had sized her up and guessed that she was open to a little fun, he began to tease her, trying to lure her into impropriety. He would stand against the parlor wall, where the others could not see him, and make faces or imitate their lovelorn looks, until finally she did laugh, unable to explain why to the others; for as soon as she laughed, Teddy immediately sat down again and behaved himself.

Soon his games became verbal. He would pass her in the street or sit next to her at someone's dinner party or dance past her in the Virginia reel and whisper something in her ear to make her blush, innocent compliments at first, then real words of love, then more intimate confessions that she blushed at even as she tried to laugh them away. The truth was that they thrilled her. She would go home at night and remember them, and her body would behave imexplicably at the thoughts that ran through her head. She looked forward eagerly to seeing Teddy again, to hear what outrageously improper thing he would say next.

When he began to touch her discreetly—still in public, stealing kisses like sugared almonds from the glass dish in the parlor—it seemed only the next step in the courtship. Constance had never told Maddie what she should allow, or not allow, from her beaux, and Maddie did not want to ask now. She was vaguely aware that "nice girls" did not admit to such stirrings as she felt at the things Teddy said and did. So she did not admit them, but she did enjoy them. Teddy's kisses never went beyond the gently chaste caresses she had seen depicted in romantic paintings— except once, and that had been her doing.

They had gone with a party of friends for a moonlight cruise on the river, and Teddy had lured her into a shadowed corner of the deck, away from the noisy laughter of the others. He was in one of his playful moods and threatened to throw her overboard. He even picked her up to do it, and Maddie had tightened her grip on him, pretending to be frightened. Then, as if he were aware that the mood had changed, he abruptly let her go. But Maddie would not be let go. She kept her arms around his neck and pressed her body against the length of his, instinctively fitting it into his masculine angles and hollows, and when she felt a hard, alien pressure against her middle, she was no more frightened than before. She pulled his head down to her mouth, and this time he kissed her properly, and she knew that his searching tongue was only a substitute for another, more intimate kind of exploration. Even as she reveled in his kiss, it was not enough. She wanted that other kiss.

Shaken, Teddy pushed her away. "I think we'd better get married, sweetheart, don't you?" he asked.

Maddie looked at him and for a moment could not think why they needed to bother with that. But of course, he would not go any further any other way; that was what being a gentleman was.

"Oh, yes," she said finally, breathlessly. "Teddy, can we elope?"

He laughed. "Certainly not! Your mother would never speak to me again."

"You can say it was my idea."

"Even worse! She'll think I got you . . . well, never mind, sweetheart. We'll get married as soon as it's decent, all right?"

Maddie had to settle for that and passed the next months in a fever of impatience; and when at last they set off for New Orleans and their honeymoon, it was as if a new life had opened up for her. It was not that she had been confined to St. Louis—except by her own impatience—but only that in New Orleans she felt so free. She knew at once that she loved traveling as much as Teddy did, or at least she adored traveling with Teddy, who made everything a new adventure, from browsing in the open markets along the riverfront to sleeping late and waking to huge cups of *café au lait* brought to them in bed. And visiting New Orleans was like seeing a dozen countries at once; Spain and France and Mexico and Cuba and Louisiana lived side by side on the narrow streets.

They had come by riverboat, remembering that they had become engaged on one, and they spent as much time on the river as they could. But they also reveled in the wonderful restaurants of the French Quarter, happily stuffing themselves on creole dishes rich in cream and spices and seafoods Maddie had never heard of before, and going home giddy from the champagne Teddy soon taught Maddie was the only wine worth drinking. Teddy even liked to go shopping with her and sat contentedly for hours while she tried on the most fashionable dresses in the city and he made knowledgeable comments about everything from hats to teagowns to chemises.

Oh, Teddy, I can't decide between these two gowns!
Sweetheart, it couldn't be simpler—take both of them!

It seemed that they laughed all the time in New Orleans. Everything they did they enjoyed. It was fun being with Teddy just because he was so good-looking, with his tightly curled blond hair and that dimple in his chin. And he was so pleasant that everyone they met, especially the women, stared at him in admiration. But he never looked at any other woman when he was with her.

She did not forget the hurts she had suffered at the hands of the fortune hunters she had once been foolish enough to believe were as fond of her as they were of her father's money, and she was never again quite so trusting as she had been of treacherous Richard Brokmeyer. That now well-ingrained suspicion of anything or anyone that seemed too good or too much fun made her take a deep breath and a second thought every now and then, while Teddy went full speed ahead without her, and she had to run to catch up.

Oh, Teddy, can't we just stay in today?

Certainly not! And waste this beautiful day?

It must have been this inability of hers to trust, to give herself completely, Maddie decided much later, that prevented their honeymoon from being the blissful idyll Teddy had promised her and that she had fully expected. She had waited so long, anticipated so much—too much.

On their first night together, he had been thoughtful and gentle, leading her along so that she would get as much pleasure from their lovemaking as he did. And she had—at first. Teddy's kisses had made her feel warm inside and out. The sight of his naked body, as beautiful without clothes as with, quickened her pulse. And his touch on her own bare skin made her heart race.

You're so beautiful, he told her reverently, leading her to their bed as if it were an altar where he would worship her—and he did, tracing soft kisses up and down the length of her body, making her dark eyes glow and her firm, generous breasts ache in anticipation. He had warned her, as kindly as he could, that the first time would hurt, so that she was almost disappointed when it didn't, and he slid into her effortlessly, almost without her feeling it.

Do you love me? he asked, as he was thrusting into her. *Say you love me!* So she did.

38

She didn't understand what was wrong and didn't know how to explain it to him, so she waited. Surely the next time—or at least after a little while, when she grew to know what he wanted, what she wanted—then she would feel the passion that she had anticipated, the passion that made Teddy cry out when he had spilled himself inside her, then collapse, wet and depleted, beside her, murmuring endearments into her ear before he fell asleep.

She tried to feel more, and each time she thought she would, for his caresses never failed to rouse her, his kisses to make her want more. But there was no more. After a certain point, she felt no further arousal. Instinctively, she tried to do it differently, to lie on her side or even in some other room, but Teddy liked their own bed and his way of making love. So she began to pretend, to echo his cries and whispered endearments. After all, it was not Teddy's fault that she had expected too much. There was no reason to deny him his pleasure.

Teddy never questioned her about it, so she thought he must not have noticed her lack of response. Perhaps that really was all there was to it.

They went home to St. Louis and everyone thought they were happy. Maddie thought so, too, except for that one little thing, except for . . . no, that had nothing to do with Teddy. John Jerome died suddenly, a year after his daughter's marriage, of a heart attack. Constance sold the house and moved back to her family's home in Charleston, and Maddie had no one left—no one else—to talk to. Teddy's attentions to her were no less ardent; but they were all she had, and he was not always home. He did not work, but he always had something to do, always had friends to meet at the racetrack and other places she could not go with him. She gave him money to do it, because that seemed all she could give freely. It was the only excitement he had, and Teddy craved excitement.

Teddy didn't work because his grandfather, like Maddie's father, had been a self-made man, building a fortune quickly in the days when such things could be done in America, and his father had taken over a chain of furniture stores that had begun with one in Kentucky and then spread across the South. But by the time Teddy was old enough to join the family firm, there were no challenges left in it. Teddy did not see why he should work if he did not have to, and finally he thumbed his nose at the stern visage of his grandfather staring down from the portrait over the fireplace, shrugged off his father's threat to disinherit him, and left home declaring he would find his own fortune.

Then he had met Maddie and had not needed to make a fortune of his own after all. And eventually he had run away from her, too.

Maddie reached for one of the hotel's huge white towels and rose slowly out of the bathwater. *What had made her think of that?* It had been her own behavior that had sent Teddy away; she had become jealous of his friends, his other interests. She had been horrid to him—that much was clear now—and when a man received no sympathy in his own home, he could scarcely be expected to remain there. The very night Teddy left for Lexington—or so she thought—she had accused him of taking more interest in his stupid horses than in her. She knew it was not true; poor Teddy had tried to coax her out of her sullen fit, but she had been selfish, hugging the hurt to her.

It had never, until now, occurred to her that he might have been running from something else, something more deeply rooted that she had never even seen, much less understood.

Maddie put the towel over her head and rubbed furiously, as if to force such morbid fancies out of it. Teddy never let such considerations trouble him; he had much more likely gone off on some tremendous lark, thinking no more of it than as a night on the town and expecting to come home any day to tell Maddie of his adventures. He would not have expected her to be concerned, Maddie had told Devin Grant, but she *had* been concerned—and selfish enough to wish Teddy preferred her company to anyone else's. And yes, a little jealous, too, of the freedom Teddy did not feel he needed to give up, even when she had sacrificed her own.

She splashed cologne all over herself, then dusted her long legs and smooth arms with talcum powder. Wrapping her silk negligee around her newly softened and scented body, she went into her bedroom, where Louise was waiting to brush her hair dry and put it up for dinner. She sat down at her dressing table and turned her back so Louise could begin, and only then did she catch sight of her scowling reflection in the mirror. She took another deep breath, placed her fingers against her forehead to smooth away the lines, and smiled up at Louise.

"Mother used to tell me to erase a frown that way. Did it work?"

"It seems to be gone, at all events," Louise said, adding with a rare touch of affection, "but I suspect a smile would have done the job just as well."

"Yes, I'm sure you're right, Louise," Maddie said, catching Louise's hand and giving it an affectionate squeeze. "Thank you."

"Mr. Drummond would like to have a word with you," Louise said, as if regretting stepping ever so slightly out of her place. She always referred to her husband as Mr. Drummond, even when Maddie addressed him as Oliver or Ollie, as if it were up to Louise to maintain a standard of polite behavior for her mistress to follow.

"Tell him to come in," Maddie said, violating yet another of Louise's standards.

"Now, ma'am? You are in . . . you are not dressed."

"I am, as Aunt Charlotte used to say, 'in my disability,' which is not quite *not dressed*. Anyway, you are both practically family and have known me to be far less proper, haven't you?"

Louise did not reply to that, but opened the door to signal her husband, who was waiting in the sitting room. A slight, middle-aged man with the kind of bland looks one scarcely remembered five minutes after meeting the man attached to them, Oliver Drummond slipped into the room so quietly that Maddie was unaware of his presence until Louise had returned to do her hair and Maddie looked up into the mirror.

"Hello, Oliver. Have you had a busy day, too?"

"Yes, Mrs. Malcolm, although not so profitable perhaps as your own. As requested, I attempted to verify Mr. Devin Grant's references. I found nothing against him."

"But?"

"But I found very little for him, either. He obviously exists, for we have both seen him, I from across the street as he approached his office this morning. His agency does in fact perform the services expected of a detective firm, but it does not seem that Mr. Grant himself takes a very large part in them."

Maddie's frown reappeared. "Do you mean to say he is some sort of imposter?"

"No. As you know, the Pinkerton agency has dealt with him in matters one might expect such a firm to handle. Furthermore, he is accepted by everyone employed by him as the head of the agency. But that appears to be a nominal position only."

"Why do you say *appears*?"

"Because I have been able to peruse a number of confidential police files, which specifically mention his name as assisting the police in their inquiries, or as providing a significant clue in an investigation. And yet, none of this appears in any public account of the cases in question, as if Mr. Grant did not wish the publicity that would ordinarily be invaluable to a firm seeking to expand its clientele, or even simply to stay in business. And there was an odd thing this afternoon . . ."

"Yes?"

"I observed the office after you left, to see where he would go at the end of the business day. His clerks had all left by six o'clock, and the last of them locked the door. Mr. Grant himself, however, appeared never to leave the building."

"It does have two entrances, you know."

"Yes, but from where I stood I had the door you left by in my direct line of vision and the main entrance reflected in a window across the street. No one left by either door after quarter past six."

By this time, Louise, who gave no indication of having heard a word of this conversation, had nearly finished with Maddie's hair. There was a brief silence as she slipped in the last of the hairpins; then Maddie turned around to look directly at Oliver Drummond.

"Do you wish me to continue this line of inquiry, Mrs. Malcolm?" he asked when she remained lost in thought.

Maddie sighed. "Yes, I'm afraid we must. It is all too irregular. I'd rather get on with something more to the point, but I cannot now simply drop Mr. Grant and look for another agency, not so long as these little mysteries hover around him. Perhaps it might be best to wait and see if he actually does any work on my case, and what sort of work it is."

"Very well, Mrs. Malcolm."

"Oh, by the way, Ollie, I have *snagged*, as Florence Wingate would say, an introduction to Peter Kropotkin. Wasn't that clever of me?"

She smiled when Oliver did look surprised. "Very

clever, indeed, Mrs. Malcolm. You may soon be doing my work for me.''

''Not at all, although I'd rather do that than try to figure Devin Grant out,'' Maddie remarked tartly.

Oliver left so that Louise could dress Maddie for dinner—yet another supper for two with Louise, since as Florence had told her with a martyred sigh, the Wingates were engaged to dine with cousins of Geoffrey's in Kensington.

Maddie stood still while Louise fastened the back of her favorite black satin evening gown, trimmed with jet on the full sleeves and at the hem, and watched herself in the mirror as Louise's ministrations narrowed her waist and brought out the white curves of her breasts at the low, wide neckline. She wondered idly what Devin Grant would think of her in this gown and was suddenly conscious of a stab of regret that he was not at this moment waiting for her in the lobby. She could almost see him there, tall and handsome in evening clothes, watching admiringly as she made her entrance and took his arm to be led into the dining room, the focus of every other woman's envious gaze.

She sighed. ''Well, Louise, shall we go down?''

Chapter
Four.

AS good as his word, Laurence Fox sent a note around to Maddie's hotel to say he had "located" Peter Kropotkin, and much to her amazement, he added that the great theorist would be at Newmarket the very day Maddie was to attend the races with the Wingates. She did not question this wonderful coincidence. Certainly it was the first promising development in a search that thus far had resulted in no more than Maddie's falling into bed exhausted each night, Oliver Drummond's wearing an increasingly gloomy frown every day, and Devin Grant's sending frequent but ever more cryptic messages to her hotel that he was "pursuing inquiries."

And so it was that on a sunny Tuesday morning, the party of four, accompanied by Florence's maid and a large picnic basket, departed from Liverpool Street Station in a private compartment in a Great Eastern railway carriage for the sixty-mile trip to Newmarket town. There, thanks to Mr. Fox's prescience, they found a hired carriage waiting to convey them in comfort to the racetrack, where they arrived unwearied and comfortable and eager to plunge into the activity going on all around the Rowley Mile.

"Oh, look there," Florence said, as soon as she had arranged her pale gray walking skirt gracefully around her on her chair and raised her silver field glasses to survey the surrounding boxes. "There is Mrs. Keppel in the royal enclosure. That means that Alexandra won't be here today. And there is, I believe, Sir Ernest Cassel, but I do not see the Prince of Wales. . . . Oh, do look what a dreadful hat that other young woman has on, Madeleine. She must be one of Mrs. Keppel's protégées, but Alice ought not to allow her out in public until she has learned to dress!"

Maddie, however, had put down her own glasses after finding herself being stared at in return by a shady-looking person with a black mustache.

She was aware that she made a lovely picture, in her dark-blue and white princess dress with white lace at the throat that fell to the waist and made her dark hair look even richer under her straw hat trimmed with blue ribbon. She had, after all, spent nearly two hours that morning submitting to Louise's fussing to make herself beautiful, so she could not complain if men looked at her. But she did not have to look back.

She turned instead to watch Mr. Fox, who was setting up his camera to take in a general view of the course. The Rowley Mile course, he had informed them in the train on the way to Newmarket, was named for King Charles II's favorite hack. The track itself was shaped like a V, the last part of which ran downhill after the turn and uphill again. In long-distance races, Laurence said, little of the beginning could be seen, giving rise to the joking complaint that spectators were obliged to hang about in Suffolk in order to see a race that is run in Cambridgeshire, the course being situated just on the border between the two counties. Today, however, most of the activity was centered on the one-mile point, where a considerable crowd had gathered close to the fence and below the stands.

They were orderly on the whole, possibly due to the presence of the prince at today's meeting, but Maddie preferred to think it was the lovely spring weather that made them all—or nearly all—look like such pleasant people. She scarcely tried to suppress her own rising excitement at . . . she wasn't sure at what, but it was the kind of day when anything could happen.

All at once she had an inkling of what attracted Teddy to race meetings. It wasn't the race itself, but the occasion. It may have been the excitement, too, the suspense of not knowing what the outcome of the race would be, but she suspected that most of all, Teddy liked being with so many people like himself, all enjoying themselves at what was, after all, just another kind of game.

Laurence Fox was surveying the crowd, too, but with a professional eye. Maddie noticed that he looked differently at people when he was considering them as subjects than when he was merely making conversation with them. He shaded his eyes with his hand as he stared intently across the course, made up his mind about his composition, and turned to set up his camera.

She should have insisted on going to the races with Teddy, Maddie could see now. At the time, she had thought he would dislike having a clinging wife always hanging on his sleeve, so she let him have his independence. Perhaps he had not really wanted it, but it was too late now. She had let him go and had stayed home by herself, more confined—and lonely—than she had ever been as an unmarried girl.

It was Julia Brokmeyer who came to her rescue one day a week after Teddy had gone off to Newport for a yacht race. Julia had taken up politics—her husband, Richard, was running for a city office at the time—and she wanted Maddie to go with her to hear a speaker on women's suffrage. Maddie had no interest in getting the vote but went along to keep Julia company. In the end it was Julia who lost interest in politics, and Maddie who found a new cause. But it wasn't the vote.

"When a woman becomes a victim, where is she to turn?" the speaker, a beautiful but also forceful woman from Boston, had demanded after speaking at length about the lack of representation for women in government. "When she becomes the victim of crime—crime within her own home!—who will care about her? Who will even listen? The police? All men. The government? All men.

"Do you know, ladies, where the expression 'rule of

thumb' comes from? It is derived from the supposed right of a husband to discipline his wife with a rod no thicker than his thumb. In this country there are husbands who still believe in that right and abuse it—as they abuse their wives. Women cannot call for help because they have no voice!''

Maddie had poked Julia in the ribs at this point and asked, ''What does she mean?''

''She means we must have the vote to protect ourselves,'' Julia whispered back.

But that was not what Maddie had heard. Surely there were not such men, men who beat their own wives? But even as the thought came to her, she knew that if she said it aloud, Julia would laugh at her innocence. And if she asked how getting the vote sometime in the dim future would help such women now, Julia would tell her to help them the way Constance had helped her African missions and earthquake victims—by attending committee meetings and raising money at church raffles. That was not enough, just as the vote was not soon enough. Maddie wanted to do something at once.

After the meeting, Julia went back to meet the speaker and to boast about Richard, who, she assured the speaker, was in favor of granting women the vote. Maddie asked her instead where the women she had spoken of lived and how she could help them. The woman studied her face for a moment, then took her card and promised to send someone to see her. Two days later, Louise Drummond knocked at Maddie's door.

Plain, taciturn Louise Drummond, in her practical brown

wool dress and stiffly starched collar and cuffs, her graying hair parted in the middle and pulled back into a tight bun, was the last person Maddie would have expected to take up the cause of unfortunate women. It was not until she had worked with Louise at a hospital in St. Louis for three months that Maddie learned Louise had once been one of them. Her first husband had beaten her and stolen money from her. But she was, Louise said, one of the lucky ones. She had found the courage to report him and the presence of mind to pick someone who would really be of use. Oliver Drummond was a Pinkerton detective and did not usually deal with such cases, but he took on Louise's. He also took on Louise, and after her first husband hanged himself in jail, they were married.

It had not taken three months, however, for Maddie to realize how small her own problems were compared to those of the women she tried to help, and how good Teddy was to her compared to those other husbands she tried to speak to but could not reach because they would not speak to a woman as an equal. For a time, Maddie was never so happy as when she went home, tired and discouraged, to find Teddy with his feet up on the porch railing and the racing forms in his hand, waiting for her with a smile and a kiss.

Hello, sweetheart. I missed you.

I'm home now, Teddy.

It was Louise who first sensed Maddie's growing frustration that nothing she did seemed to make much of a difference in the lives of the women she wanted to help. After she helped heal their bruises, they returned to their men, only to come back to her with fresh hurts, in an endless cycle. If she gave them money to pay the rent or buy their children clothing, their husbands took it and drank it away. Maddie tried not to hate those men, because that would not help either, but her frustration was building again. Almost without realizing it, she began to take her pent-up feelings out on Teddy, goading him about his lack of a job or any kind of useful interests. To Teddy's credit, he did not retaliate; instead, he took a job with Richard Brokmeyer, who had won his election and was in a position to give his friends jobs that were both lucrative and, more important to Teddy, that enabled him to spend those nights when Maddie came home angry—again—with his political cronies in their favorite tavern.

It was only after Teddy disappeared that Maddie found out Richard had fired him a month after he hired him.

By then, Maddie had found a new way to do something definite and lasting for her cause. She bought a large house in downtown St. Louis and had it converted into a hotel for abused women and their families, where the women could live free of worry about money or fear of their husbands. Pleased with her efforts at last, she was ready to try yet again to make Teddy happy, too. But they had drifted even farther apart without her noticing it.

"Maddie, I hope that when you stop running around in circles, you end up at home again."

"How can you say that? I must have something to do or I shall go mad!"

"You can stay at home. That's your job!"

"But you're never here!"

"And who told me to get out and find something to do?"

It was true. Everything that Maddie had done for her own good had been the worst thing she could have done for Teddy. Conscience-stricken, she tried to apologize, to assure him that she would never relegate him to second place again, that she would never take his love for granted again.

She was never sure later if he believed any of it.

"Mrs. Malcolm?"

Maddie's wandering attention was drawn by Geoffrey Wingate's voice behind her. She looked around to see that Laurence Fox had disappeared under his black cloth again and that Florence was still fixed to her field glasses.

"I'm so sorry," she said, smiling up at Geoffrey. "The sun must have made me doze off for a moment."

"Have you no burning desire to spy on your neighbors, Mrs. Malcolm?" he asked and, indicating the empty space beside him, offered to move her chair into the shady part of their box.

"I have no doubt that your wife will pass on the most interesting gossip about all the fashionable people here today," she said, accepting his offer and a glass of champagne. "And Mr. Fox will do the same—with illustrations—about the less exalted folk obliged to stand to view the horses. Is there going to *be* a race, by the way? Nothing seems to be happening at the gate, and there are people wandering around on the course. Surely they will be in the way of the horses if they are not warned off.''

''The next race is not scheduled for nearly half an hour, I'm afraid. Are you bored waiting? We might take a stroll.''

Maddie would have liked to stretch her limbs but knew that she would have to wait until Laurence was ready to accompany her. She was not sure she would recognize her quarry, despite the photograph Laurence had shown her of Peter Kropotkin, and in any case, she could not very well march up and introduce herself to a notorious anarchist when she was supposed to be just strolling with an unsuspecting Geoffrey Wingate.

''Thank you,'' she said, ''but I believe I should wait to watch at least one race. If it proves too tiresome—or too exciting, for that matter—I'll have fulfilled my obligation to look at it and may make my escape afterward. Is this your first visit to Newmarket, Mr. Wingate? *Is* there anything else to see here?''

''I'm afraid I can be of little help there; this is my first visit as well. I obtained the use of the box from a friend I ran into at my club who was obliging enough to provide the carriage as well. Everything else has been young Mr. Fox's doing.''

''Then you can't tell me about the races, either? Shall I place a bet?''

''The Prince of Wales has a horse running today. You may bet on it if you wish, for the sake of Anglo-American friendship. My friend informs me that the prince's horses generally do well, although my brother-in-law says precisely the opposite and invariably bets against the prince.''

''Your brother-in-law? I didn't know that Florence had a brother.''

''Oh, yes. His name is Frank, but as he is something of a black sheep in the family, it's no wonder that she hasn't mentioned him. It's been several months since we have had any word from him, in any case.''

''Thank you for warning me, then. I won't embarrass Florence by asking about him.''

Geoffrey smiled. ''Oh, Frank is not so bad as all that. At any rate''—he leaned back in his chair and added, in the most off-hand tone possible—''not when you consider Florence's Aunt Louella May Falcone, who conjures up the spirits of her dead ancestors on her Ouija board. Or her Grandmother Hartwell, who claims to have been a spy for Jeb Stuart. Or her cousin Josiah Giddings. *He* keeps his dead mother's embalmed corpse on display in the parlor.''

Maddie, appalled, stared at Geoffrey until, looking closer, she saw the sly twinkle in his kind eyes.

''Oh, you are dreadful to tease me that way!'' she said, laughing. ''I almost believed you!''

He smiled. ''Oh, some of it's true.''

Maddie resisted asking which part and changed the subject to something less provocative. But Geoffrey treated every subject as if it were something he had never considered before and found novel, and Maddie discovered that she enjoyed talking to him. He was very much at ease and made no demands; he did not expect her to be witty or to flatter his male pride. She thought she could understand a young woman being tempted to marry someone as kind and reliable as Geoffrey, although she did not quite understand what Florence in particular had seen in him.

They turned to perusing the racing calendar then, deciding on bets that they could both bear to lose but would not be embarrassed to have to report winning, and Geoffrey sent the messenger who came by for the purpose to place their bets for them. Having taken her host's advice not to bet on the showiest animal in the running, which would very likely not "stay the course," Maddie was pleased when the horse she chose did indeed win the first race but declared that she would quit while she was ahead. She interrupted Laurence Fox in the act of stowing some glass plates in his traveling photographic case to ask if he would take her to the window to collect her winnings. Mr. Fox, recalled to his escort duty, readily agreed.

"You are a cautious gambler, Mrs. Malcolm," Geoffrey observed admiringly.

"It's her only major fault," Florence countered. She had bet on the showiest horse and was totting up her loses with an annoyed scowl.

"I take chances only when the prize is worth the risk, Mr. Wingate," Maddie said with a smile. "Shall we bring you back another bottle of champagne?"

"No, there is more than enough here, thank you. Florence, as you may have noticed, does not stint on the important things in life."

With that, Maddie took Laurence's arm, and they turned out of the box in the direction of the paddock. The crowd around them included small groups of Jockey Club members talking blood lines, and, as they walked on, fathers of families and younger bloods calling to one another across the stands about this or that horse's chances in the next running.

"I spotted our quarry in the crowd by the oval," Laurence told Maddie. "We should meet him if we go on this way."

"How very efficient you are, Mr. Fox."

"One sees many things through the camera lens," he replied, patting her arm with his hand in an avuncular way that made her laugh.

They exchanged small talk as they strolled across the green, as if making for the refreshment stand, although they were in fact gradually edging toward the fence separating the grass in front of the stands from the track. Maddie was trying to guess which of the men standing around the fence might be Kropotkin when, still with no more effort than any accidental encounter might require, Laurence raised his hat to a gentleman nearby and said, "Mr. Kropotkin. How do you do, sir?"

A large man with gold-rimmed spectacles and a bushy brown beard turned toward them, his preoccupied frown changing into a genial smile as he raised his hat to Laurence. He smiled even more broadly when he looked at Maddie, and he made a little bow to her. Maddie felt herself stiffen, but the contrast between Kropotkin's manner and what she had expected was so great that he disarmed her considerably even before he spoke. She had to force herself to remember that this was a dangerous man—the more so, no doubt, for his geniality.

"Mr. Fox," he said. "Well met, indeed, young gentleman. Are you here at Newmarket in your professional capacity? You do not have your machine by you."

He spoke with only a slight accent that did not sound to Maddie particularly Russian, but Peter Kropotkin had lived in London since he fled arrest nearly thirteen years before in his native Russia for his anarchist activities. She did not know whether it was his life in the tranquil English countryside or merely a clever adaptation on his part, but he seemed far more the geographer he had been earlier in his career than any kind of revolutionary. Indeed, he might have passed for a village schoolmaster, except for the traces of his aristrocratic heritage that lingered in his posture and his speech. He had been born a prince, after all.

"Mrs. Malcolm, may I make Mr. Peter Kropotkin known to you? Sir, this is my American friend, Mrs. Edward Malcolm, of St. Louis."

Kropotkin bowed and took Maddie's hand to bestow a light kiss on the glove, in the Continental manner, before professing himself pleased to make her acquaintance.

"St. Louis is, I believe, in the state of Missouri and on the banks of your great Mississippi River, is that not correct, Mrs. Malcolm? I regret I have never visited America, but naturally, like all envious Europeans, I have made a fascinated study of it."

"You shame me, sir," Maddie said. "I fear we Americans are much less knowledgeable about your country."

"But I have several countries, dear lady. Surely your ignorance is not quite that broad?"

"Perhaps you will be good enough to tell me about them."

Mr. Fox took this hint and excused himself to go and collect Maddie's winnings. Kropotkin took Maddie's arm in his own to continue strolling in the direction she had been going.

After a moment, she said, "I must make a confession, sir. I asked Mr. Fox to introduce us, so that I might ask a favor of you. I hope you are not offended?"

"Not at all, dear lady. Nothing would please me more than to be of assistance if I can be."

Maddie hesitated briefly, then explained in as business-like a way as she could about her search for Teddy and her belief that he might have become involved with an anarchist group. She did her best not to seem to condemn such an involvement on Teddy's part and to appear open-minded about, if not actually ignorant of, anarchism in general. Kropotkin seemed to understand her hesitation but nevertheless could not resist the temptation to lecture her on the theories of anarchism that he had been largely responsible for formulating.

"You must understand, dear lady, that not all anarchists wish to blow up Nelson's Column. Your husband may be as safe with such a group as at any political meeting in your own country. It is only that the term anarchist has, regrettably, come to be used by the ignorant general public to refer solely to the authors of certain violent acts—to those who call for class warfare and the overthrow of established society. Not every anarchist believes in such things."

"But surely it is not just the, so to speak, lay public that identifies anarchists with violence," Maddie said. "The anarchists themselves have taken the credit—or rather the blame, as one must say—for these acts."

"I am ashamed to say that some do," Kropotkin replied. "But just as there are persons who deliberately misinterpret church or civil or military law for their own ends, there will also be anarchists who lose sight of their ideals. There are also a few, I am sorry to say, who take up the cause because it offers the only excitement they have in their lives. If your husband has fallen in with such as these, then I fear he may indeed be in some peril."

He paused, as if to see how she would take this, but Maddie had learned quickly enough from Devin Grant not to be goaded into defending her motives—or Teddy's.

"The pure theory of anarchist communism has no place for acts of violence," Kropotkin went on. "Rather, it envisions a society in which harmony is maintained—much as it is here at Newmarket—by voluntary associations among human beings to bring about what each group desires, not by force, but by cooperation."

"It seems to me that it is the anarchists who wish to *force* cooperation on the rest of us," Maddie said.

"Alas, popular fiction has painted such a vivid picture of the bomb-throwing anarchist that even a person of your intelligence accepts it. We in fact only make proposals. . . . That since control by a central state is wrong, everything needed for human life should be owned in common and distributed according to need. That every man should be free to act and speak as he likes, within the limits set down by his natural respect for others.''

"Forgive me, sir, if I say that I understand why some of your followers might become impatient. Such goals must be almost impossible to realize, human nature being what it is.''

"You have a low opinion of human nature, Mrs. Malcolm.''

"Not at all, sir. Like you, I daresay, I believe people are naturally good . . . if they are allowed to be. If, however, they must struggle against poverty, prejudice, or misfortune, then I think it is too much of us more fortunate beings to expect them not to prefer more violent means to improve their lot, whatever innocents they may hurt in the process.''

"And are these your views, dear lady, or those of your husband?''

Maddie hesitated, a little taken aback by the question. She had been thinking more of her own cause than Teddy's. In fact, she had never discussed Teddy's beliefs with him, and she was struck for a moment with a doubt about what precisely Teddy *would* have answered for himself. She had to force her mind back to its goal—getting Kropotkin to help her—almost as if it were a horse that had balked at a jump. *Lie if you must,* she told herself, *but get him on your side.*

"We share them, sir," she said, as confidently as she could, "and it is for that very reason I appeal to you." She came to a halt to look up at him. "I don't suppose you ever encountered my husband personally, and in any case

I'm certain you would tell me if you had. But Teddy was—is—an idealist, and I cannot imagine that he would have leapt into anything so dangerous as an assassination or similar violent plot if he had not first convinced himself of the soundness of the ideals you describe so eloquently.''

The Russian studied her for a moment before answering. Maddie turned her most trusting and candid gaze on him, suspecting at the same time that he was not taken in by it. But whatever her momentary doubts about Teddy's motivations, she was certain of her own determination to find him. That fundamental truth must show in her face.

Kropotkin smiled and nodded, as if to concede the argument to her. ''I will make inquiries for you, dear lady. But I must warn you not to expect too much, for even I cannot prevail upon persons to whom secrecy is a way of life to reveal their secrets. Surely, you must have learned that from your husband, who has kept at least one secret from you, has he not?''

He patted Maddie's gloved hand as he spoke, but the faint echo of disbelief behind his words came through to her despite his exquisite politeness. Indeed, although his manners were infinitely better than Devin Grant's, she could see that he clearly believed her no more than Grant had.

But at least he had promised to make inquiries. She had sought no more than that, so she made up her mind to accept the favor gracefully and then changed the subject of conversation. They were discussing the best source of Russian sables in London—a subject Kropotkin doubtless considered more likely to interest a lady than political theories—when Maddie spotted Laurence Fox across the lawn from them and smiled at him to signal that it was all right for him to approach them again. But Laurence shook his head faintly and made a slight motion of his hand to his left. Maddie's eyes followed his direction, and her stomach gave an uncomfortable little lurch.

Coming toward her, with an easy stride and an expression of barely suppressed ill-humor that Maddie had no doubt stemmed from something she must have done, was Devin Grant.

Chapter Five

"YOU know the most unexpected people,"
Devin Grant remarked five minutes later.

They were walking in the direction of the
viewing boxes, Mr. Grant having detached Mrs. Malcolm
from Mr. Kropotkin after an exchange of polite inanities
that had very nearly caused Maddie to lose her temper. But
if she could be friendly to Peter Kropotkin, she told
herself, she could certainly be civil to Devin Grant.

"You knew him, too," she objected, putting up her chin
and looking straight ahead in a way that she hoped would
put this mere hired detective in his place. She hoped also
that it might banish her first, instinctive reaction to his tall
figure, fashionably dressed in dark green trousers, a green-
trimmed gray coat, and a gray top hat that did not quite
shade the angry flash of his dark eyes. It was that anger
that quickly cooled the blush that rose inexplicably to her
cheeks.

"I knew who he was," he said, "which is not quite the same thing as being intimate enough to be seen strolling around a public place hanging on his arm and chatting as if he were an old friend."

"Mr. Grant, are you by any chance about to lecture me on how I may behave? I should warn you that I will not only not take kindly to it, but I'll more than likely do just the opposite. And then I'll probably fire you."

He had no doubt that she would do just that. Taking her firmly by the elbow, Grant had all he could do to keep his own temper in check. She had made it clear on their first meeting that she was not going to sit at home—or in her posh hotel suite—waiting for him to bring her a report, but he had assumed that when he did come around to doing so, she would be there to receive it. Instead, she had gone jaunting off to the races; and there, when Devin did finally seek her out, she seemed not in the least interested in hearing what he had to tell her. Conscious of the injustice of such an assumption, not to mention the ridiculous schoolboy disappointment he felt at her not being overjoyed to see him, only added to his annoyance.

Fortunately duty had obliged him to accompany the Prince of Wales to today's race meeting; otherwise, he might not have prevented her from doing something entirely foolish, if not actually destructive to his own plans. He wished he knew what she was up to with Kropotkin.

He was not particularly concerned that Kropotkin might be up to anything. The old man was a theorist, not an agitator, and although Grant might not agree with his theories, he had no quarrel with Kropotkin's largely social, and always open, activities. It was the people Kropotkin knew, and to whom he might introduce Madeleine Malcolm, that gave Grant reason for concern.

Oddly enough, it had been the prince's latest joke about Devin's conscientious adherence to his duty that brought Mrs. Malcolm's meeting with the anarchist to his attention. He had accompanied the prince's party from Sir Ernest Cassel's country house near Newmarket to the racecourse, ostensibly as escort to Mrs. George Keppel, his employer's new mistress. It was not an unpleasant duty; Grant genuinely liked Alice Keppel, who had a remarkable gift for knowing exactly what to say and how to behave toward anyone, and who always looked delightful.

Devin supposed that she had spent hours that morning having her soft brown hair styled and being dressed in that becoming pink silk gown, which seemed to have lace trailing from every seam. The prince liked to have beautiful women to look at, and most women were flattered enough when he looked at them to feel beautiful. Having once left her maid's hands, however, Alice seemed to give no further thought to her appearance, and she turned her remarkable turquoise eyes to her escort with no need to see her beauty reflected in his own eyes.

She even commented on Grant's own clothing, declaring dark green to be very *à la mode* this season. This made the prince laugh.

"My dear Alice, you cannot have said anything more likely to make Grant send that jacket straight back to his tailor. He much prefers to be inconspicuous, indeed, invisible if at all possible. Although how he contrives to disguise his six feet two inches never fails to amaze me.''

"I dare not reveal my methods, even to you, sir,'' Devin replied, falling in with the prince's customary light-hearted banter. He was always in good humor at the racecourse. Much to Grant's relief, he had agreed not to drive onto the course this time to give the lesser enclosures a better look at him, but he still wandered about from viewing box to paddock and back again, his field glasses hanging from his neck and his protuberant blue eyes sparkling like a child's. People who never saw "their Bertie" except at such jolly social occasions sometimes thought the prince less than bright, but Devin knew how very clever he could be when the occasion warranted, so at other times he went along with whatever his prevailing mood might be.

Grant had originally come to work for the prince by chance. Most of what had happened to him in his life had come by chance, he realized, but chance had always been good to him, so he did not complain. Still, he did not take his fortune for granted.

Grant had joined the army at eighteen, mostly to get away from home and the strict supervision of his widowed father. The army, Devin thought, couldn't be half so regimented as his life up to then. What he hadn't expected was that it would be boring. He never saw active service and was never even sent abroad; his regiment moved out of its headquarters in the south of England only to see the old queen home from her summer sojourn on the Isle of Wight, to accompany one of the royal princesses when she launched a new ship at Plymouth, or to parade itself on the Salisbury Plain, usually in the heat of summer, in front of the prince and any foreign dignitary who might be impressed by red uniforms. So when Lieutenant Grant, quite by chance, was on the spot to rescue a female member of the prince's party from a runaway horse, the prince offered him a position in his household as a reward. Grant took it.

As his mother, the queen, grew older and less inclined to have any contact with her subjects, the now middle-aged prince released his frustrations over the long wait to inherit his throne in even more hectic rounds of social and ceremonial activities. Grant found himself serving as a kind of advance guard, going ahead of the royal party to look over the accommodations, the dinner menu, the sleeping arrangements, and the entertainment scheduled for the prince. Later, as the prince attempted to put in place the household he would need when he finally did become king, Grant's job evolved into securing the prince's safety, as well as his comfort, on his travels. Three years into his service he suggested setting up the detective agency as a cover for such activities. No one was more surprised than Grant when the agency flourished. The prince joked about it in private, but he knew as well as Grant did that the prince came before any case the agency took on, however fascinating.

Which was why, when chance brought Madeleine Malcolm to his office, Grant did not tell the prince about it. He was still convinced that there was more to her search for her husband than she had told him, but he had even less evidence to support that theory, only the instinct that Madeleine Malcolm would prove yet another complication in the plot that had begun with the murder of the earl of Southington's valet.

Grant had followed the trail of that mysterious stranger in the pub, but like an underground stream that surfaces only in hidden places, it was elusive and unrewarding. He had more success in tracking down the valet, who had been truthful in his references at least to his French origins, and along whose trail that mysterious underground stream would occasionally surface. Grant followed it to Paris and found enough evidence there to report back to the prince the danger of a plot against him.

That had been his first error. The prince did not believe in plots; more specifically, he did not believe that vague threats should interrupt his pleasures. He told Grant to do whatever he could that did not interfere with his usual duties, but not to become obsessed by it. If the plot was that tentative, he said, it was unlikely that anything would come of it.

"No, no!" the prince protested now, when Alice Keppel wondered aloud how detectives "shadowed" their suspects without being seen. Did Mr. Grant adopt disguises? "I beg you will not tell us anything! It is bad enough, dear Alice, that he sees anarchists with pistols behind every bush, without his telling us that he spends his spare time memorizing their likenesses and vital statistics, so as to be sure to recognize them in the street.''

Sir Ernest, who had been surveying the track through his glasses, remarked just then that some anarchists did not trouble to hide themselves away from polite society. ''There is Peter Kropotkin himself, playing the boulevardier with a stunning creature who I hope for your sake, sir, does not represent the next generation of anarchists.''

Curious, Devin raised his own glasses in the direction Sir Ernest was looking, stifled a curse, and disappeared out the back of the enclosure without so much as begging anyone's pardon. Mrs. Keppel looked after him astonished, but the prince only smiled and said, ''Duty, presumably, calls.''

''Where are we going?'' Madeleine Malcolm asked, when Devin steered her in the direction of the striped tent that housed the prince's supply of claret and the baskets of food for his ''simple little picnic,'' as Mrs. Keppel had blithely called it.

''It will be private in here,'' he said. ''We can talk undisturbed.''

He held the flap open for her and followed her into a spacious area that looked as much like an office as a storage facility. There was a desk and chair at one end, and all around the canvas walls hung paintings, in numerous styles and mediums, but all depicting horses. There were horses posed between carriage shafts, horses romping in fields, horses peering over stall doors, and horses garlanded in roses after a race victory. They walked around the collection, the display of which Devin explained had also been Mrs. Keppel's idea, in case the weather should be inclement and the royal party be reduced to taking their luncheon under the tent where there were no natural views to make conversation about. At least Alice stopped short of inviting the prince's favorite horses to lunch, he thought.

"Who are the artists?" Maddie asked.

"No one of note. One or two are by gifted amateurs, local Suffolk and Cambridge people. Some are by Mrs. Keppel's and Sir Ernest's daughters, I shouldn't be surprised."

Maddie paused without comment in front of an obviously childish watercolor of a favorite horse who seemed to lack hindquarters entirely, then passed on to another which she could not let go unremarked.

"Hangin' 's too good for that one," she observed in a perfect imitation of Florence Wingate's honeyed way of registering aesthetic horror. Devin laughed, then kicked himself for it; he would have preferred to keep his righteous anger burning. He had intended, too, to berate her for associating herself so publicly with Kropotkin, but none of these intentions had survived his first contact with her—with the firm slenderness of her arm beneath the sleeve of her dress, the sweet soapy smell wafting gently from her hair, the narcotic effect of the faint sound of her breathing as they walked among the pictures in silence. She had, he realized now, the same kind of unfluttery, unselfconscious femininity that Alice Keppel did—and a similar reserved sensuality that promised a good deal while revealing little.

He was more disconcerted to discover that the attraction he had felt toward her on their first meeting was stronger than ever, as if it were the most important thing to come out of that meeting, far outstripping the common sense that told him it was too soon—if it would ever be soon enough—to do anything about it. Now it was more likely that she would rebuff any advance he made or, worse, take advantage of it in much the same way she had wielded her checkbook on that last occasion. He would have to curb his impatience. He ought to know how by this time.

"How *did* you meet Kropotkin?" he asked finally, dragging himself back to duty but barely arriving there intact.

"We were introduced by a mutual acquaintance." She gave him a sidelong glance from those deep brown eyes, and he consciously had to straighten the smile from his own mouth. "Why do you ask?"

"I thought you might have been pumping him for news of your husband."

"And if I was? I see no reason that I should not pursue my own inquiries."

"Then I don't know why you hired me."

She laughed, showing a flash of white teeth in, he thought, a maddeningly triumphant smile, as if she knew he disliked her meddling and delighted in provoking him. He took a step closer to her, but she moved on, almost as if the slight pressure of space narrowing between them propelled her away from him.

"Then tell me what you have been doing in my behalf," she said, pausing again in front of a watercolor of a horse and its jockey. "When you have had time off from whatever you do for the Prince of Wales, that is."

"That is another matter. It has nothing to do with your case."

"Obviously," she said, acerbically. He winced, but he could not reply to that one.

She turned to look up at him, then seemed to decide against pursuing that. "Have you read the Pinkerton report?" she asked instead.

"I have. Furthermore, I have written to the Paris police officer in charge of the case of the body in the Seine, to make an appointment to discuss the matter. I assumed you would not object to my incurring the expense of going to Paris in pursuit of information?"

"Not at all. I agree that is the most logical place to start, . . . which is precisely why I plan to go there myself within the week."

"And what, *precisely,* do you plan to do when you get there, Mrs. Malcolm?" he said, feeling his temper rising again. Why was it that she could rouse his anger so easily and for so little reason? "I ask, you understand, only so that we do not inadvertently waste time in duplicating each other's activities, or worse yet, that my inquiries are not jeopardized by your causing my sources to be wary of all this interest in a long-closed case."

"I assure you, Mr. Grant, that if I should find out anything of interest, you will be the first to know."

"Permit me to doubt that, Mrs. Malcolm, on your record thus far."

"I beg your pardon?"

"You have not kept me informed, either, of all your activities here in London."

She raised her eyebrows and gave him an ingenuous look. "I have done nothing worthy of reporting . . . apart from the quite accidental meeting with Mr. Kropotkin just now."

"Allow me to be the best judge of that, Mrs. Malcolm. I doubt, for example, that your visit to the records department of the *Times* yesterday was to look up the court calendar for the third and fourth of August last year . . . something my clerk could surely have looked up for you, had you chosen to confide in him. I should also be very surprised if the reason that you were in Bow Street was to report to the police anything so mundane as a burglery or missing portmanteau."

He took a certain satisfaction in her look of genuine astonishment, tinged with what he liked to think was grudging admiration, at his knowledge of her activities. He took his advantage further, detailing all of her movements outside her hotel for the past four days, until suddenly it was borne in on him that her look had turned to one of amusement. He stopped in mid-recital, wondering what he had said. Had he got something wrong after all?

"I am impressed by your diligence, Mr. Grant," she said. "But you needn't rub it in, or as I believe the saying goes here, flog a dead horse. I wish rather that you would tell me what it is you suspect me of, that you must shadow my every move.''

''Not quite every move.''

She said nothing, using silence in that disconcerting way she had to elicit the response she wanted. Absurdly, he felt himself blush, as if she had known what he really meant before he did.

''It was obvious from the first,'' he said, unjustly, ''that you did not trust me to do the job you hired me for. I must therefore, in addition to my own investigation, make certain that your activities do not interfere with what I had assumed to be our mutual interests.''

She lowered her head for a moment, pretending to read a stud book left open on the desk. He realized that he liked looking at the back of her head, where she could not see his expression—or mock it. A few feathery strands of hair floated on her neck below her hat, and for a second that was all that seemed to move in the room. She looked—or the back of her head looked—as if she were considering her next words, and when she raised her eyes to him again, they were no longer laughing at him. He immediately suspected that she was acting again.

''I do beg your pardon, Mr. Grant. I had no such intention, believe me.'' She smiled again, apologetically this time. ''No, perhaps that is too much to expect. But let me tell you that I had no intention of interfering—only of assisting you in your inquiries. Perhaps if we talked more often in this way, to compare notes, our activities need not, as you say, duplicate themselves. You must understand by now that I am not the sort of person who is content to sit back and let someone take complete charge of her life—for that is what this search is about, after all—*my* life. Also, I can't promise to refrain entirely from interfering, as you call it. On the other hand, it seems to me that part of your job is to keep *me* informed, rather than I you. Do you suppose we might begin again, on a more mutually trusting basis?''

He had to admire the way she lectured him without seeming at all to censure him; the maxim about honey catching more flies than vinegar had been well drilled into her. He had to keep in mind, however, that her honeyed words did not signify approval, even less esteem toward him. Why he should seek her esteem, he did not quite understand, and he suspected that putting their relationship on any but a strictly businesslike basis was not going to make it any smoother or more trusting. Nevertheless, he did not hesitate to take her up on her suggestion.

''Very well, Mrs. Malcolm. In that case, we should meet at least daily, more often if I have—if either of us has—anything new to report. Perhaps you would be good enough to receive me tomorrow evening for that purpose?''

''I'd be delighted to dine with you tomorrow for that purpose,'' she said unexpectedly. When he gave her a questioning look, she added, ''I'm paying for your time in any case, Mr. Grant; I might as well pay for your supper as well.''

Feeling thoroughly put in his place once again, he accepted, and they agreed to meet in the lobby of the Savoy the following evening at eight o'clock.

Chapter Six

MADDIE woke up earlier than usual the next morning, impatient to begin the day. Her second encounter with Devin Grant had been less draining than the first. In fact, it had been stimulating in a way she did not quite understand but did like. Not that she disliked Grant himself any less, but he presented a challenge that she was now eager and ready to take up.

Oh, she would cooperate with him all right. She would even be nice to him. She had proved to herself yesterday that she could be ladylike and still best him in an argument, and she had liked the feeling of satisfaction that gave her. Not that he was what her father would have called a pushover; she always had the feeling that he was holding something back from her, the way some of her beaux used to let her win when they played tennis or croquet. But she would goad him until he did not have any reserves left.

"Oliver," she said to her secretary after she had bullied Louise through dressing her in less time than Louise thought quite proper, "Mr. Grant has some position on the Prince of Wales's staff. Do you know what it is?"

"I'm sorry, Mrs. Malcolm, I don't. I had not thought to look into anything of the sort."

"Do so, would you please? My guess is that it is connected with his detective work, possibly even with the unsolved mystery of how he got out of his office that day. I confronted him with it yesterday—that is, with his not having time to work on my case if he is also employed by the prince. Naturally, he evaded answering me."

"Naturally."

Maddie looked at Oliver and laughed. "You needn't talk like that, Ollie. I know I'm too inquisitive; the equally inquisitive Mr. Grant told me I was. But as the headmistress of my school once said, 'one does not learn if one does not ask.'"

Oliver allowed himself a slight smile and said, "One will ask, Mrs. Malcolm."

"Thank you, Ollie. Oh, by the way—"

"Is there something else, ma'am?"

Maddie hesitated, reluctant to make the request but knowing it had to be done. "I'm afraid you will have to meet with Mr. Grant."

"Of course."

She raised her eyebrows at that. "Do you trust him, then?"

"I won't know that until I know him better," Oliver

replied reasonably. "May I ask, Mrs. Malcolm, why you do *not* trust him?"

Maddie sighed. "I don't know. I suppose it's only a . . . a difference of personality, perhaps. And he is so secretive about what he is doing, as if I weren't paying him to do it for me. Perhaps you will be able to get more out of him than I can."

"I will see what I can do. Is there anything else?"

Maddie smiled. "Isn't that enough?"

Oliver went off to carry out Mrs. Malcolm's request, shaking his head over her odd reaction to Devin Grant but glad that she recognized that they must work together rather than in competition. Yes, that was what was odd— she had never struck him as a competitive sort of woman. In fact, that was what he had liked about her even before he met her.

Louise had talked about her, of course. At first he had seen her as just another society matron who wanted her own way and her husband under her heel, where most of her kind thought the poor devils belonged. But it was not long before he saw the changes she wrought in Louise, who, although she remained outwardly as stiff and undemonstrative as always, had softened noticeably behind that shell of hers, something she had not been able to do, even under Oliver's care, since her first husband died. Then, when Mrs. Malcolm bought the house in St. Louis as a refuge for abused women, Louise had come home positively glowing, and not, Oliver was fascinated to learn, because she was happy for the new tenants of the Elm Street Residency.

"She'll be able to get back to her own life now," Louise had said. "She'll make it up with that husband of hers, have children, and be as happy as she deserves."

It didn't work out that way, of course. A month later, Mrs. Malcolm came to the Pinkerton agency and asked to see Oliver. She told him that her husband had disappeared and, without resorting to tears or emotional appeals, gave him the facts and asked him to take on her case. But it was the fragility behind that brave exterior—so unexpectedly like Louise's, in fact, however much the exteriors differed—that prompted the short, unprepossessing little agent also to take on the role of knight errant for the tall, gloriously beautiful Mrs. Malcolm.

Louise moved into Mrs. Malcolm's house and began calling herself a "dresser," a position that Oliver had never heard of before but that Louise obviously considered an honor. Thereafter both of them had devoted themselves entirely to Mrs. Malcolm's service, and neither had regretted it since.

Oliver kept his private opinion of Mr. Edward Malcolm even from Louise. It was not his place even to have an opinion, only, because Mrs. Malcolm requested it, to find the missing gentleman for her. He went about his new assignment with his customary diligence, but with a frustrating lack of results, and when the agency threatened to take him off the case and declare it unsolved, Oliver took the unprecedented step of resigning to go into private service.

When his investigation came to a halt in St. Louis, it was Mrs. Malcolm's idea to go abroad. Louise had been reluctant—she still was—but loyally agreed to go. Oliver was grateful, and he personally looked for a suitable detective agency in London that might be of help.

But Devin Grant couldn't help if Madeleine Malcolm didn't trust him, so Oliver was relieved when she finally allowed him to act as go-between. Besides, there were things he should tell Grant that he had never told Mrs. Malcolm. And he was curious himself about Grant. There hadn't been any hint in the records about this business with the Prince of Wales, and Mrs. Malcolm was right about his being secretive. Moreover, he hadn't missed a certain similarity between Mrs. Malcolm's account of her first meeting with Grant in his office and his own first meeting with her. But neither had he missed the major difference. Grant had doubtless sensed something of the real woman behind that confident, competent exterior—but had he reacted as strongly to her as she had to him?

Oliver had a feeling that monitoring the relationship between Devin Grant and Madeleine Malcolm was going to prove far more engrossing than this wild-goose chase after Teddy Malcolm.

Personally, Oliver would be glad when they proved once and for all that he had drowned in the Seine.

* * *

Maddie had always made it a point to repay her debts, and she owed something to the photographer Laurence Fox, so after Oliver left her, she had Louise send a message that they would come to his studio that afternoon.

She was not particularly eager to have her face preserved for posterity, but curiosity made her look forward to seeing his studio as she and Louise departed the Savoy in a hansom cab. Louise, as usual, disapproved—even before Maddie told her, as best she could from her own inexperience of such things, what Mr. Fox intended—but it was her duty to chaperon her mistress whenever Mrs. Malcolm ventured out into the commercial world, and nothing would induce her to forego her duty on this occasion.

Mr. Fox's studio was located at a respectable, almost fashionable, address in Wigmore Street, for which Maddie suspected he paid more in rent than he could strictly afford, for the sake of his clients who were in the main fashionable ladies who did not care to venture east of Covent Garden nor north of Marylebone Road, even to have themselves immortalized on celluloid film. Nevertheless, no sooner had the cab halted at the door than Louise insisted on descending first, to scrutinize the neighborhood with her critical eyes before allowing Maddie to set foot in it. Laurence answered the bell himself, which did not meet with Louise's approbation, but he was respectfully delighted to see both ladies, which did.

"Mrs. Malcolm, how prompt you are, and how perfectly dressed for the occasion! Light colors, you know, make such a more cheerful picture than any other and do not make unbecoming shadows on the face, which is of course the focus of the exercise. Do let me take your wrap, and if you will follow me upstairs. . . ."

The studio, it turned out, occupied the whole of the first floor, and Maddie began to revise her estimate of Mr. Fox's net worth. He did, however, apologize for the lack of a lift, saying that he would have preferred the top floor, which boasted a skylight, but he could not ask his clients to climb four flights of stairs for the sake of a lighting effect he had learned to duplicate in his present location.

There were, indeed, several large, undraped windows in the half of the room where Mr. Fox's camera was set up, and an elaborate system of wires and electric globes gave evidence of the eager photographer's experiments in supplementing natural lighting by that means.

Louise took in the entire room in one comprehensive and disapproving glance, then sat down in a straight-backed wooden chair—despite Mr. Fox's offer of a more comfortable upholstered armchair—from which she did not move for the rest of the morning, except to attend to Maddie as required. Maddie, however, was intrigued by the paraphernalia that covered several shelves and hung from pegs on the walls. Laurence obligingly—and with some pride, Maddie noted, guessing that very few people troubled to ask about it—explained what everything was, from the mysterious little bottles of chemicals resting in cotton nests to the dozens of glass plates, each plate in its separate narrow wooden sleeve, to the enclosed darkroom which, for the sake of Louise's scruples, Maddie declined to enter, only peering around the door frame as Laurence explained how he developed his photographs.

At one of the windows stood his most recent acquisition, something he called a panoramic view camera, with which he was experimenting by taking views of Wigmore Street.

"And the windows of the office across the street, I see," Maddie said. "Have they any pretty little secretary-typists to make it worth your pains?"

"Oh, yes," Laurence said, unaware that he was being teased. "Several of them have come over on their luncheon break to have their photos taken, and to take some of their own."

He showed her a wall covered with lopsided views of empty corridors and circular likenesses of giggling girls taken with someone's old Kodak, as evidence. "This is why I purchased the panoramic view camera," he said. "Every shop girl and earl's daughter may now take a respectable photograph with the new Kodak. 'Pull the string, turn the key, press the button'—and presto, no one needs me anymore. I must therefore keep ahead of the new inventions if I wish to make my living as a photographer."

"Do you do so?" Maddie asked. "Forgive my Yankee crassness, but I did wonder about it."

"Any photographer who does his work well can succeed at it," he said, adding with a smile, "but only those who choose the right subjects can make a vocation of it."

"Of course. And here I am keeping you from your work. Shall we start? Where do you wish me to stand, or sit, or whatever is customary?"

"There is one little ritual to perform first," he said, disappearing into the darkroom. A moment later, Maddie heard a muffled clatter of china, and Laurence emerged with a tray holding a large flowered tea pot, two cups, and a plate of little cakes. He poured a cup of tea and handed it to her. "Now we may begin," he said.

Maddie laughed but accepted the tea gratefully. Even if this really were a ritual of his, for "shopgirls and earl's daughters" alike, she thought it a charming one.

He posed her first on a high stool, in her hat, and took a number of plates, all the while talking to her of this and that inconsequential matter to put her at her ease. Then he asked her to remove her hat, and after Louise had tidied her hair, he posed her on a sofa near the window, still talking steadily as he worked.

"You must have a sobriquet by which you will be known," he said, "just as Lillie Langtry is called the 'Jersey Lily,' because she is from the island of Jersey. Something like, for example, the 'Missouri Magnolia.' "

Maddie laughed at that. "I'm afraid magnolias are few and far between in St. Louis, Mr. Fox."

"What other flowers are common there, then? What is *your* favorite?"

"I admit a partiality to rhododendrons, but the name lacks a certain romance, I'm afraid. We also have a great many May apples, sweet Williams, and goldenrod, but those are very common, everyday sorts of plants. The state flower is the hawthorn, but that is much the same as the flower of that name here in England. We are also known as the 'show-me' state."

Mr. Fox came out from under his black cloth to give her an aggrieved look.

"And for our mules," she added.

"I don't suppose you would consider moving to California or Mississippi?"

Maddie laughed. "I *am* sorry, Mr. Fox, but I warned you that I'm not prime material to become a 'famous face.' "

"Nonsense," he said, vanishing under the cloth again. "Raise your chin a little. Yes, that's it. We will think of something, ma'am, if we put our minds to it."

Not being able to catch Mr. Fox's eye again, Maddie glanced toward Louise and was pleased to see a slight smile softening the stiff line of her mouth. Not wanting to spoil the effect, however, she pretended not to notice and concentrated instead on Mr. Fox's instructions, submitting herself to being photographed from several angles, in various kinds of light, and draped in an assortment of silk scarves and velvet cloaks.

It was a little like sitting for a portrait painter, except that the time seemed to go much more quickly. She was asked to change her posture or her expression several times and was posed before a variety of backdrops, from a velvet drape to an artificial rosebush, rather as if she were a display in a shop window.

"What happens to these images that you produce?" she asked him.

"Whatever you like, Mrs. Malcolm. I shall make up twenty or thirty pictures to sell to the illustrated magazines and the picture postcard companies, which will be responsible for the distribution."

"Distribution?" That sounded not quite respectable, so she asked what it entailed.

"Oh, it's perfectly respectable, I assure you. Ladies are generally eager to have their likeness made up in this way. Naturally, there are always some less—er, some ladies who, perhaps from motives of jealousy, insist that a lady who poses is no lady, but I trust we have got beyond that little prejudice."

"So do I," Maddie said. He laughed.

"Nothing will be reproduced that you do not approve, ma'am. Along with the proofs, I will send a contract specifying some possible uses for the prints, from which you may choose those you wish, or do not wish, implemented. You may also choose which poses you prefer to see in print, and of course, you may have any you like to give to your family and friends."

That made Maddie remember the real reason that she was submitting to this faintly absurd ordeal. She had a sudden vision of Teddy walking down a village street somewhere and catching a familiar face out of the corner of his eye. He would stop to examine her picture in a tobacconist's window, perhaps, then go in and buy a postcard. He would stand in the street and stare at it for a long time. . . .

Maddie could not imagine what Teddy might think in such a situation. Would he make up his mind to drop everything and come right back to her? Perhaps he could not because he was in debt or some other trouble and did not want to apply to her for help yet again. Perhaps he could not because he was ill or hurt. What if he were lying

in bed somewhere and someone else—a woman, certainly—
brought him the photograph, but he could do no more than
prop it on his bedside table and gaze wistfully at it?

Why are you suddenly so foolishly sentimental? Maddie
scolded herself. *Scenes like that happen only in novels.*
Still, she could not prevent tears pricking the backs of her
eyes when she thought that she might never see Teddy again.

But why was that easier to imagine than finding him?

It was more than an hour before Mr. Fox decided he had
enough to go on, apologized for keeping her sitting for so
long, and thanked her profusely for coming.

He insisted on making a fresh pot of tea for all three of
them before they left, and when he went off to attend to
this, Maddie submitted to Louise's replacing her hat and
coat. She noticed as she was confirming her appearance in
the wall mirror that there were more photographs displayed
on the far wall of the studio, and she walked over to study
them.

These were obviously Laurence Fox's own work, dating
back to his early experiments. Most were portraits, many
of the subjects well known even to Maddie's foreign eyes.
But she liked those of ordinary people best: a child with
huge dark eyes, a boy in his school uniform, a group of
kitchen maids caught in the middle of laundry day, two
ladies in Russian blouses paused in front of a shop window, a stout gentleman walking his equally broad bulldog
in the park.

But then her eye was caught by a photograph of a party of holiday makers on a boat. The subject of the composition was a family of four, but leaning on a railing in the background was a familiar figure, slightly out of focus but unmistakeable. It was Teddy.

Of course! That was why she could not imagine Teddy in England. He had gone to France, after all. Hope surged in her again. She had told Devin Grant that she had to take action for her own peace of mind, but it was hope that fueled her actions.

"Fortunately, it was a smooth crossing," Laurence's voice said from behind, startling her. "I was able to set my camera up on deck long enough to take several shots." He handed her a cup of tea, which she took automatically, turning back to the photograph.

"When was it taken?" she asked.

"On the cross-channel packet, last autumn. I believe there is a date on the back." He unpinned the print from the wall and turned it around. "Yes, twenty-one October."

Maddie took it from him and stared at the image for a moment, forgetting the tea that was rapidly cooling in her other hand. "May I purchase this print from you, Mr. Fox? As a memento of this morning."

He made a little bow and said, "It is yours, Mrs. Malcolm, with my compliments and gratitude."

She smiled up at him then, realizing how kind he was not to question her reasons for wanting that particular image, and for giving it to her so freely. He smiled back, his dark blue eyes reflecting his good nature. He really was, Maddie thought, a very sweet boy. She was glad she had come.

Chapter
Seven

OLIVER Drummond walked up Fleet Street at a pace that exactly mimicked that of the bowler-hatted businessman in front of him and harmonized with the darting movements of newspaper copyboys and the sweeping gestures of the cabbie at the corner helping a monocled peer into his vehicle. Oliver liked to blend in with his environment, but this world was still new to him, and his eyes were alive with interest. He had grown up in Chicago, but hadn't realized until now how much he had missed the bustle and excitement of a city.

He found the pub easily enough, although it was down a narrow alley off Whitefriars. It took him a minute to adjust his eyes to the smoke and dim light inside, but then he saw Devin Grant at a table near the back, his head silhouetted against a window. Although Oliver couldn't see Grant's eyes, he guessed that the detective had been watching him since he came into the public house.

Grant didn't get up, but he took Oliver's hand and motioned for him to sit down. Only then did Oliver remember that Grant towered over him, and in such a confined location his standing up would have made that even more obvious. Oliver was conscious of such things, but he wouldn't have expected it from Grant.

"Was this your idea or hers?" Grant said, when he had ordered a pint of bitter for each of them. Oliver did not pretend to misunderstand.

"Hers."

Grant raised an eyebrow but said nothing more. Oliver thought he was testing him and decided that honesty would be more useful at this point than retaliating with a test of his own.

"She recognizes the need for us to cooperate with each other, Mr. Grant. We do have the same objective, after all."

Grant didn't respond to that either, but Oliver thought there was an ironic twist to his smile.

"Don't you agree?" Oliver pressed him.

"I should tell you that I am more accustomed to working alone," Grant said.

"And I prefer to make my job easier by getting as much help as possible. You needn't be concerned, however, that I will insist on accompanying you everywhere you go. I realize that your undercover work for a certain important person does not lend itself to confidences."

It was a shot in the dark, but Oliver could see that it hit the mark. Grant did not, oddly enough, seem concerned that Oliver knew more than he was supposed to.

"How do you suggest we work out our differences, then?" he said, lobbing the ball back into Oliver's court.

"We need only be aware of them, I think. You may continue to work in the way you are accustomed to do—"

"Good of you."

"—and I shall do likewise. We need only meet regularly to compare our findings and decide on the next step—on *my* next step, if you wish. I am at your disposal."

"At Mrs. Malcolm's request?"

"At her wish."

"A fine distinction."

This time it was Oliver who held his tongue. Grant was touchier than he had expected. Did his attitude stem from his assignment from Mrs. Malcolm or the prince? Oliver could hardly ask, however, at least not at this point in their relationship. He would have to go slowly.

He took a swallow of his beer, and the taste of it registered on him for the first time. His expression registered on Grant, who smiled suddenly. "Haven't you been in a pub since you came to London?" he asked.

"I always just asked for ale."

"There are ales . . . and ales."

"So I perceive."

Oliver looked at Grant and decided he had passed the test—for today, at any rate. Grant was going to be wary for some time, yet.

"Tell me how Mrs. Malcolm's husband became involved with the anarchists."

If this was a further test, Oliver was glad to take it. This was the one thing he had never told his employer because it would have hurt her. He had told himself there was no point in her knowing, but keeping it to himself had weighed heavily on him.

"He went to work for a local politician in St. Louis but was fired for taking bribes. Mrs. Malcolm knows he lost the position, but she was told it was because Mr. Malcolm had been offered a better one. He had been—by his lights. He became a back-room assistant to a less scrupulous councilman in another ward. This man had a wide acquaintance with the underworld, and through him, Malcolm joined an anarchist group based in Pittsburgh. He used to go there regularly, more for the excitement of the forbidden, I suspect, than because he believed in what they did. He never told his wife about it either, possibly for the same reason."

"Do you know the names of any of this group?"

Oliver reached into his pocket for a notebook and wrote down the names, which he had memorized to avoid carrying anything incriminating around with him. Grant glanced at them, and Oliver thought he looked disappointed.

"Have you contacted any of these people?"

"The first two in Pittsburgh, yes. The others had dispersed to various parts of the world. The last two are supposed to be here in England."

"Don't waste your time looking for them. Briggs is dead, and Parker was in Rome last year but hasn't been heard of since. Here, I'll give you two other names to look for."

Oliver glanced at the names Grant wrote in the notebook.

Frank Hartwell and Michel Lamont. "Where have you looked already?" he asked.

Grant shook his head. "I won't tell you, simply because if you start from scratch, you're less likely to overlook anything. I know a little about these men, but I need more."

"Do they have anything to do with Edward Malcolm?"

Grant smiled. "You're right, I'm getting help wherever I can, too. But yes, they do have to do with Malcolm. I'm just not sure how yet."

Oliver tore out the notebook page and lighted a match to it. Then he stood up and held his hand out again to Grant. "I'll start right away. Shall we meet here again tomorrow?"

Grant shook his head. "In two days, at the King's Arms in Chancery Lane."

"How is their bitter?"

Grant smiled. "Try it for yourself."

Maddie had put the photograph Laurence Fox had given her in her evening purse as soon as she returned to the hotel from her session at his studio, so that she'd have it with her to show to Devin Grant at dinner. She was unsure of the photograph's significance, but it appeared to confirm their conclusion that Teddy had left England for France last October. At least inquiries might be reinstituted at Calais, now that they knew the precise date of Teddy's arrival in France.

"Where is Oliver?" Maddie broke the silence to ask

Louise as she was being dressed. "Has he returned from that errand I sent him on—and has he forgiven me for it?"

"I believe he is next door having his tea, ma'am," Louise said, responding only to the first question.

Maddie waited until Louise had finished buttoning up the back of her black satin-and-jet evening gown, then reached into her handbag for the photograph. "Take this to him, if you would, and ask him to come to see me."

"I haven't finished your hair yet, ma'am," Louise of the unalterable priorities objected.

"Never mind. You can do it while Oliver and I talk. Take this to him, please."

Five minutes later Oliver Drummond came into the room and raised his eyebrows into Maddie's mirror.

"Is it any help?" Maddie asked.

"Well, it is certainly a confirmation . . . if this date on the back is accurate?"

"Yes, apparently Mr. Fox dates all his work by the day it was made. I notice that he also wrote down the name of the packet."

"May I keep this?"

"I'm afraid not. I really must give it to Mr. Grant tonight or risk yet another accusation on his part that I am hampering his investigation. How did your meeting go?"

Oliver looked at the photograph once more, as if committing it to memory. Then he handed it back to her and gave her a brief summary of his conversation in the pub with Devin Grant; it was briefer than he would have liked, since there was very little he felt free to repeat. He tried to give the impression that he was cutting his report short because she was going out and would see him again soon in any case. She seemed to accept that, making no comment as Louise finished her hair, carefully fastening it with diamond-studded combs and black feathers to match Maddie's gown.

"Someone has been making inquiries about you, too," Oliver told her.

"Mr. Grant?"

"I thought so, at first. But the duty officer at Bow Street described someone quite unlike him. He also complained that I was the second man to come around asking about anarchists, and the first one was looking for a woman. I pressed him for more information, and he repeated the woman's description. I'm afraid it sounded very much like you, ma'am."

"Dear me!" Maddie said, thinking it best to make a joke of the matter. "I trust I shall not be apprehended in the street. Did you tell this to Mr. Grant?"

"No. I found out after I had met with him."

Maddie struggled with that for a moment. "Very well," she said at last. "I'll tell him. At least I'll be well protected tonight. I can't imagine anyone attempting to wrest me away from the formidable Mr. Grant."

"Nevertheless, Mrs. Malcolm," Louise interposed, repeating herself for the third time that day, "I don't feel easy about you going out alone in any man's company."

"I'm sure Mr. Grant will behave himself, Louise."

"Shall I make sure of that?" Oliver asked, meaning, Maddie knew, that he would shadow their movements. But she thought the potential for danger too slight to chance the greater likelihood of Oliver's being detected. Besides, she was looking forward to even one evening's worth of private life. Much as she loved Louise and Oliver and was grateful to them for their solicitude, there were times when she just had to get out from under their protective wings.

"No, thank you, Ollie. I think I can risk it. Anyway, you and Louise haven't had an hour to yourselves since we arrived in London. Why don't you go out to dinner somewhere yourselves? Go to the music hall, if you like."

Louise protested, but Oliver smiled and overruled her for once. "Thank you, ma'am. We'll do that."

"Good!" Maddie tucked a handkerchief under her sleeve, picked up her purse and the cloak that was lying across her bed, and kissed Louise on the cheek. "Well, I'm off, then. And for heaven's sake, Louise, don't hurry back, and don't wait up for me! I'll see you both in the morning."

Maddie descended by the red-upholstered lift to the lobby, trying to keep her mind off her strangely beating heart. This was only a business engagement, she told herself, even if it was evening. Devin Grant was only her employee, however attractive he might be, and however long it had been since an attractive man had taken her out to dinner . . . escorted her to dinner, she supposed she ought to say. _Oh dear, could she have wounded his masculine pride by taking the initiative? She hadn't considered that._

Turning her mind to the ethics of the situation, she lost her nervousness by the time the lift reached the ground floor, and she stepped out of it confidently. Emerging into the lobby, however, she realized she must be early after all, for Devin was nowhere to be seen. She sat down on a sofa to wait.

Five minutes later, she glanced at her watch. It was precisely eight o'clock. He should be here any moment.

Ten minutes later, she was tapping her satin-slippered foot irritably on the carpeted floor. Where *was* the man? She glanced around the room again, even knowing she could not possibly have missed him. To her left, a man in a bowler hat was watching her in a rudely intent manner; he lifted his hat to reveal fair hair parted in the middle and a pair of gold-rimmed spectacles and tipped the bowler insolently in her direction. Maddie stared back in a way she had found effectively discouraging in the past, but the man seemed oblivious to hints. Instead, he grinned at her.

It was then that Maddie realized why he looked, as well as acted, overly familiar. She let out a gasp. It was Devin Grant!

He got up then and approached her.

"How long have you been sitting there like that?" she demanded.

"Good evening to you, too, Mrs. Malcolm."

"Oh, don't be so absurd. Sit down and tell me what you are doing dressed like that." He had on a straw-colored topcoat of the sort worn by stagecoach drivers in the country, which he removed, laying it and the bowler hat on the back of the sofa. Maddie was relieved to see he had on evening clothes underneath, but he retained the spectacles, and when he sat down, he crossed his legs and prissily picked an imaginary spot of lint off his knee. Maddie was fascinated to see how these tiny differences in his dress and mannerisms altered him so completely that she had looked right at him at first without recognizing him at all.

"*That's* how you knew everything I had done. You followed me in disguise!"

"I would not like you to think I lacked resourcefulness in your cause, Mrs. Malcolm."

"Well, I confess I am all admiration. But I'll be much more observant in the future."

"And I shall be that much more resourceful."

She laughed at that, and he grinned, much more in his own style, then stood to offer her his arm. Leaving his "disguise" with the porter, he led her into the Savoy Court to hail a cab, and they set off in a mood that Maddie was surprised to find easy, even companionable.

The mood did not soon dissipate, and even the night seemed friendlier. Lights blazed all along the Strand from the restaurants and music halls, and music and laughter came to them from the street buskers entertaining patrons waiting to get into the Tivoli and the Adelphi and the Gaiety. The road was thick with hansom cabs, and the doorways with men-about-town in opera cloaks and white gloves.

Devin took her to a discreet little restaurant in Covent Garden, where she would not be recognized and which was both quiet and of high quality. The small round tables were well separated from one another, and the white cloths beneath the softly flattering shaded lamps were immaculate. And, Maddie thought, sniffing discreetly, whatever was being served smelled delicious.

Devin kept his spectacles and his altered hair style, and after thinking about it over the soup course, Maddie excused herself to go to the ladies' cloakroom, where she darkened her eyebrows with a pencil she carried with her and tucked the curls Louise had so carefully loosened from her coiffure back up into the pins securing it. When she came out again, she walked with deliberately smaller steps and cast her eyes modestly down at the floor.

When she sat down and looked up again, a glint of mischief in her eye, Devin was applauding silently. "Well done! You've caught the trick of it nicely. Most people, you know, go in for false hairpieces and putty noses, but such extremes are rarely called for."

"I may be less resourceful than you, Mr. Grant, but I am not unobservant."

He grinned. "I should mention, however, that the demure look was less credible than the cosmetic pencil."

She threatened to throw a roll at him, and he put up his hands in mock horror. "Next time I'll do my imitation of Florence Wingate," she threatened him. "That should impress you."

"Who is Florence Wingate?"

After Maddie's description, he remarked, "She sounds very American. Unlike you, which is why you would have less trouble disguising yourself here."

"If that is meant as a compliment, Mr. Grant, it's

103

misplaced. Perhaps I'll begin wearing a little red-white-and-blue flag on my hat to prove my nationality."

"Our flag is also red, white, and blue," he said.

But she only laughed, making up her mind to enjoy herself and not let him provoke her, so that by the time her *supréme de volaille au paprika* had arrived, she had forgotten the problem of how to slip him the banknotes to pay for their dinner. Presumably he would include it in his accounting for his other expenses, she told herself, dismissing the matter. She had become almost unconscious, too, of his looks and undeniable masculinity, although she wished he would comb his hair back into its usual style before she gave in to an impulse to do it herself. As long as their conversation was confined to small talk—her impressions of London, his slight knowledge of the United States—the meal passed in mutual amity.

"My father loved to travel," she said, "but he never got outside the United States."

"Mine wouldn't set foot outside Britain," he said. "No, outside England. He had no use for the Welsh or the Irish either, and the Scots only because his mother was, much to his shame, Scottish."

"I'm sorry. He doesn't sound like a very pleasant person to live with."

"I suppose he wasn't very comfortable. But he did have strong views on his duty, and he was a particularly conscientious landlord and a just, if not always merciful, magistrate—not much liked, perhaps, but very much respected. The county people even lobbied to get him a knighthood, but the government in power at the time disliked him as much as he hated them, so he never got it.''

''What was your mother like?''

''I don't remember her. She died when I was two.''

''Then you were an only child, too?''

He smiled. ''Yes. You see, if we really look for it, we can find something we have in common.''

She laughed, but over their coffee he realized again that it was impossible to forget the most important difference between them. She looked as if she would like to forget it, but with the coffee, she too remembered that their meeting had another purpose. She reached into her purse and wordlessly handed him a photograph—her husband's. He studied it, using the few seconds to marshal his thoughts and control his emotions. He turned it over to read the notations on the back, then looked at her again.

''Where did you get this?''

''A young photographer I met took it. You may remember him—the young man I was with at Newmarket. Laurence didn't know who Teddy was at the time—as you can see, his focus was on the family in the foreground. He was kind enough to give the photograph to me.''

''You are quite sure this man by the railing is your husband, then?''

She nodded. ''It's the way he stands, leaning one hip against the rail and putting both hands in his pockets. Teddy always hated to wear gloves, even on formal occasions when they were required. In cold weather he preferred to thrust his hands in his pockets like that.''

''Did he have any other such identifiable mannerisms?''

"I don't think so, but I must confess that I had forgotten about that one until I saw the photograph. You're not always conscious of such things when you live with . . . when you see a person every day."

She did not meet his eyes, concentrating instead on her coffee cup, and he wondered what was in them. Sadness, perhaps? She had lately adopted the use of the past tense when speaking of her husband. Or was that unconscious, too?

"What do you suppose he was doing on the packet?"

She did look up at that, and he was irritated to see her eyes shining with incipient tears. *Damn her.*

"I presume he was on his way to Paris. The Pinkerton report said he had gone there, but there was no information about his means of travel. Do you think he might have been going there for some other purpose? Or that this was not his only channel crossing?"

He didn't know what he meant. He had no idea why Malcolm should have made regular—or even irregular— trips to the Continent. Unfortunately, he would now have to take time to pursue the question. He would have to stop interrogating her just to sound as if he were doing his job. He hadn't wanted this evening to be tainted with business; and up until the time she had shown him this photograph, they had been getting along better than he hoped. But now, with the introduction of the cursed husband, a constraint had fallen between them. Not knowing what to do to reestablish the earlier mood, however, he continued his cross-examination.

"Presuming the connection with the anarchists to be a

fact . . . he might have been a messenger of some sort, carrying news or instructions between the Paris and London groups.''

''Oh, yes!'' she said, a little too eagerly, he thought. ''That is the sort of thing Teddy would be good at. He never looks as if he is in any hurry or on urgent business; he would pass for a casual holiday traveler, whatever sort of possibly incriminating papers he might be carrying. Also—''

''Yes?''

''Well, I can't see Teddy engaging in any kind of dangerous or violent or even illegal activity. Carrying messages, on the other hand, would satisfy his desire to be active while not jeopardizing his ideals about the anarchists, for I am certain he has them or he would not have become involved.''

Not only was she using the present tense again, she was mouthing the same platitudes she had plied Kropotkin with to convince him of her husband's sterling qualities. Did she imagine Devin did not know what she and the Russian had said to each other at Newmarket? He wished she did not so underestimate his intelligence.

''Does he speak French?''

''Teddy? Yes, in a schoolboy sort of way. He's very quick about that sort of thing, though. I'm sure he picked up a good deal in just his first week in France.''

Devin wondered uncharitably if Malcolm ''picked up'' his French in the classic masculine manner—by sleeping with a Frenchwoman. But even he balked at suggesting this to Maddie, however much he would have liked to shake her loose from her obsession with her husband. But his inclination to badger her with questions, never strong tonight, had worn itself out.

He called the waiter for the bill, deciding on the spot to assert himself in at least a small way by not billing her for the meal as she doubtless expected him to. Or would she even notice? Oliver Drummond, who paid him, probably never showed her the itemization. Well, he would know he did it.

"Shall we go?"

He laid her cloak regretfully over her beautiful creamy shoulders, trying not to touch them as he did so, then preceded her outside to hail a cab. He had to touch her arm to hand her up into it, and he was aware that every time he did so was that much more disturbing than the last. Inside, he sat as far away from her on the seat as possible, but even then, he was subjected to the play of the streetlights on her exposed bosom, where they made provocative shadows, then erased them, only to bring them up again when they rounded the next lighted corner.

She was very quiet. He coughed, hoping to prompt her into speaking, or at least into moving so that the light did not hit her just that way, but when she did, she was face-to-face with him so that all he could see now was her ripe mouth. He leaned forward suddenly, putting his hands on her satin shoulders and lowering his mouth to that tempting redness.

She made no move to resist him. In fact, for a moment she responded, letting him enter the softness of that warm, welcoming mouth. But suddenly he pulled himself back and turned his head away from her. *Damn*. He couldn't do it, not until he discovered precisely what her relationship to her husband had been. Even if it was not what he feared, even if her loyalty to him stemmed from guilt rather than love, Devin was still selfish enough about her to want all of her or nothing.

He leaned back against the upholstery again, not looking at her until they reached the Savoy, where he escorted her silently inside, and she, businesslike once again, shook his hand and thanked him for a pleasant evening.

She may even have meant it.

Chapter Eight

SOMEWHERE between sleep and waking, Maddie thought she heard a voice calling to her.

"Teddy, is that you?" she murmured.

There was no answer, so she knew she was dreaming. But perhaps he heard her anyway. She tried again.

"Teddy, do you forgive me?"

A whisper of wind seemed to blow over her, like a summer evening's breeze off the Mississippi. She had thrown off the bedclothes, as she had that night on the river, because it was too hot to sleep under them. And because the film all over her body from perspiration left by lovemaking made their slight weight intolerable. The breeze cooled her gently.

She could sense the weight of Teddy's body in the bed beside her, but she did not turn to look at him. Had it been all right that time? Had he been pleased with her? She almost thought she had enjoyed it, too. Perhaps it did only take time, time to learn to read his moods, to make the connections between the anticipation and the act itself. She thought of how he had kissed her that night after dinner, and the flesh on her arms tingled in remembrance; she could feel the tips of her breasts tense imagining his hands gently cupping them, his tongue teasing the smooth, taut skin.

As if he sensed her thoughts, he turned back to her. In the dim light his dark skin seemed even darker, and the muscles of his back stood out in graceful relief as he moved slowly from her breast to her neck, his mustache leaving feathery caresses along her neck. Then he lifted his head to look at her, and his gray eyes gleamed with a light she had never seen in them before. . . .

Oh, God!

Maddie sat up abruptly and for a moment could not think where she was. The river? No, the room was still. But the moon was reflecting off water somewhere. . . . Oh, yes, it was the Thames. She had drawn back the curtains after she turned the lights off, to look at the view.

What time was it? She snatched up the bedside clock— six o'clock. Not the moonlight, then; it was dawn. She moaned and pulled her knees up to her chest and laid her head down on them. She knew now what she had dreamed.

Damn Devin Grant.

An hour later, she had made up her mind. Let Oliver deal with Devin Grant. He seemed to be able to do it; he didn't need her. Whatever made her think she could get the better of a man like Devin Grant, anyway? He'd been trained to get what he wanted out of people. Painless extractions, like the dentist's advertisement in the window next to the Elm Street Residency. That was Grant, all right.

And she was a woman who couldn't even talk her husband into staying home!

"Louise!"

Did he make love to all the women he worked for, or was she special—a tougher nut to crack, requiring special treatment?

"Lou—" Her maid was standing in the door to the little dressing room where she and Oliver slept, her pale blue wrapper clutched around her, her hair hanging unbrushed to her waist and an anxious look on her face. "Oh, Louise, I'm so sorry. I don't know what possessed me to startle you like that. Go and get dressed. I'll ring down for some breakfast."

"But Madeleine—Mrs. Malcolm—what's wrong?"

"I want to leave for Paris."

"When?"

"Now! As soon as possible! I want to get out of London."

Louise looked bewildered. "But it will take at least a day to pack. . . ."

"Yes, all right . . . in two days, then." Maddie shoved Louise gently back into her room to get dressed and then closed the door behind her, leaning against it with a sigh.

She should have said she had had a nightmare. That was

what it was, after all, and Louise would have understood that. She was right, of course. They couldn't just pack up and go at once, leaving Oliver behind to take care of business.

Perhaps in two days she would be able to face Devin Grant herself.

Perhaps, for just two days, she wouldn't have to see him at all.

But three days later, Maddie was still in London, looking down at yet another calling card that had just been handed her and saying, "Well, Ollie, I suppose I should be grateful that I am saved from going out to be accosted in the street by everyone's calling around to see *me*."

Laurence Fox's photograph of Maddie had appeared in the *Illustrated London News* that morning. The Savoy had been obliging enough to send a copy up to her even before Laurence himself bounced into her sitting room waving the magazine in the air and asking her how she liked it—the photograph, not the magazine. Maddie had expressed some reservations about being labeled the "American Beauty Rose," but admitted that the photograph—one of those in which she wore a pink taffeta cloak, its collar held up behind her head—was very well done indeed, and she openly expressed her admiration for Mr. Fox's talent.

"No, no, dear Mrs. Malcolm, the subject is all," he said, obviously pleased with himself. "And I am happy that my subject is satisfied. Here, I have brought you a copy of that print and several of the others, which also do you justice—or at least come close to it.''

At his eager insistence, Maddie examined the pictures, feeling very strange, and not a little embarrassed, to be looking at her own image, which stared back at her, occasionally giving her flirtatious looks or an impudent smile. In one, there were tears in her eyes. What could she have been thinking of then?

It was like looking at herself in a mirror, except that it wasn't really herself, somehow. Or perhaps she had never really looked at herself. No, she remembered examining her reflection all the time when she was young, wondering when she was going to become a swan. She hadn't had to do that after she married Teddy, because she could see her own beauty in the way he looked at her. And she was older now—that much was certainly evident in the photograph—and ought to be less concerned with her looks.

She wondered what Devin Grant would think about the American Beauty Rose.

Nevertheless, Maddie thanked Laurence profusely, told him to apply to Oliver Drummond about their contract and for written permission if he wished to have some of the other photographs reproduced, and handed the whole boxful of them to Louise to put away in some dark drawer. Louise, however, chose this opportunity to assert her independence, and later that night Maddie again found herself staring at herself, this time from her dressing room wall. Only by the gentlest persuasion was she eventually able to get Louise to put the pictures up in her room instead, where she could cluck over them as much as she liked without making Maddie blush every time she walked past them.

Of course, she had to expect that Florence, too, would call the instant she saw the *News* to congratulate her and to announce that she had already called Mr. Fox to make an appointment for herself.

"I must say," Florence gushed into the telephone (for it was only ten o'clock in the morning, long before she was ready to stir from her dressing table), "he was very sweet about doin' me at once. I expect he felt he couldn't refuse, having already done you, but I'm not proud. Besides, Geoff and I are off to Paris on Thursday—did I tell you we'd decided to go sooner, after all?—which means I won't be here for my own debut, but you will look out for me, won't you, and bring stacks of copies with you when you come. Will you be stayin' at the Bristol, by the way?"

Maddie was uncertain afterward about the impulse that made her say she would be, when she had in fact instructed Oliver to book rooms at the Ritz instead, or even to reveal that she would be leaving on Friday herself. Florence had been kindness itself to her, and Maddie did not want to desert her now that she had made a few more friends. But Florence could be so . . . exhausting, was the only word for it. She did agree to come down and help Florence pack the next morning, and to hear all about her own photographic session, and she told herself that she would *not* be disappointed if Laurence offered his tea and cakes to Florence, too.

The next, more unanticipated, result of Maddie's appearance in the national press was a rush of telephone calls, which Louise began routinely to answer with, "I regret, sir, that Mrs. Malcolm, does not endorse beauty products, not even Your Soap [or Somebody's Lotion or the Other's Tooth Powder], although she is obliged to you for your offer. Good day."

Thanks to a sympathetic hotel switchboard operator, such calls dwindled to a trickle within twenty-four hours; but then private individuals whom the Savoy could not always distinguish from salespersons began to telephone, and Oliver took over the screening duty. Finally, people began to call in person. This at least was within Maddie's control, so that when the desk rang up to say a Mr. Kropotkin wished to see Mrs. Malcolm, she agreed to receive him.

Kropotkin, dressed like a Parisian boulevardier, appeared a few minutes later. He bowed and removed his hat, which he handed to Louise, who eyed him suspiciously for a moment before he bowed to her, too, and kissed her hand, leaving Louise staring at it instead, as if the hand no longer belonged to her. Maddie invited him to sit down.

"It seems we are now members of the same club," he said to Maddie, after accepting an offer of coffee from the slightly flustered Louise.

"Which club is that, sir?" Maddie asked.

"Why, Mr. Fox's Famous Faces Fellowship, to be sure! I confess, however, that I cannot imagine why he troubles himself with such as I when beautiful roses such as you consent to pose for him."

"You flatter me, sir. But I believe Mr. Fox is not so young that he does not consider posterity. You will be far better remembered in fifty years' time than I will, and our young friend's grandchildren will be able to point proudly to your photograph in the encyclopedia and say, 'Our grampa took that.'"

Kropotkin laughed. "I had not thought of it precisely that way, but perhaps you are right. Nevertheless, we live in the present age, do we not? And you have a pressing need with which I may perhaps help you."

Maddie leaned forward eagerly. "Have you heard something about my husband, then? I am sorry to press you, but we are leaving for Paris sooner than anticipated, and I am grateful that you even came to see me."

"Not at all, dear lady. Alas, I fear I have no direct news. I shall naturally send any further information I may receive to your hotel in Paris. Nevertheless, I have—"

Maddie interrupted when Oliver appeared just then and introduced him. "I trust you will not object if my secretary joins us, sir? He is my confidant and adviser in this matter of my husband."

Kropotkin waved Oliver to a seat and waited until all three were supplied with a cup of coffee before observing, "You will forgive me, dear lady, but am I misinformed that the gentleman who escorted you at Newmarket, Mr. Devin Grant, is representing you in this matter?"

Maddie saw no point in denying that Devin had been with her that day but decided that attempting to explain why he was would be futile. "He is assisting us, yes. But as I trust I made clear to him as well, Mr. Kropotkin, I am not one to leave such a personally important matter entirely to a stranger. Naturally, I'll pursue my own inquiries in the hope that pooling our mutual resources will bring results more quickly.''

"I see." Kropotkin glanced at Oliver, who maintained his usual bland policeman's expression. Kropotkin seemed to come to a decision.

"Then I am willing to include Mr. Drummond in the information I am about to reveal to you, Mrs. Malcolm. But at the risk of causing friction between you and Mr. Grant, I must beg that you not reveal it to him."

"May I ask why?"

"You may ask," Kropotkin said, reassuming his most charming manner, "but I fear I will not tell you."

"Very well," Maddie said. "You have my word that I will not discuss anything you say with Mr. Grant."

"Unless Grant discovers it on his own," Oliver interposed.

Maddie nodded. "Yes. Mr. Drummond respects Mr. Grant's abilities . . . and does not wish to cause any more friction, as you call it, than necessary. We'll maintain this confidentiality as best we can, then, if you do the same, sir."

Kropotkin considered this, too, between leisurely sips of coffee. Maddie felt convinced that he knew about the less-than-trusting relationship she had thus far maintained with Devin Grant. Perhaps it was as well that he did; she did not want to deceive him, but she did not want to attempt to explain to him something that she could not adequately explain to herself. She hoped only that he did not know Devin Grant well enough to share secrets with him that he kept from her.

Kropotkin put his cup down on his saucer and reached

into his pocket. "Very well. What I have for you is a list of names and a letter—two letters—of introduction. Any one of these people may provide just the clue you need, or none of them may. But they may also be able to refer you to other persons whose names—because I have been so long out of touch on these matters—I do not know."

He produced a folded piece of paper from his wallet and handed it to Maddie.

"Who are these people?" she asked, perusing the list of about a dozen names, none of them familiar to her.

"Things have changed considerably in Paris, you may know," he replied indirectly. "Incidents involving violent anarchists reached a peak there some five years ago, and the government cracked down on the activities of all anarchists. Those such as my colleague Jean Grave, whose philosophy does not condone violence, also suffered repression. But since that time, little by little, the anarchist press has reestablished itself. The names I have given you are in the main those of the editors of such periodicals, whose own contacts are widespread.

"I have marked the names of men whom I consider, with all respect, dear lady, would be more responsive to businesslike inquiries from Mr. Drummond. The others are more—shall we say—Parisian and thus more susceptible to an appeal from a lady in distress. These letters—" he handed her two unsealed envelopes—"are introductions for you and for a gentleman. I did not specify whom, but Mr. Drummond may make use of it."

"Thank you, Mr. Kropotkin," Maddie said, passing the list to Oliver. "You have been very helpful."

She rose and reached out to shake Kropotkin's hand. "I am grateful to you, sir, for giving me hope that I may yet find my husband not in danger at all, but in association with gentlemen such as yourself."

They exchanged farewells, and Oliver accompanied Mr. Kropotkin to the lift. Maddie sat back to mull over their conversation. Was she really hopeful because of anything Kropotkin had said, or was she deluding herself? She knew Teddy well enough to think it more likely that he would be attracted by the excitement of scheming to plant a bomb or knock down a statue than by talk and ideas, however revolutionary. A group of anarchists who skirted the edges of the law, but were in no real danger because the government had removed their claws five years ago, might be doubly attractive to him. She could only hope that among those men was one who would see Teddy's weaknesses and protect him for her.

But what still nagged at the back of her mind was what Peter Kropotkin had not said. What did he know about Devin Grant that she did not? He obviously distrusted Grant, too, she thought, although very likely for different reasons. She would have to consider this possibility very carefully before she saw Devin again.

Walking back from the lift, Oliver unfolded the list Maddie had given him. All French names, although Michel Lamont's was not among them. He hadn't expected it to be, of course. Grant must have known he would find out quickly enough what had happened to the earl of Southington's valet. The elusive Frank Hartwell was harder to pin down, however. Grant must have known that, too, and Oliver had no doubt that he was Grant's real objective.

Oliver looked at the list again. No François or Biencoeur, either. Oliver smiled as he put the slip of paper back in his pocket. He had been a whiz at puzzles when he was a boy, but it had been years since he had tackled a really challenging one. It would give him great satisfaction to beat Grant to the solution of this one.

Chapter
Nine

IT seemed weeks rather than mere days before Maddie was at last standing on the platform at Victoria Station watching Oliver direct the loading of her bags and trunks into her Pullman car compartment. Louise had already gone in to look over their accommodations. Before allowing her mistress aboard, Louise always examined every form of public transportation—even a first-class compartment on the British section of the Orient Express—to remove from it any stray bits of picnic lunch, forgotten novels of dubious moral content, and other remnants of the previous occupants, which mere employees of the railway could be expected to overlook.

Maddie was content to wait outside, under the domed roof of the huge station. It was a lovely day to begin a journey, although she scarcely noticed the beams of light streaming onto the platform from the glass roof. She could feel her weariness, now that she had a moment to stand still and let it catch up to her. She had deliberately exhausted herself each day so that when she fell into bed at night, she could sleep dreamlessly until she awoke, too early, the next morning to begin again.

At least she had not thought again about Devin Grant and that last picture she had of him, looking at her that way in the streetlight, his eyes so close to hers that she imagined she saw her own reflected in them. He had sent a note to the Savoy the next morning to thank her politely for her invitation to dinner and to remind her that he had planned to travel to Paris, too, and in fact would be gone by the time she read his note.

He hadn't wasted any time. At least, away from his disturbing presence, it was easier to be confident of her goal. Maddie could only hope that her self-assurance would be strong enough by the time she got to Paris to prevent him from weakening it again.

A middle-aged couple passed her on the platform, and Maddie felt the man send her a sidelong glance, then nudge his wife in the ribs, at which she turned to stare too, although less subtly. Maddie was becoming accustomed to these attentions, having had to leave her hotel room on one or two occasions since the publication of her likeness in the national press—she had even seen it in the shops in the Savoy—but she was not sorry to be leaving the stares behind and hoped they would not follow her across the channel. Since she had also offered, on an impulse, to take the author of her newfound fame with her, she could not, of course, be absolutely certain that *tout Paris* would not soon begin to recognize her face. Laurence Fox's claim to make faces famous had turned out to be no idle promise.

Fortunately, not every Islington Lizzie and Bertie from Bow was allowed on the first-class platform, so that Maddie was spared any really unpleasant encounters, although the formidable lady approaching her now might be awkward to dismiss. It was only when this large, almost perfectly square creature in brown taffeta stopped in front of her that Maddie noticed she was accompanied by a young girl—presumably, from the unfortunate shape of the girl's nose, the gorgon's daughter—who almost literally hid behind her parent's skirts.

"Come along, Elfreda, and say your piece to the lady," said the stout matron unexpectedly, hauling the girl by the arm out in front of her. Elfreda, who despite her childish ringlets must have been seventeen or eighteen, bobbed a curtsey to Maddie.

"I do beg your pardon, ma'am," she said in a voice that fortunately carried none of her parent's stridency, "but you are the lady whose photograph appeared in the *Illustrated London News*, are you not?"

"I'm sorry to say, I am." Maddie had to smile at the worshipful look on the girl's face. "I am Mrs. Malcolm. Are you also traveling on this train?"

She held out her hand to shake Elfreda's, rendering that young woman speechless, so that it was left to her mother to announce that she was Lady Jervis and she was pleased to introduce her daughter, Miss Elfreda Jervis.

"Elfreda has something to ask you," she proclaimed then, and leaving Elfreda to accomplish this, her ladyship went off to supervise the loading of her trunks into a compartment several doors down—Maddie was relieved to see—from her own.

Miss Elfreda, having detached her hand from Maddie's, found her voice again and asked in an urgent whisper, "Oh, please, Mrs. Malcolm, can you tell me who made the photograph in the *News*?"

Now this was something new. People had asked Maddie any number of odd and rudely personal questions, but no one had yet come up with this one, and Maddie was for once happy to satisfy a stranger's curiosity.

"It was a very talented young man named Laurence Fox," she said.

Elfreda clapped her gloved hands together and laughed. She had a delightful little laugh that almost made up for her nose and the dreadful olive green traveling outfit her mother must have ordered for her out of some department store catalogue.

"Oh, I knew it must be! I see Mr. Fox's photographs everywhere and never fail to recognize the style. Laurie— that is, Mr. Fox—once came to our home, you see, to photograph my father. He is a knight, not a baronet, and when he was given the honor he thought it would be a good thing to have his portrait taken, but since he is too busy to sit for a painter. . . . Well, anyway, that is how I know Mr. Fox, although of course—that is, I regret—we have not met since."

An unmistakable blush spread over Elfreda's already rosy cheeks, and Maddie took genuine delight in telling her that Mr. Fox was traveling with her party. For a moment, she was afraid that Elfreda would fall to the middle of the platform in a dead faint, but it seemed she was only holding her breath in wonder.

"Why don't you come visit me when we're underway, and renew your friendship with Mr. Fox," Maddie suggested when Elfreda's speechlessness became prolonged. She then released her breath all in a rushed sigh.

"Oh, thank you, Mrs. Malcolm! I will do so . . . or rather, Mama and I will, if that is all right."

"Of course, Miss Jervis."

Elfreda excused herself then in response to a summons from her mama, who apparently considered her to have been independent long enough. Maddie was left in entertaining speculation. Plainly, the girl had a crush on the lamblike Mr. Fox. Was he aware of it? She was a sweet thing—no beauty, but her features were delicate and her complexion that perfect English peaches-and-cream kind. She was a little on the plump side, as well, but Maddie thought that would be less obvious in another style of dress. She began to look forward to an unexpected source of entertainment on her journey.

Her new line of speculation made Maddie suddenly aware, as she entered her compartment and saw Mr. Fox assisting Oliver Drummond in stowing her hand luggage, that he might be getting far too attached to her for other than professional reasons. His eager greeting, as if he had not spoken to her by telephone just that morning, even made her wonder if she had been wise after all to have invited him to go to Paris with her. Miss Jervis, she decided, had arrived on the scene just in the nick of time.

"Mr. Fox, please don't bother with that," she said, smiling but removing a hatbox from his hands and passing it to Oliver, who placed it in the overhead rack. "Mr. Drummond may suspect you want his job."

Laurence glanced at Oliver, whose bland expression did not change, as if there might be some truth in this, and, when Maddie chose a seat by the window, he sat down opposite her, abandoning his attempts to be useful.

"I think I am learning to recognize when you are teasing me, Mrs. Malcolm," he said, with his disarming smile, "but as yet I am at a loss to know why."

Maddie put out her hand to pat his in what she hoped was a big-sisterly gesture. "I do beg your pardon, Mr. Fox, but you must not think that because you have, so to speak, been responsible for my presentation to British society, you must concern yourself with my welfare for ever after. I invited you along because I enjoy your company, not because I am in need of a cavalier."

"I am justly rebuked, ma'am," he replied. "I will henceforth concentrate solely on keeping you amused rather than attempting to shelter you from the world. On one condition, that is."

"And what is that?"

"That you call me Laurie, as my other friends do."

Maddie smiled and turned his hand over to shake it. "Agreed!"

Just as she sat back again, the train gave a little lurch, and her excitement at beginning a new journey, which she had not yet learned to disguise no matter how worldly a pose she adopted, bubbled up, and she clutched the window sill. "Oh, look, we are moving!"

It was only minutes before the crack train had left the brick façades and paved streets of the capital and was gliding smoothly through the countryside toward the channel coast. Laurie pointed out landmarks and explained that those flimsy wooden structures in that field supported hop plants, and that those oddly cone-shaped roofs in that village were traditional in this part of Kent. Louise came into the compartment with a light lunch just as Lady Jervis and her daughter—who had taken the time, Maddie observed, to change into a slightly more becoming dress—knocked on the compartment door.

"Come in, please," Maddie said, as Laurie jumped up to open the door. In the limited space Elfreda had to pass close to Laurie to seat herself, and she glanced up shyly at him—just slightly, becomingly flirtatious, Maddie noted approvingly.

Lady Jervis shook Laurie's hand heartily, condescended to remember him, and assured him that his photograph of her husband held pride of place on their fireplace mantel, right under the framed print of Winterhalter's portrait of the queen. Laurie looked grateful just the same.

"You are just in time to join us for lunch," Maddie said. "That is a lovely frock, by the way, Miss Jervis."

"Oh, thank you, ma'am. I'm afraid Mama thinks it a bit—that is, too gay for me, but I saw it in a shop when she was not along and bought it on impulse."

Elfreda glanced at her mother, who pretended not to

hear, so absorbed was she in helping Louise to lay out the lunch paraphernalia.

Good for you, little Elfreda, Maddie thought. There is hope yet.

She introduced Laurie as if they had not met before and was gratified to hear him say he remembered her, and how was her father? This led to a promising, if hesitant, conversation between the two young people, and Maddie considered her newly hatched little scheme off to a good start.

Within two hours, they had reached Folkestone and boarded the cross-channel steamer for a smooth crossing, which was just as well, for Elfreda confessed privately to Maddie that she was a very poor sailor. Maddie advised her in that case to spend the time with her mother, so that if she became indisposèd, Laurie would not know about it and Elfreda would have done her duty to keep her mother company and might therefore be able to escape to be with them guiltlessly at another time.

Laurie, unfortunately, forgot all about her much too quickly when he set up his camera to take more photographs of Maddie on deck; then, when she declared that enough was enough, he went off cheerfully to subject some of the crew to his lens.

Maddie, left alone at last, leaned on the railing and let the sunlit waves mesmerize her, but the image of Teddy at perhaps this very railing kept intruding between her eyes and the sunny sea. But no, she remembered then; he would not have been traveling first class. It struck her that it must have hurt Teddy's pride terribly to be so dependent on her for money, even for those little comforts she took for granted. It was his pride, after all, that had prevented him from telling her, until after their marriage, that his father had finally made good his threat to cut Teddy off without a penny.

Hot water in hotel rooms, cushioned seats in railway compartments, hansom cabs, and champagne were not so easily come by for most people in the world. She ought to have known that only too well. If she were a rose, she was a hothouse creation, pampered from birth, with someone else always there to draw her bath, clean, starch, and press her clothes, prepare her meals. It was strange that none of the women at the hospital or the residency had resented her for her privileges; instead they had looked up to her and spoken to her with respect, even reverence. Maddie smiled, wondering what Peter Kropotkin would make of that.

Teddy had never complained, either. But he had never, now that she reflected on it, seemed to care how much he took from her, nor balked at asking for more. Well, why should he? What she had was his, and she had more than enough for both of them. She could scarcely expect him to be ashamed of that, much less to pretend that he was. The first thing that had attracted her to him, after all, had been his blithe refusal to be intimidated by money.

Nevertheless, she could not dismiss the idea that Teddy might have left her deliberately to escape his sense of obligation to her and the relentless hammering away at his pride that came from having no means to support himself independently. Perhaps that was why he gambled, to try to make a fortune of his own with one turn of the cards.

Perhaps that was what Devin Grant had meant by her feeling responsible for Teddy's disappearance. He had recognized her guilt before she did.

In Boulogne they were transferred to one of the elegant blue-and-gold Wagons-Lits carriages of the Continental section of the rail line, just in time for afternoon tea. But this they were destined never to enjoy, for as they were leaning out of the coach window at Boulogne to watch the colorful, multilingual crowd milling about in the station, the Wingates suddenly materialized.

"My dear, I *knew* you would be on the train, and I told Geoffrey so . . . didn't I, my love?"

"So you did, Florence."

"And here we are!" Florence gushed, hugging Maddie as if she had not seen her for years, but interrupting herself to say, "No, that case doesn't go in here. . . . Geoffrey, be a dear and show all these people where our compartment is."

"All these people" were a trio of station porters struggling with Florence's endless train of luggage, which Geoffrey, on the way to do his wife's bidding, compared favorably to Napoleon's at the start of his Russian campaign. As soon as it had gone on its way down the corridor, Florence closed the door on it and sat down to talk. When Maddie introduced her to Elfreda, Florence smiled graciously, then paid no further attention to her, devoting herself instead to Laurence Fox.

"What a charmin' coincidence to see you here, too, Mr. Fox! Am I being too bold to ask if you have brought my photographs with you?"

"I'm so sorry, Mrs. Wingate, but I had no idea you would be on this train—or that I would either, for that matter—so I sent them by express to Paris. They will be at your hotel when you arrive."

"Well, I can hardly wait! Shall I become as famous as Mrs. Malcolm?"

"There are different kinds of fame," Laurie answered diplomatically, "just as there are different styles of feminine beauty."

He smiled at Elfreda when he said that, for which Maddie could have hugged him. Florence appeared not to notice.

"I tell you what," she said, after she had rummaged about in her purse for some francs. "This calls for a celebration—a reunion party! And not only with tea, either. Oh, there you are again, Geoffrey, just in time."

"I do my best," he said and winked at Maddie. He must have known he would be sent on another errand, however, because he did not trouble to sit down.

"Geoffrey, you must go and find us some champagne and nice things to eat . . . let me see, some caviar, I think, and some of that lovely smelly cheese we had at the inn last night, and . . . oh, whatever would be nice for a friendly celebration."

"Here?" Geoffrey asked, looking at Maddie who, knowing protest was useless, nodded. Geoffrey went obediently off again, and Elfreda attempted to excuse herself as well;

but Laurie said, "Nonsense. You stay here, and I'll go fetch your mother to join us."

Elfreda smiled gratefully after him, and Florence made use of the intervening time to tell Maddie that she and Geoffrey had found the most charming little inn outside Boulogne and decided to stay there overnight.

"And then this morning, I had a premonition. 'Maddie Malcolm will be on that train today,' I told Geoffrey. 'Mark my words.' And see if I wasn't right! I'm sure it's a sign that we'll have a lovely time in Paris. What are you goin' to do there, by the way? Geoffrey and I are going to Versailles and Chantilly and Fontainebleau. . . . I adore castles, don't you?"

Happily, since Maddie did not want to admit that she had no defined schedule lest Florence include her in her plans, Lady Jervis arrived just at that moment to announce that she lived in a castle, and it was cold and damp and impossible to keep clean. This made Elfreda giggle but effectively silenced Florence on the subject. Indeed, Lady Jervis's presence served to dampen Florence's spirits down to a level that allowed everyone else to enjoy the little party after all. Even Elfreda, although her mother allowed her only the occasional sip of champagne, confessed to having a jolly time and was, as Florence grudgingly remarked to Maddie, the only girl she had ever seen whose looks improved as the champagne went to her head.

An hour later, the party moved to the bar car, which, Florence said, boasted piano entertainment and the most talented barman imaginable. Elfreda and Laurie, supervised by Lady Jervis, retired to a far corner of the car with one last glass of champagne between them, a plate of several kinds of caviar and foie gras to sustain them until they reached Paris, and a backgammon board to amuse them. Maddie sat back to listen to Florence's highly colored description of her stay in Boulogne, where she had discovered not only an inn, but the most exquisite lace handmade by a sweet old lady who charged a ridiculously low price for a whole shawl of it, which Florence then sent a waiter to fetch from her maid to show off to Maddie.

In this way, they arrived at the Gare de l'Est before they even noticed that the sun had set behind them. When the train had come to a hissing stop inside the station, Maddie took Oliver's hand to step down from it, grateful, now that they had arrived, that Florence's unexpected appearance had distracted her from any further reflections along the way on things past and best forgotten.

They left the station to find Paris just turning on its lights for the evening ahead. There had been a rain recently, and the lamplight reflected off the paving stones, making the city twice as bright and twice as light, as if it floated on water.

"Oh, look!" Elfreda exclaimed. "It's as if Paris is glad to see us."

"And so it should be," Florence agreed, as Geoffrey gave the porter an especially large _pourboire_ for muscling Florence's luggage off the train and to the taxi rank outside the station.

But for Maddie, the sense of excitement in the air and the hint of exciting things happening in the bustle of traffic and staccato footsteps on the pavement stones had, strangely, just the opposite effect. An unexplainable stab of dread went through her, and for a moment, she thought she could see beyond the lights to the dark corners they did not illuminate and hear beneath the quick chatter of cabdrivers and newspaper vendors the whispered speech and muted cries of anguish of a more shadowy world.

Oh, Teddy, where are you? Are you alone here, somewhere in the dark? Help me find you.

There was no answer. She shivered a little as she stepped into the smart, well-sprung fiacre that would take her to her comfortable suite at the Ritz, where she would be out of sight and sound of that other world.

Chapter Ten

PARIS and springtime impressed themselves finally and forever on Maddie the next morning as she sipped her coffee in the window seat overlooking the Place Vendôme, but not quite in the way she had anticipated. Inside, her suite was elegantly furnished and spacious and cozy, all at the same time. Outside the window, the sky was blue and cloudless, the air was warm, the square was filled with sunshine and people—but Maddie could not bring herself to feel part of it. She responded to Louise's concerned questions with automatic, and doubtless unconvincing, assurances that she was only a little tired from the journey from London. The truth was that now that she was here, she wanted to be somewhere else. In Paris, she would have to find Teddy or go home in failure.

She had to blame Paris. She had never felt like this before, had never been at all moody. It was not just that she was alone. She had learned long ago to enjoy her own company when it was all she had, and she had always been able to make new friends. She had done that at home and in London and would do it in Paris. And it was not just that she missed Teddy. She still worried about him, especially here in Paris, where she felt instinctively that he was in some danger. But she no longer missed him only for his company, as she had done when he first left her. No, there was a new hollowness inside her. Something was missing that she hadn't known was ever there, and it left a deeper hurt than anything else had.

She ought to have learned about that long ago, too, but the first time Teddy left her to her own devices, she hadn't seen the implications. It had been at a party, a friend's engagement party. All of the boys were friends of Teddy's, and one night he had gone off with them for an hour down to the lake in back of the house. It was a small thing, but Maddie had felt deserted. They had been married only a month then, and she still believed he would always prefer her company to anyone else's.

Of course he had laughed when he came back, his hair slicked back and a grin on his face.

"Sweetheart, we went swimming in the lake—naked. You couldn't have come anyway. And I'm back now, aren't I?"

Teddy's explanations were always so sensible that Maddie could only suppose she was being selfish. He had sat down on the sofa next to her and kissed her and given her all his attention; and when he asked her what she wanted him for, all she could say was that she was lonesome, which was

nonsense. She had always assured him—bragged even—
that as an only child, she had learned early on to amuse
herself. But she had thought being married meant she
wouldn't have to do that anymore.

A sound registered on her consciousness—a knock. She
brought her wandering mind back home.

"What is it?"

"May I come in, Mrs. Malcolm?" said Oliver Drummond
from just behind the crack in the door. Maddie wondered
how long he had been standing there, trying to catch her
attention.

"I'm sorry, Ollie. Do come in."

He had come in to report that he had reached the first
of the names on Peter Kropotkin's list, but Maddie could
not bring herself to take an interest in who that might be.
She picked up her cup and saw that the coffee in it had
grown cold. Out of idle curiosity, she lifted the lid of the
silver coffeepot and discovered that what was left was
even colder. Only then did she remember that Oliver was
still talking to her.

She apologized again, and for the first time in their
association asked him to write out a report and give it to
her later, when she would be able to concentrate on it.
Then she dismissed him with sweeping permission to do
next whatever he thought best. Nevertheless, something
he said as he was leaving temporarily roused her from
her abstraction.

"Oliver!"

"Yes, ma'am?"

"You haven't heard from Mr. Grant yet?"

"Not yet."

He waited for a moment for her to say something else, but when she fell silent again, he slipped out, closing the door softly behind him, as if on a sick room.

That registered on Maddie. *Damn Devin Grant*, she thought. Where was he? After all his assurances, he was still keeping her in the dark as much as before, and she was letting him get away with it!

Well, not quite, but righteous indignation made her feel better. On the channel crossing, she and Oliver had discussed possible courses of action when they got to Paris, and Oliver was obviously doing his best for her, with or without Devin Grant's help. Her own job was less easily defined, and apart from continuing to make herself visible where Teddy might see her, she had to depend on recognizing and taking any opportunities that came her way.

The first of these she had recognized as not at all necessary, but she wanted to do it. On the train, somewhere around Rouen, it had occurred to Maddie that Devin Grant had very neatly *not* introduced her to the Prince of Wales at Newmarket, when he might easily have done so. It was not that Maddie was all that eager to exchange small talk with royalty, but she had convinced herself that the lack of an introduction was just another instance of Devin's not trusting her. He had never introduced her to anyone, now that she came to think of it, not even the clerk in his own office. So she had made up her mind to remedy that herself; and when Oliver had discovered, on registering, which suite the prince would occupy when he arrived the following week, she cajoled the hotel into letting her have it until then, when she would move into another set of rooms. Having stayed in his suite would make a perfect conversational opening when she succeeded in making herself known to the prince. And that she would do.

She poured the dregs of her coffee into a potted plant and rang for Louise to help her dress. She would *not* stay in and mope all day; she would go out and *do* something.

She rang the Jervises' suite to invite Elfreda to go shopping—without her mama, if at all possible. Lady Jervis, however, had already made plans to go sightseeing that day, to introduce herself and her daughter to Paris, in much the same way, Maddie suspected, that the British under Wellington had once done—by occupying it entirely. But she accepted an invitation to join them, if only to shake herself out of her gloomy mood and prove to herself that the sun shone in Paris, too.

Delaying only long enough to consult her Baedeker, Lady Jervis instructed the hotel to hire her a *voiture de grande remise*—"Oh, yes, madam," said the concierge when Lady Jervis underlined the phrase in her guidebook, "a fly"—and they set off on what the book called a "preliminary drive."

They had scarcely swept through the Place de la Concorde and around the Madeleine before Maddie began to feel much more cheerful. They crossed the Seine by the Pont Neuf, and Notre Dame rose up like a proud flagship from the Cité, as if to greet them. Paris seemed to be smiling at her after all, so Maddie smiled back. Even Lady Jervis turned out not to be the ogre she had seemed, although she was opinionated about the most unexpected things.

"Oh, yes, I am decidedly a republican," she said, turning her nose up at the suggestion of a stop to visit the Emperor Napoleon in his tomb at Les Invalides. "My husband is a great admirer of the Americans, particularly. He finds their way of doing business most enterprising and imaginative. We took our wedding trip in New York, you know."

"Mama!" Elfreda exclaimed, while Maddie tried in vain to imagine the Jervises' enterprising and imaginative honeymoon. "You never told me that."

"I do not recall that you ever asked," Lady Jervis said with, Maddie thought, more than a hint of impatience. But Elfreda did not seem to notice and pressed her mother for more, upon which Lady Jervis revealed that she had accompanied her husband on a number of his journeys to the United States, early in their marriage, of course, before Elfreda was born. Maddie seized on this as a way to ingratiate herself with Lady Jervis to the point where her ladyship might be willing to relax her rigid Baedeker timetable and entrust her only daughter to Mrs. Malcolm's American hands and republican tastes.

Elfreda, apparently aware that her new friend had some ulterior motive for drawing out her mother's views on everything from New York hatmakers to Chicago stock-yards, kept her silence, so that by the time they were taking a rest from their sightseeing in the Café Anglais, the older ladies were in perfect harmony with each other and Elfreda ventured a suggestion.

"Mama, did you not say you looked forward to visiting Papa's business acquaintances while we are here in Paris? If you would rather do that than drag about with me in the shops and dressmakers, perhaps Mrs. Malcolm would not be bored with doing so."

Maddie looked admiringly at Elfreda when this bold stroke actually succeeded and Lady Jervis, after a great many polite protests and slightly more sincere apologies, handed her daughter over to Mrs. Malcolm, who was only "too kind" to offer to chaperone her.

Thus it was that the next morning, Maddie, Elfreda, and Louise set off for Galeries Lafayette together. Maddie had at first suggested going to the more stylish shops on the rue de Richelieu, but Elfreda confessed that she was a little frightened of the snobbish proprietresses of such salons and, although not quite such a republican as her mother claimed to be, much preferred the democratic hurly-burly of the *grands magasins*. Maddie promised to protect her from any snubs on the part of upstart salespersons, and they compromised on first a visit to the Galeries, then a stop at Worth's, where Maddie wanted to be fitted for a new evening dress, thus encompassing both ends of the fashion spectrum in one day. Elfreda could then decide where, between those extremes, she would be most comfortable, and they would have her measured and fitted the next day.

Resigned to living with Elfreda's unbecoming leg-of-mutton sleeves and ugly purple batiste walking dress for another day, Maddie then had a surprisingly enjoyable morning rummaging among the gloves, ribbons, buttons, parasols, artificial flowers, and silk stockings on display at both the Galeries and Le Printemps across the street, so that by the time they had settled in for lunch at Richard-Lucas, they were burdened with dozens of little paper-and-string-wrapped parcels, with which Maddie sent Louise back to the Ritz, assuring her that they would wait until she returned before going on to Worth's.

"Now then," Maddie said in a conspiratorial tone over the soup course, "we are alone at last and can have a cozy little chat. But you must first tell me, for I am not entirely sure I understand, why precisely your mother has brought you here to Paris."

Elfreda sighed. "Oh, dear. We have been having such a jolly time this morning that I quite forgot about that. You shall have to think of someone you may have introduced me to, so that the day will not seem a total waste."

"I beg your pardon?"

"Paris is only the first stop, you see," Elfreda explained. "As you may imagine, Mama does not go traveling to enjoy herself. No, she has a *mission*. She is determined that we will do the entire grand tour in the hope, however vain, that I shall meet some eligible gentleman, preferably titled, who will wish to marry me."

Maddie put down her spoon and stared. "Good gracious, do you still do things that way here? What about your mother's republican principles? And are the men at home so unsuitable that you need to travel abroad to find a husband?"

Elfreda looked as if this required a lengthy explanation, so they waited until their first course had been cleared and a very fine looking *escalope de veau* laid before them before delving into it.

"Mama's principles are, you might say, flexible," Elfreda explained, after she had done justice to the veal and begun nibbling at her carrots. "She is all for conducting her own life according to them and, for Papa's sake, dealing with people from all sorts of undistinguished backgrounds. But for me, she insists on only the best—or at least, the most expensive. The real reason she let me go out with you today, I believe, is that she does not wish me to get to know the same people she and Papa know, for fear one of them will be an attractive young bank clerk or dry goods salesperson. Instead, I am to be put in the way of counts and princes, if at all possible . . . even if they, too, must be purchased."

"And what does your papa say to all this?"

Elfreda smiled fondly. "Oh, Papa doesn't say very much—well, he can't when Mama holds forth—but I know he wants only what will make me happy."

That struck a familiar chord in Maddie, whose father had been much the same. But otherwise she suspected her youth had been as different from Elfreda's as she was from Elfreda. She couldn't help being impressed by the girl's eloquence, for one thing. Maddie could not recall that she had ever been so outspoken at that age. Her first impression of Miss Jervis as a shy, unprepossessing child overshadowed by her mother had not survived the channel crossing, but now Maddie began to see in Elfreda the makings of an intelligent and witty woman—if she were ever allowed to grow up and be herself.

"I take it you do not care for a title?" Maddie said.

Elfreda shrugged. "It does not matter to me one way or the other. Papa's title, even if it is only a knighthood, and not a hereditary title, has had its uses—even I have seen that—but I think a coronet is unimportant if one's husband has other qualities."

"Such as?"

Elfreda concentrated on her food for a moment, as if considering this. "Well, he need not be wealthy if he is industrious, or at least imaginative, so that he may one day gain wealth, even a title. Sometimes I think Mama has forgotten that Papa was not a knight when she married him, but worked for that honor."

"She probably hopes you won't have to go through the same struggle for recognition."

"Oh, but one may be recognized for one's talent without having such formal ceremony made of it. Also, I think a profession which allows one to come in contact with what Mama calls the best people is even better than a title which means that those people must recognize you whether they like you or not. I should very much dislike any more . . . that is, I should not care to be tolerated only for my wealth or position. People who do that really only want to lower you to their level."

Into Maddie's mind came the picture of Laurence Fox, charming Lord This and Lady That into posing for him, offering them cups of tea and in turn being offered a weekend at their country houses or trips to Paris. Of course! she thought. Elfreda might speak in generalities, but she had someone very specific in mind.

"Was there no one at home with such qualifications?" she asked.

Elfreda raised her light blue eyes. Maddie made a mental note of her long lashes and a need for a little artificial darkener, but otherwise she kept her expression interested, if impartial.

"There were very few eligible young men in our circle," Elfreda equivocated, "and none of them proposed marrying me. I am not entirely sorry, for myself, but it would have saved Mama a great deal of bother, I'm sure, if I could have induced one of them to have me. But since I did not know how even to bring them to the point of proposing, there was no question of accepting."

"You don't seem the kind of girl who is comfortable flirting with boys at dances."

Elfreda sighed. "I'm not. Well, Mrs. Malcolm, just look at me. I am not bad-looking, I suppose, but I'm not one of those delicate butterflies to whom coquettishness comes naturally. I would only look silly if I tried to flutter my eyelashes and pretend to be stupid."

Maddie reached across the table to press the girl's hand. "Look here, Elfreda. You *are* pretty, and very sweet, and delightful to talk to. You have more than enough qualities of your own that need only be brought out to make you the belle of any ball."

Elfreda looked dubious. "How do I do that?"

"*We* will do that," Maddie declared. "In fact, we can start right now, by thinking of something more interesting to call you. That is, if I am right that you do not especially care for your name?"

Elfreda sighed tragically. "I *hate* it! But I was named for my grandmama on Father's side, who set him up in business when he was a young man. As long as she was alive, I had to be called Elfreda as often and as loudly as possible; she grew quite deaf in her old age, you see. Grandmama died when I was sixteen, and by that time no one ever thought to call me anything else."

"Do you have a middle name?"

"Yes. That is, my whole name is Marguerite Elfreda. Marguerite was my papa's favorite aunt, but Mama never liked her and said the name sounded like a parlor maid's."

"Oh, but it's perfect!" Maddie said. "Do you know what Marguerite means in French?"

"It's a flower of some sort, isn't it?"

"A daisy! And that's what we'll call you. It's not just Laurie Fox who can bestow names on people. From now on, you are Daisy."

Daisy blushed at the mention of Laurie's name, then smiled. "Yes, I think I like that. And Mama would never guess. She refuses to learn French and will have no idea that a daisy is a marguerite."

"If she should ask, we'll tell her you remind me of my sister Daisy," Maddie said in a conspiratorial whisper, "so I call you that because I like to think of you as a sister."

"Do you *have* a sister Daisy?"

"I have no sisters at all, but your mama doesn't have to know that."

Daisy giggled, a sound Maddie thought indicated she was getting into the spirit of the thing.

"You can also tell your mama that we ran into Prince Kropotkin today, and, let me see, his grandson should do, although I have no idea if he has one. That should appease Lady Jervis's sense of mission."

"Who in the world is Prince Kropotkin?" Daisy asked, as her eyes widened at the pastry cart being rolled in their direction.

Maddie told her, and Daisy decided the story had enough truth in it that it wasn't quite lying; then, when Maddie suggested that if they did not, in fact, run across any counts or princes during their stay in Paris, they would just make up one or two more, Daisy lost her remaining qualms about relative truthfulness. She ordered an éclair *and* a napoleon and agreed that even a lie could be justified to make Mama happy.

"Not that we will not meet some perfectly charming young men anyway," Maddie assured her, warming to her own mission. "Florence Wingate will see to that, even if I fail to do so. How do you like your young men, by the way? Tall and fair or dark and slim and romantic looking?"

"Oh, well, I hadn't really thought of it that way, as if one could order one from a catalogue. But . . . I suppose I like dark hair and eyes. I met a poet once. He was terribly ineligible, of course, but what really made me uncomfortable was that he was so fragile-looking I was afraid to shake hands for fear of knocking him over."

"I know exactly what you mean," Maddie said. "That is one of the disadvantages of being tall. Well, let me see.

We are looking for a dark-haired, well set-up young man, not necessarily foreign, preferably handsome . . . eligibility negotiable.''

Daisy giggled again, and Maddie was certain that she too envisioned Laurence Fox as just filling the bill. They were making plans for the third step toward making Daisy into a belle—having her hair styled by a real French *coiffeur*—when Louise returned and joined in the discussion. Soon even Louise sounded as if she were almost enjoying herself, and by the time they set off for Maddie's fitting at Worth's, she thought Daisy had shed the last of her shyness.

The almost oppressively elegant atmosphere of the House of Worth awed Daisy at first, but by the time they had been shown into a private salon and had the house's latest creations paraded before them, she was so fascinated that she forgot to be self-conscious. Maddie asked her for her opinion, and together they chose two morning dresses and an evening gown for Maddie, and perhaps—well, she would have to think about it—that charming walking dress that would suit Daisy beautifully made up in pale green.

Afterward, Maddie invited her into the fitting room, where Daisy looked on with interest as Louise helped Maddie off with her outer garments so she could stand in her petticoat to be measured from every conceivable angle. The tiny seamstress, herself dressed in severe black except for a white pincushion fastened to her wrist with a ribbon, exclaimed with delight over Maddie's height and perfect proportions. Maddie winked over her head at Daisy, who had to put her hand over her mouth to keep from giggling.

Since she had to stand still, Maddie passed the time watching Daisy and reflected that there might be a good deal of satisfaction to be gained from easing the passage into womanhood of a girl like Daisy, helping her avoid some of the disappointments and difficulties Maddie herself had experienced and to find happiness sooner in life. She began to understand, too, why so many of her supposed friends in St. Louis had turned a deaf ear to her pleas for help with the Elm Street Residency women. It was not, as Maddie had supposed, that they blamed those women for their own misfortunes, but that they did not want to think it could happen to them ... or to their daughters. Maddie would be reluctant to expose Daisy to such things, even if the knowledge might make her a stronger woman.

It was the first time in her memory that Maddie had felt anything that might be described as maternal instinct. How odd that it should surface now.

Chapter
Eleven

LAURENCE Fox, having overindulged himself already by accepting train fare from Mrs. Malcolm, refused a room at her expense at the Ritz and instead installed himself and his photographic equipment in a room in the less fashionable but more picturesque quarter of the city called the Marais. There he amused himself by taking candid photographs of the more colorful local denizens before finally turning up, full of apologies for not having reported sooner, at the Ritz. Maddie promptly told him he could redeem himself by escorting her and the Jervises to the opera and Maxim's the next night and gave him a handful of francs to buy tickets and make arrangements for them.

She had no need to mention anything more about Daisy than that she would be coming, but it was impossible to expect Daisy to greet the plan quite so calmly.

"Oh, Mrs. Malcolm . . . the opera! Maxim's! And I haven't a thing to wear!"

"You will," Maddie reminded her, "if you'll only put on your hat and come with me to Worth's. They will be able to finish your new evening gown in time for Friday."

There followed two days of frantic fittings, searches for just the right evening wrap to go over their new gowns, and just the right shoes and stockings to go under them, activities which served Maddie well enough to forget her momentary lapse into self-pity over having no one to share the spring with. Daisy's delight at her "new look" would do nicely—for now—as a substitute.

So it was that Daisy Jervis entered the most famous restaurant in Paris on Laurence Fox's arm looking so radiant that even Laurie commented on it, which made Daisy look even lovelier and left Maddie grateful to the young man for his sensitivity. It also made her feel her loneliness even more acutely, and when they were shown to their table on the exclusive upper level, where they had an excellent view of the lower floor and the prettiest women and handsomest men in Paris—all in pairs—she felt even more *de trop*. But she did her best to seem at ease.

"However did you manage this?" she whispered to Laurie as the waiter pulled her chair out for her. Polished crystal glinted in the soft light of the miniature pink lamp at their table, and behind them the wall gleamed with wood wax and reflected glory.

"It was simple," Laurie said and grinned. "I sent them

your photograph. Naturally, they would want to place you where you can be best admired by everyone else.''

''Oh, dear.'' Maddie sighed and, glancing around the room, realized that many of these elegantly dressed people *were* staring at her, some discreetly but others quite openly. ''I do wish you hadn't told me that.''

''Oh, how can you say so, Mrs.—Madeleine,'' Daisy exclaimed. Maddie had asked the younger girl to address her by her first name, but Daisy was not yet comfortable with the habit. ''They all admire you so much. It must be thrilling.''

Maddie did not like to disillusion her, for it was obvious that Daisy had never enjoyed such heady attentions, and she envied her for them. At least Daisy was not as a result self-conscious about her own looks and did not fuss over her new, lace-trimmed silk gown and the string of pearls Maddie had persuaded her was all the jewelry she needed.

At the opera, too, Daisy had attracted almost as much attention as her companion. Maddie thought it best, for the sake of Daisy's self-confidence, not to point this out to her. Laurie Fox's notice was all she cared about, anyway. Happily, Lady Jervis seemed to be capitulating to Mr. Fox's charm, as well, so that when he gallantly offered to escort her back to the hotel, she declined the offer—a little coyly, Maddie was amused to observe—and went off in a taxi by herself.

Midnight came and went over their *ostendes* and *marennes vertes*, but none of them grew in the least sleepy. The level of wine in the gilt-necked champagne bottle in the ice pail beside them went down, but Daisy said she could not possibly grow more giddy than the laughter and excitement all around had already made her. But then the red-uniformed band struck up a waltz. Laurie and Daisy looked at each other as if wondering whether to dare convention and dance. And Maddie looked away from their flushed faces and saw something that sobered her with a shock.

Standing in the entrance, looking lethally handsome in top hat and evening cloak, stood Devin Grant. He was scanning the room for someone, and Maddie found herself holding her breath, terrified that it might be someone else. But it was not. He saw her, and for an instant their glances met over the heads of the golden young couples on the lower floor. Devin removed his cloak and hat and handed them to the doorman, all in one graceful motion; then he came toward her, cutting his way smoothly through the crowd, and before she could adjust even to the idea of his presence, he was standing in front of her. Neither spoke.

Laurie stood up, however, and Devin introduced himself to him. "Mr. Fox, I believe? How do you do." Laurie introduced Daisy, who, entranced by this unexpected arrival and clearly intrigued by his possible relation to Maddie, boldly invited him to join the party.

"Thank you. I will." He smiled at Daisy in a way that Maddie was glad he had never used on her and that clearly completed Daisy's capitulation to his charm. Then he signaled the waiter for a chair and pulled it up next to Maddie's.

"I see you are enjoying Paris, Miss Jervis," he said, and Maddie thought, why *hadn't* he ever smiled at her like that?

"Oh, yes!" Daisy exclaimed and revealed, "we've already been to the opera tonight," as if indulging in two forms of amusement in one night represented the height of dissipation.

"What was it?" Devin asked, and when Daisy looked puzzled, added, "the opera, I mean."

"Why, it was—" Daisy glanced at Laurie, who supplied, "*The Barber of Seville.*"

"Yes, all about a lady who is in love with her music teacher and writes a great many letters. Mama fell asleep in the second act and was too tired afterward to come here with us. Mad—Mrs. Malcolm and I got lost looking for the ladies' cloakroom, and we saw *dozens* of statues and paintings and gilt mirrors and . . . did you know, Mr. Grant, that the grand staircase is *all* marble?"

"So rumor has it."

Maddie stepped on Devin's foot, but he showed no sign of repentance for teasing Daisy, encouraging her instead into plying him with questions. He answered cheerfully, if, as Maddie suspected, not always truthfully, but at least Maddie had a little time to get her breath back.

She had been startled at just how breathless she felt merely sitting next to him. He had not yet spoken to her, nor touched her save to shake her hand in greeting, but she was acutely aware of his tall, masculine presence. Worse, she had been delighted to see him, a delight not at all diminished by the anger she had conjured up against him over the last few days. She needed those few moments Daisy provided her to recall that anger, but then it came out as simple, and unattractive, petulance.

"Have you been shadowing me all the way from London?" she asked him when Laurie finally asked Daisy to dance and took her away.

He laughed. "No, I expect you've learned to take care of yourself by now. I see you've even adopted a protégée, in fact. She's a nice girl."

"*Nice?*" Maddie's sense of humor surfaced to restore her equilibrium. "Is that all you can say after the effort I've spent on her? You should have seen her before I took her in hand."

"Very nice, then. Are you going to have her under your wing forever?"

There was something behind the question that Maddie wasn't quite sure she understood, but that unbalanced her again. She tried to disregard it. "Well, for as long as we're in Paris, I suppose."

"That's what I meant."

It was still there, that something.

"Not that I want to lose her, of course. I like Daisy."

"Of course."

He wasn't going to give anything else away, Maddie could see, and much to her own surprise, she found herself explaining, "I can't leave her alone with Laurie, for propriety's sake, but I do feel sometimes like the well-known fifth wheel."

He took the hint, letting her know he recognized it as such by grinning maddeningly at her. "I am at your service, Mrs. Malcolm, should you wish for an escort yourself on your . . . on whatever it is the three of you do together."

"Thank you, Mr. Grant. But may I remind you that you are also in my service for another reason? Perhaps you will be good enough to tell me what you've been doing about that . . . all this time."

She thought she saw a flash of anger in his gray eyes, and for an instant her heart leapt to her throat. She should not have prodded him like that. But he said only, "I have already seen your secretary." When she looked surprised, he added, "How do you suppose I found you tonight?"

"I should have guessed. Do you mean I'll have to wait to talk to Oliver before I hear whatever it is you have to report?"

"My dear, no one, not even an American, comes to Maxim's to talk about business. Get up. We're going to dance."

She ought to have refused, Maddie supposed, or at least exhibited some reluctance, but just then she wanted nothing more in the world than to waltz with Devin Grant at Maxim's, to join those dazzlingly beautiful lovers—for so they all seemed to be—on the dance floor. This was Paris, she told herself again, and believed it this time. She was going to enjoy it.

She gathered up her ivory satin skirts, glad now that she had endured the hours of standing still for them, for the look in his eyes when they took all of her in, from her upswept hair, studded with ivory and pearl rosettes, to her unadorned décolletage to the elegant folds at the waist of her gown and her high-heeled satin shoes. She felt herself preening like a cat and glanced up at him, smiling.

He took her hand in his, placing the other firmly around

her waist, and even through his glove and her satin she could feel the warmth of his fingers pressing into her back. She scarcely heard the tune the musicians struck up; she did not have to listen, for he led her effortlessly, pulling her a little closer in a turn, tugging at her other hand to guide in the other direction. It was like riding an ocean swell, and she reveled in the sensation of being carried along with no effort on her part.

It was warm in the room, and the air was heavy with the fragrance of the flowers massed in huge vases against the walls. The movement of the dance made Maddie's pulse race, but it was Devin's warm breath in her hair that made her feel as if she were floating weightlessly somewhere above common earth.

"You are magnificent," he whispered into her ear.

"What?"

She had closed her eyes, and so absorbed was she with the movement of the waltz and the multitude of sensations it roused in her that she was not certain she had heard him, only that his husky voice added yet another sensation. He laughed softly but did not repeat what he had said, and a moment later the music died, and with it the warmth and the movement and the sound of his voice.

Only the memory of his hands on her did not fade, even as they went out into the cool night and walked home silently, no longer daring to touch each other, even with Laurie and Daisy walking in front of them, unseeing and unhearing as they exchanged their own secrets in the night.

* * *

She was only a client, Grant kept telling himself. He could send written reports, or telephone her, or deal with her secretary. He had never mixed business with pleasure before, and now he knew why. He had, in short, not expected to want to see her—if only to look at her—so much.

He had certainly not expected to be so distracted by her heady perfume, her delicious skin so tantalizingly exposed above that unbelievably becoming gown, her magnificent body so little hidden beneath it despite the layers of satin and petticoats. But he *was* being distracted, and curse her and lecture himself as he might, he wasn't getting anything else done. At least not well.

Only too aware that he would never to able to sleep after that waltz at Maxim's, Grant had made up his mind to try to forget Madeleine Malcolm by doing something that needed to be done, something physical that would make him forget those other sensations she had imprinted on his body.

The Prince of Wales would be in Paris in six days, and Grant had done nothing about it. He would be staying at the Ritz, of course; when Cesar Ritz opened his magnificent new hotel the year before, the prince had been the first to change his allegiance to the new palace-away-from-home at 15, Place Vendôme.

"My dear fellow," the prince had said when Grant vainly suggested somewhere less ostentatious, "I ask of a hotel only that they treat me like a prince, but the Ritz does better—there I am already a king! The food is superb, the bath is as large as a whole room at the Bristol, and the maids are delightful.''

"And your suite faces the square—and a hundred windows that might hide an assassin.''

"I shall stay away from the windows.''

And that was as much as the prince would promise him, for talk of assassins never failed to make him peevish. So Devin had his work cut out for him.

His own room was on the floor above the one reserved for the prince and afforded him the same view across the square and precluded—he hoped—the possibility of anyone's breaking into the prince's suite immediately below. But to be certain of the security of the location, he decided to try himself to get into the reserved suite from the roof, to see if he could do it without being spotted. Attempting to think like a criminal, he dressed in black with a cap covering his hair, darkened his face with charcoal, and went up to the roof armed with a rope and some jeweler's tools to cut the glass with. He intended to replace the windows with shatterproof glass, in any case, so the Ritz could not complain about his little experiment.

The door to the roof was unlocked, already a bad sign; he made a mental note to inform the management. Once outside, however, he realized that the steep slope of the roof would probably discourage any but the most determined burglar, although assassins were notoriously single-minded, not to say foolhardy. It was all Devin could do to maintain his balance as he tied one end of his rope around a pair of chimneys. He glanced down as he took hold of the rope with both hands and adjusted his footing. He couldn't see the square from here, and he could not be seen; he would have to make a note to station a man on the roof across the way, or better still, at the top of the Vendôme column.

Letting rope out cautiously, Devin lowered himself as far as the gutter drain pipe and had another look down. Four stories below, the cobblestones of the Place Vendôme were now clearly visible, damp from the street cleaners' activities and gleaming in the lamplight. There were only two men in the square, walking unsteadily across it, as if on their way home from some late revelry; they did not look up. He checked the rope for firmness and let himself over the side of the building. The night was warm and still; if he dropped anything, the noise would echo from every corner of the square.

Directly below, as he had calculated, was the ledge of one of the windows of the prince's suite. The ledge, he noticed, was nearly as steeply pitched as the hotel roof; something as simple as greasing it might be sufficient to prevent anyone getting enough purchase to break in. He began to feel a little more satisfied with the building. It was a fortress, a formidable obstacle, all by itself.

Nevertheless, he let himself down gingerly until his feet touched the ledge, where there was just enough space for him to crouch down enough to reach the latch. He tested it, and it moved. No need to use the glass cutter, which was just as well because he wasn't sure he could reach his pocket from this position. He eased the window open and slid his body in over the sill, hips first for purchase.

Guessing that there was thick carpeting even just below

the window, he jumped in. His landing made no sound, and he let his breath out in a sigh of relief.

He listened and heard nothing. But instinct told him—too late—that there was something alive in the room.

"*Haut les mains!*"

Too startled to do anything else, he raised his hands automatically, still clutching the rope, however, so that it did not slide back out the window. Peering into the darkness, he could just make out a figure in a long white nightshirt, its arms stretched out in front of it. The metal of a pistol barrel glinted in the dim light. *Damn. There wasn't supposed to be anyone occupying the room!* The thought passed through his mind that someone had been posted guard without his knowledge. But then the draft from the window made the nightshirt move slightly, and he realized that the garment was too long and too flimsy to be a man's.

Unthinking, he tossed the rest of the rope coil at the figure and jumped to one side. But the gun didn't go off. The woman dropped it, muttered something, recovered, and made a lunge for the gun on the carpet.

Devin got there first, slamming one hand down over the weapon and the other over the woman's hand. She fell onto her side with a muffled cry, and when he touched her, she made a quick movement to roll over out of his reach. He let go of the pistol and took hold of her other hand, pinning her to the floor.

Still she said nothing, but the echo of a familiar perfume rose from her dark hair.

"Good God! Maddie!"

He couldn't see her face clearly, but he knew without a doubt it was she. She drew a sharp breath, confirming his instinctive recognition. She knew him, too.

"What are *you* doing here?" she hissed.

"I should ask you the same thing," he countered, still holding her to the floor.

"I paid for the key, which is more than you did!"

"This suite is supposed to be empty."

"Well, it isn't!"

That much was obvious. He almost laughed at the joke on him and made a move to release her. But then, realizing suddenly that she had nothing on under that delicate, almost transparent nightdress, he hesitated. She stopped wriggling, as if aware at the same time that the movement of her breasts against his arm had aroused him.

"Let me go."

Her voice was wary, but low and husky; she wasn't ready to scream for help yet. Unable to resist the temptation, he lowered himself on top of her again, feeling the whole of her long, luscious body along his. She moved her head, but he followed the movement, capturing her mouth easily with his own. Hers felt soft, yielding. He tested it lightly with his tongue, and the lips parted just long enough to let him enter. For a moment he thought she would let him go deeper into those delicious depths; he thought that she must know, too, that his body was meant to lie with hers like this, fitting so perfectly with it. He let one of her hands go to move his own down over the length of her, lingering at her breast and at the soft mound of her abdomen, before she began suddenly to struggle.

She tore her mouth away, and for a moment he could think of nothing but reclaiming it, tasting more of that sweetness that fired his imagination until he knew exactly what making love to her would be like, and he wanted it more than anything he could imagine.

But there was nothing flimsy about the woman beneath the soft silk. She stopped struggling, and he could feel her stiffen in readiness. She raised her knee abruptly, and he only just stopped her from hitting him in the groin. She did succeed in knocking him off balance, but he rolled over, leaping to his feet like a cat. But she was quick, too. Her hand reached out and found the pistol, and when he looked at her, she was on her knees and pointing it at him again. She was breathing hard, but he knew she had the advantage, and not just because of the pistol.

"Get out of here or I'll call for help."

Her voice was steady, but for some reason she was giving him a chance to get away unseen by anyone else. He hesitated only an instant. Far better to be thought a thief than a rapist.

But what a waste! he thought, then grinned and picked up the rope as he backed toward the window. In another ten seconds he was hanging off the side of the building again. This time he didn't wait to look down.

Chapter Twelve

GRANT never did get any sleep that night. He spent the remaining few hours before sunrise alternately cursing his stupidity for not checking to be certain that those rooms were in fact unoccupied and trying to rid his mind of the sensation of Madeleine Malcolm's all-too-desirable body under his.

What would she have done if he had gone right back— by her front door this time—and demanded to be let in? *Fool! What makes you think she wants you as much as you want her? God knows, she has no reason even to trust you.*

He spent an hour pacing his own room and wasting energy in useless conjecture and even more useless, if irresistible, fantasies about her. He had felt oddly protective of her, even when he'd had her in his physical power, as if he had been a third presence, watching her about to be violated by some fool who had stumbled into her room and was taking advantage of what he found. That protectiveness, that urge to guard her from himself, was all that had kept him from taking her there and then.

Finally, he pulled aside the dark curtains on his window to see that the sky was getting light over the rooftops, so he changed his clothes for the work he expected to do that day and went down to the desk to find out what he should have done in the first place.

"*Oui, monsieur*," the clerk told him, "the suite of the prince is reserved for the week coming, as arranged, but *pour maintenant* Madame Malcolm is using it. *Oui*, she is aware that she is required to change her rooms within the week, so that His Highness's usual suite can be made ready for him."

Devin hadn't shaved, and he had put on an old tweed coat and vest, with a frayed black tie knotted around his neck, so he was not surprised that the clerk eyed him suspiciously. He knew who Grant was, but he nevertheless maintained his professional discretion as far as refusing even to mention the number of the suite, much less to divulge why Madame Malcolm was in there in the first place. Devin had no desire to rub his nose in his own inefficiency by pressing him, so he let it go. At least he could be confident of the Ritz staff's remaining close-mouthed.

Then he went out into the cool morning air to do something else he should have done sooner. He paid a call on Claude Fournier.

* * *

Devin had met Fournier when he was a young, idealistic reporter for one of Paris's most popular daily newspapers—too idealistic to be satisfied for very long with having to report on social events and civic happenings. Their first encounter had been during Grant's first trip abroad with the prince, the year the Eiffel Tower was completed. The prince of course wanted to see the tower, and the newspapers of course wanted to report what he had to say about it, and Claude was among the more aggressive reporters who dogged the prince's every movement.

As the prince's trips abroad grew more frequent, Devin got to know and enjoy both Paris and his most useful contact there. He watched Claude's career blossom—if a career dodging libel suits and policemen's clubs could be said to blossom—with keen interest. When Jean Grave, the great leader of anarchist thought in France and editor of the influential weekly newspaper *La Revolte*, invited the young Fournier to join his staff, Claude leapt at the chance. And he picked just the right time to join the anarchist cause, which would reach its peak in Paris a few years later. Bombs rocked the city in those years, and violent verbal blasts from the anarchist reviews did nearly as much damage. Philosophers like Grave and revolutionaries like Vaillant, who was guillotined for throwing a bomb in the Chamber of Deputies, had little in common, but at the time neither group was above using the other as a means to an end.

Fournier started his own newspaper, *l'Indépendant*, in 1892 and used it the way small boys used slingshots, to tease and goad the adults on the street into paying attention to him. Devin had thought at the time that Claude positively reveled in the excitement and that it made him feel more alive to be constantly in danger of being closed down or thrown into jail.

But then the adults did sit up and take notice. In 1894, in the wake of the assassination of France's President Carnot by an Italian anarchist, emergency laws were passed to control the press. Fournier had a last moment of glory during the Trial of Thirty, when the best-known anarchist theorists were put on trial to try to prove they were responsible for the bombings. Claude's witty and satirical speech against the futile efforts of the authorities to find the real instigators made headlines in papers other than his own.

Claude kept his newspaper, but something happened to it after the trial. It lost many of its best writers, but what was worse, it lost its spirit. Rivals jeered at it, renaming it *Le Dépendant* when Claude actually wrote an editorial in support of the new government. Devin knew that Claude had simply decided to try to change what he did not like in France by working with the established authority instead of against it, but few of Fournier's other friends saw the change as anything but a betrayal. *L'Indépendant* changed, too, from an inky, slapdash, but lively weekly broadsheet to a slick, tired monthly review that was in greater peril of closing down from lack of revenue than from removal of its editor on sedition charges. And Claude was no longer a zealous young reporter; he was tired too.

The last time Grant saw Fournier was when he was in

Paris tracing the infamous valet Michel Lamont, and it was Claude who had discovered Lamont's background and connections and had put Devin on to the man called Frank Hartwell. Grant had attempted, in disguise, to infiltrate the anarchist group led by Hartwell and found himself being interviewed—as if he had applied for a position as a clerk in a bank—by the man himself, who spoke English with an accent Devin couldn't place, but well enough to be suspicious of this too-eager recruit. He was rejected for the "job" and never got to Hartwell again, although God knew, he'd tried.

Devin tracked Claude down having breakfast with two of his colleagues in a workingman's café on the boulevard Saint-Martin. They had been there since the café opened, judging by the pile of saucers growing on the marble-topped table, and seemed in no hurry to get back to work, although it was more likely that there was no work to get back to. Marius Galembert, a middle-aged man with un-kempt hair and wire-rimmed glasses, sat next to Claude, reading *Le Matin*; Jean-Pierre Landy, a good-looking young man with long hair and a scar on his chin, was playing solitaire at the next table. Devin had met Galembert before but knew Landy only by sight. None of them was talking to the others. Fournier was smoking a cigarette and staring off into space.

Devin walked into Claude's range of vision and saw his

presence register on the sleepy eyes. They widened in surprise, and Claude jumped up to embrace him.

"*Bonjour, mon ami! Comment allez-vous?* When did you arrive in Paris?"

"Two days ago," Devin said, and Claude looked pleased that he had come to see him so quickly.

Galembert got up, shook Devin's hand without saying a word, and removed himself to Landy's table. Landy looked up, nodded, and went back to his cards.

"Sit down, sit down," Fournier said. "What will you take? Coffee, yes?"

"Coffee, yes," Devin said and signaled the waiter who, with a quick balletic movement, brought them two large cups and a plate of rolls. Fournier downed the coffee at once but ignored the food.

"Why aren't you dead yet?" Devin asked. "You never eat anything, that I can see."

Fournier smiled. "But this is Paris, my friend. You breathe, and nourishment enters by the nostrils. Take a deep breath and *regardez!* You see my meaning."

He suited the action to the words, but Devin preferred the coffee. "I know what you mean, Claude; it becomes clear, or rather not so clear, as soon as one steps off the train. But I'm afraid we English cannot live on air, however potent."

"Since you have so little air in your great, clumsy London," Claude countered, replaying an old theme between them, "I am not surprised you come to Paris. You are here for pleasure this time, I hope?"

When Devin did not respond, Fournier glanced at him. "So. Business, is it? Not the same as before?"

"I'm afraid so. Things have got more complicated. I need your help again, Claude. I need information."

Fournier shrugged. "*Hélas*. I might have guessed. If I can tell you, I will . . . on condition."

Devin smiled, knowing what was coming. "What condition this time?"

"You must take me to dinner at a new little bistro I have discovered on the rue Caulaincourt. There is a little waitress there who is—" He kissed his finger to his lips in the classic Gallic compliment. "And she has no doubt a sister or a friend. They always do."

"I will buy you dinner, my friend, but I must decline the sweet."

Claude raised an eyebrow. "What is this? You cannot have had a surfeit of—what do you English call them?— crumpets, since you arrived?"

"No, rather an insufficiency of *madeleines*."

Claude's black eyes lit with curiosity, but when Grant offered nothing more, he shrugged. "Ah, well, I will not make you explain that. The ways of the English in love have always been incomprehensible to me . . . and yours the most mysterious of all. You are too discreet, *mon ami*, too English. *Eh bien*, I do not even know why I call you a friend. You are everything I am against."

"I'm a workingman, too, Claude."

"But see whom you work *for*! You have been in the army, too. The archbishop of Canterbury is no doubt a cousin. It is the poor, like us, who lead real lives, not the privileged like you and your—hah!—employer.''

"Put it in an editorial, Claude.''

Fournier laughed, with no rancor behind it. "And too sure of yourself also, like those equally useless friends and cousins. But what can I do with you? You are too old to teach. Tell me instead what information you need. I warn you that I have not the resources I once did.''

"You have just grown lazy, my friend," Devin said. "You may not have any new resources, but I cannot believe you have lost contact with the old ones, and those will suffice. I am looking for an American, an innocent who has become involved with the more dangerous kind of anarchist. The rumor is that he is dead, but I must prove it.''

"What is this innocent's name?''

"Malcolm. Edward Malcolm, usually called Teddy.''

"Bah! Such an English name!" Claude pulled a battered reporter's notebook out of his pocket and handed it to Devin, who wrote the name on a blank page. The Frenchman glanced at it, then handed the notebook over to Landy.

"*Connaissiez ce type?*''

Landy glanced at the name, shook his head, and passed the notebook to Galembert, who said, "*Anglais?*''

"*Americain.*''

"*Non.*''

Fournier tore the sheet out of the notebook, lit his cigarette to it, and turned back to Devin. "I am sorry, my friend. But I will keep this name in my head and make inquiries for you.''

"I would be grateful." Devin took a swallow of the bitter coffee and added, "I'm also looking for information about a plot—an assassination."

Landy and Galembert, who had given no indication of hearing any other part of the conversation, raised their heads in unison at that. Fournier laughed.

"*Mon Dieu*, Devin! Have I not just reminded you that this is not London? We are not so free as you imagine to speak of such things here. Such as we especially must take care."

"Nevertheless," Devin said, leaning closer to Fournier and lowering his voice, "although you may not speak of them, you know about them. What have you heard?"

Fournier glanced quickly around him. The tables immediately next to them were empty, but Landy and Galembert picked up their chairs and pulled them up to the single table just the same.

"There is nothing new," Galembert said. "No one has the energy to start that again."

Landy said something rude that even Devin could not translate. There was no keeping up with the young and their slang, he thought, and asked Landy, "What about you? Have you heard something?"

"Yes," Landy replied in English. "Yesterday I hear a rumor of a foreign group that is come to France. Who they are and who their leader is, I do not hear. But it is said they plan . . . what you said."

"The target?"

Landy took Fournier's notebook and drew a little symbol on it, then turned the paper around in Devin's direction. He had drawn a miniature crown.

Devin looked into Landy's eyes, decided he could trust him, and said to Fournier, "I will take you all to supper tomorrow, Claude. And if any one of you finds out anything else, I will do more. I will pay for the printing of a new number of *l'Indépendant* each time one of you brings me some piece of information that I can use. Agreed?"

Galembert's eyes lit up behind his wire-rimmed glasses, and he was the first to reach out his hand to shake Devin's. "*D'accord!*"

Landy shook his hand, too, and Fournier smiled. "*Mon ami*, you come like a much-needed new broom to sweep the cobwebs out of our minds. We will help you. It is a promise."

They parted then, after making plans to meet the next night at Fournier's little bistro. Landy and Galembert got up and went off in the direction of the Place de la République. Grant went the other way, whistling softly to himself.

In another café, on the other side of the street, Oliver Drummond crossed Claude Fournier's name off Kropotkin's list. It was just as well he had not approached the editor of *l'Indépendant* at once. Now he would have to find out what had been said in some other way, but at least he had something interesting to report to Mrs. Malcom. . . . if she wanted to hear it.

Oliver turned his chair slightly so that his back was to the street and gave in to a sigh. He wasn't quite sure—and if Louise knew, she was keeping it to herself—what Mrs. Malcolm's attitude toward Grant, and for that matter toward finding her husband, was any more. She seemed to swing between extremes of wanting to take some definite action, to drop the whole case, to force Grant to tell her what she wanted to hear—whether he knew what that was or not—and to have nothing further to do with him. Oliver could only try to read her moods and tell her what she wanted to hear when she asked to hear it.

And then there was Grant. For a man who said he preferred to work alone, he had a large number of friends. And Oliver, who would have liked to talk to some of them, was on his own until Grant decided to let him in on what he was finding out from Fournier and God knew whom else. He hadn't mentioned knowing Fournier before, and when Grant came to the hotel last night, looking for Mrs. Malcolm, he hadn't said anything about meeting Fournier today.

Presumably, Grant also preferred to act on whatever opportunities arose, without having to consult anyone else. Oliver wished he would make the first move to restore their mutual trust, but for the time being Oliver could only be observant—and patient.

"Oui, m'sieur?"

Oliver looked up. He must have signaled the waiter without even being aware that he had done so. He looked down again at his coffee cup. It was empty. It was also very early in the morning, but he suspected it was going to be a long day.

"A pernod, *s'il vous plaît*."

Chapter Thirteen

MADDIE tried not to remember, but the mystery of it teased continually at the back of her mind, and when it sometimes came to the front, she gave in, not entirely with reluctance, to remembering.

There were two mysteries, really. What *had* Devin Grant been looking for in her hotel suite in the middle of the night? She could not imagine it had anything to do with his search for Teddy; he had been genuinely surprised to find her there. Or did he believe she was keeping some evidence about Teddy from him and, thinking for some reason that she was out, had decided to look for it instead of asking? That seemed more likely, even though she had nothing—that she was aware of—that he could possibly find useful.

Perhaps he had known she was there. He was wearing one of his disguises, after all, in which she would not have recognized him if he had not . . .

· Surely he had not come to . . .

Her mind drew circles around that second mystery, afraid to focus on it too clearly. She had awakened that night without really knowing why. There had been no sound to disturb her sleep, only an instinct, possibly the same instinct that had made her decide earlier to keep her pistol underneath the bed. She had reached down very carefully and run her hand along the carpet until it came to the cold black metal, then had drawn the weapon slowly up and clutched it to her nightgown.

She listened. Still there was no noise, so she pushed the bedclothes aside and stood up, back against the wall to steady herself, and focused her eyes on the square of the window. It had become a ritual for Louise to pull the heavy nighttime drapes across the windows and for Maddie then to pull them aside again, for she hated sleeping in a closed room, like a cell. So only the flimsy white outside curtains covered the window, and it seemed an eternity that she stood there, holding the gun, before suddenly a figure appeared through them. The movement had been so quick, it hadn't even registered on her widened eyes.

"Raise your hands!" She hadn't even noticed at the time that she had said it in French.

The man obeyed but did not seem frightened. He was very self-possessed, in fact, and stood perfectly still waiting for his eyes to adjust to the darkness so he could make her out. She thought she ought to say something more, to make a move, but then he did, lunging at her so suddenly that she dropped the pistol even before he reached her. She fell to the floor, with the intruder on top of her, and when she tried to reach for the gun, his hands had clamped down on hers, pinning her to the floor.

It was then that she recognized him. But strangely, instead of relief, she felt fear for the first time. She drew in a sharp breath and retaliated the only way she could, with anger.

"What are you doing here?"

Devin didn't release his grip, and she felt an unreasonable panic rising in her throat. She had to force herself to remain absolutely still, hoping that he would let her go if she didn't struggle or scream for help. But even then, she knew what he would do next.

At least, her body knew. She could feel the tingle start in her stomach and radiate outward, and her breasts, as if of their own volition, tightened against his chest. For an instant she could see his eyes gleam in the darkness, and she gazed up at him, unable to speak. The light in his eyes shifted as he looked down at her mouth. Then his head followed his gaze, and his own mouth grazed her lightly, went away, then came back and lingered a little longer, still barely touching her.

Involuntarily, she raised her head a fraction to meet him, to offer him more. He took the invitation, probing with his tongue, then invading her, exploring and seeking the secrets she kept from him there; and she wanted at that moment nothing more than to tell him, to show him, everything he wanted. He felt so good, so close to her. His hands released hers and began to stroke her gently, moving down her body leaving a trail of longing until every inch of her wanted what her mouth had.

He lifted his head from hers and she moved slightly, just enough to see the metal of the pistol that lay inches away from her outstretched hand. She stiffened, brought back to reality by the sight of the weapon, and this time she was able to act almost quickly enough. She jerked her knee up suddenly, and he barely escaped the insulting blow she aimed at him, cursing and rolling over to get out of her reach. She reached out to snatch up the pistol and was on her knees pointing it at him almost before he had regained his feet.

He looked at her for an instant, as if judging how likely she was to shoot him, then guessed correctly and backed toward the window.

"Wait!"

The word came out before she knew she was going to say it. She didn't know why she did. But it was still too late. He was gone.

Maddie drifted through the next days as if she had no connection with anything going on around her. She heard what was said to her and did what was expected of her, but it was as if she were watching someone else perform the motions. She could not understand why no one else seemed to notice that she was not really there, but they behaved as if everything were perfectly normal.

"Florence has decided to set up a _salon_," Geoffrey Wingate was saying to her and to Daisy and Lady Jervis one afternoon, perhaps two days later. Maddie looked around and saw that she had dressed herself in a perfectly suitable, even attractive, new teagown in pale peach with cream-colored lace trimming, that her favorite hat with the peach-dyed feathers seemed to be securely fastened, and that she had somehow got herself to the garden restaurant of the Ritz without stumbling. She even remembered that they were waiting for Laurence Fox to join them for tea.

It was a warm, lazy kind of afternoon, such that Maddie thought her lethargic mood probably seemed natural to the others. Good. They wouldn't mind, then, if she did not talk very much. Lady Jervis, who was taking the opportunity to catch up with her travel journal, would certainly not notice. Geoffrey, who was watching her out of the corner of his eye, may have been concerned but would not press her to join in the conversation.

Fortunately, Daisy was still capable of ordinary polite small talk. "What is a salon?" she asked in her ingenuous way, and Geoffrey Wingate explained that many of the old Parisian aristocrats held salons, or open house, once or twice a week in order to keep up on the latest gossip, introduce their friends to some new musical or literary talent, and generally keep better days alive in their fading memories. Maddie wondered vaguely why Florence would want to do such a thing, but when Geoffrey explained it to Daisy, that young woman at least thought it a splendid idea.

"It seems to me an excellent way to meet people," Daisy said. "One begins by inviting one's friends on the condition that each brings a guest, and the next time, the guest brings a guest, and *voilà!*"

"Is it customary in Paris to do such things in one's hotel suite?" Lady Jervis lifted her pencil long enough to ask.

The Wingates had, despite everyone else's being at the Ritz, remained at the Bristol, for which Maddie had been grateful, even if she also felt a little mean for being content with a little less of Florence's company. Still, the Bristol was only across the square from the Ritz, and Florence could come to see her, too.

She had been glad earlier that morning when she encountered Geoffrey by himself, however, while she and Daisy were having coffee at the Café de la Paix. Geoffrey had been out walking, and with his malacca cane and pale blue coat and white hat had looked very much the Parisian *flâneur*. He had stopped to chat, in that pleasant way he had, and he seemed to sense something of Maddie's mood, for after one acute glance at her, he did not attempt to draw her into the conversation. Instead, he expressed a wish that she might feel more like herself later, and they agreed to meet for tea.

"I did suggest that renting a small house might be more suitable," he was saying now, "but Florence said we would only waste time redecorating and hiring servants. And you know, just between us, that it is as likely as not that Florence will become bored with this new idea as quickly as she has taken it up—so the hotel remains the best venue for the time being."

Geoffrey passed the plate of macaroons to Daisy, who declined a second one, having made up her mind to slim down to do justice to her elegant new clothes. Today she was dressed—"delightfully *jeune fille*," Geoffrey told her—in a blue-and-white shirtwaist dress with strips of lace down the front of the bodice and a large straw hat with a blue ribbon hanging down the back. When she and Maddie had arrived, arm in arm, Daisy had cast a comprehensive glance around the garden, where a number of elegant ladies were already seated at the round, linen-covered tables under the striped umbrellas. She had apparently decided that she could hold her own with any of them, for she had not given them a second glance since.

Maddie had to admire the quick way Daisy was turning herself into a belle, having been given only a little shove in the right direction. Daisy had not lost her charming directness, however, which only added to her appeal. Maddie decided that Laurie Fox didn't stand a chance; it was only a matter of time.

In a few minutes, Laurie arrived at their table. "Oh, there you all are!" he exclaimed. He shook hands with everyone, then pulled up one of the wicker chairs, sat down in it, and produced a parcel from his coat pocket. "Daisy, your photos have turned out splendidly. Have a look."

Daisy had taken Maddie's advice and asked Laurie to help her purchase the latest model of Kodak camera and show her how to use it. He had also offered to have the pictures developed by a French photographer who had a darkroom for the purpose. Now he spread the first batch out on the tablecloth to be admired.

"Oh, look," Daisy said, "here we are at Notre Dame. How you are scowling, Mama! I believe you thought it was somehow irreligious of me to take a picture of a church.''

''But it's a good likeness,'' Maddie assured her.

''Of the church,'' Laurie whispered to Maddie, just loudly enough to make Daisy giggle.

Nearly all the likenesses were good, since Daisy had no qualms about ''shooting'' moving objects and anything that took her fancy. Laurie had instructed her in the mechanical use of the machine but had refused to advise her on her subject matter; the result was like a family album full of Daisy's friends—and even a few perfect strangers—enjoying Paris.

''Here you are looking into Fouquet's window,'' Geoffrey said, handing Maddie a side view of her bending over slightly to examine what she remembered now was a pretty cameo brooch, which she subsequently bought to send to her mother.

''Good gracious. I don't remember your taking that one, Daisy.''

''That's what's called a candid shot,'' Daisy told her. ''Do I have that right, Mr. Fox? When the subject is unaware of being photographed.''

''That's what's known as being sly,'' Geoffrey said. ''And don't you ever do it to *me*, young woman!''

''Oh, I needn't do so with you, sir, for you pose so well,'' Daisy told him, showing Maddie a picture of Geoffrey standing in front of the Ritz.

''Unfortunately, the Vendôme column seems to be growing out of my hat,'' Geoffrey objected.

"Does it really?" Daisy took the picture back and showed it, ruefully, to Laurie. "I never thought of that."

"Well, you'll think of it next time, won't you? That's what's known as poor composition."

"That's what is known as learning from experience," Maddie said, making everyone laugh, including Daisy, so that when Laurie produced another roll of film and helped her to load her camera, even Maddie got into the merry spirit of the party posed around the garden restaurant table to have their image captured for posterity, and Daisy declared that her new efforts would be the best yet.

"Perhaps you can take some pictures at Mrs. Wingate's salon," Daisy suggested to Laurie, "and show me how to use the camera indoors."

"No, thank you very much," Laurie protested, making a little bow in Geoffrey's direction. "No offense, sir, but I offered my services to your wife as her protégé of the week, but she seemed to consider photography not a sufficiently elevated art form for her debut as a hostess. I believe I have been displaced by a Hungarian violinist."

"Good lord!" said Geoffrey. "Not that melancholy-looking young fellow whose hair keeps falling into his eyes? I can't imagine how he can see to play."

"I understand they play from their souls," Maddie said. "Perhaps they don't have to see."

"Unfortunately, we shall have to see *him*. I am instructed, by the way, to invite you all for Thursday at four in the afternoon, but if you prefer to have another engagement, I quite understand."

But no one declined the invitation, however indifferently

delivered. At least, as Maddie told Louise when she was later being dressed for the occasion, curiosity on the part of her guests would guarantee the success of Florence's first salon, if not her subsequent efforts.

Florence had improved on her spacious hotel suite by adding extra lighting and an Aubusson carpet laid over the hotel's for the occasion. A buffet table had been set up along the windows facing the Place Vendôme, for Florence had hit upon a surprisingly effective blend of South Carolina hospitality and English afternoon tea as a backdrop to her melancholy violinist. This young man managed, despite his hair and the abundance of potted palms surrounding him, to perform creditably enough that people were even pausing to listen to him now and then—between the more important business of exchanging gossip and commenting on other people's looks and social credentials. When Maddie, Daisy, and Lady Jervis arrived, their hostess was not even to be seen amid the crush.

Laurie Fox, who had brought a camera despite its lack of artistic acceptability, looked around for somewhere to set it up. Lady Jervis searched for someone who spoke English and chose a plump woman in an unfashionable hat who was sitting on a sofa by herself trying to look unconcerned that no one seemed interested in speaking to her.

Maddie looked for Devin Grant and didn't see him. She did not know whether to be relieved or not.

She finally tracked down her hostess, however, and said, "You are a resounding success, Florence. One can scarcely move without tripping over a cosmetics king or an artist's agent, not to mention their wives."

Florence sighed. "_And_ their mistresses. But they are all _Americans_, my dear, and a few English, of course. I had so hoped for a Rothschild, or at least some minor _baronne_ or _comtesse_."

"I understand that Parisians, particularly Parisian ladies of the old families, are reticent about accepting the hospitality of those outside their circle," Maddie said consolingly. "Particularly foreigners."

"Besides," Florence said, disregarding even the suggestion of her being regarded as foreign, "Viktor promised faithfully to bring some of his musician friends, but not a one has put in an appearance."

"I had no idea you wanted to become a patroness of the arts, Florence."

"My dear, you know I am an utter ignoramus when it comes to anything of the sort, but think of being able to say one was the first to recognize the next Liszt or Sardou or Seurat!"

Maddie refrained from asking how one who could not distinguish merit in an acknowledged work of art could be the first to discern such merit in the infancy of the artist's career, but she thought it best not to add to Florence's frustration.

"What about that young man by the window?" she asked instead. "Judging by his clothes and the eager way he is consuming your little sandwiches, he may well be a starving artist.''

Florence raised her lorgnette to survey the too-slender but still handsome young man. She looked annoyed for a moment but said, ''He must be one of Viktor's friends, after all. I'll go and welcome him.''

She drew a determined breath and made her way through the crowd like a ship parting the waves, and Maddie felt a pang of sympathy for her young victim, who looked startled when Florence approached him and introduced herself.

She watched them for a while, trying to view the stranger as Laurie Fox might. She had been a little surprised to see how people she knew in Laurie's photographs sometimes appeared different from her perceptions of them, and she had tried to learn from him to be more observant, to cultivate her ability to see people as keenly as he did, so that she would not be so surprised.

Despite his youth and general resemblance to every other young man Maddie had seen on the streets of Paris, there was something different about this one—a kind of haunted look, as if he had recently passed through an illness, or even some danger. He was well dressed, but his cuffs were frayed; and although his shoes had been expensive when new, they had since been repaired several times. He held himself stiffly, as if ready to run if the danger returned; yet his youth softened the posture enough that even Florence, who was talking intently to him, gave him a motherly squeeze of the shoulder.

But then Maddie saw his eyes and unexpectedly snapped

out of the lethargy that had been weighing her down for days.

"Someone you know?" Geoffrey Wingate's voice in her ear startled her.

"No—that is, I'm sure I've never seen him before. But there is something familiar about him."

"That's my wife."

Maddie smiled, but the look of sheer hatred that she had seen in the young man's eyes was still there, as if it were as fixed as their pale blue color. He was probably behaving perfectly nicely to Florence, not even aware that his eyes belonged somewhere else.

"Geoffrey, what do you know about anarchists?"

"*Dansons la Ravachole, Vive le son, De l'explosion,*" he sang softly. When Maddie looked at him, puzzled, he said, "Ravachol was an anarchist, one of the radical stripe, but like many others, not very efficient. He bungled the murder of a lawyer—couldn't find the right apartment and so blew up the whole building, fortunately with no serious injuries. They guillotined him and made a hero out of him."

"Peter Kropotkin said not all anarchists are like that, like the newspaper caricatures."

"The illustrators must get their images from somewhere. Besides, even one half-educated fanatic like Ravachol can do more damage than a dozen civilized intellectuals like Kropotkin."

"Do you think the young man standing with Florence might be such a fanatic?"

Geoffrey studied the boy for a moment. "There hasn't

been an incident of that kind in France for five years, but yes, he reminds me of someone, too."

"Who?"

"Emile Henry. He had that same cold look, although he was just a boy, too. When they asked him why he threw a bomb into a crowded railroad station café, he said he had waited until he could kill as many people as possible."

Now Maddie wished that Devin Grant were there. His solid presence would have warded off the chilly sensation, so like that she had felt the day she arrived in Paris, that now struck her again. It occurred to her, too, that she knew too much about anarchism and not nearly enough about anarchists. What sort of haunted young men were they, the Ravachols and Henrys? And how could Teddy be one of them? What could have changed him so?

Then she had an idea. She looked around for Laurie Fox and, as she expected, found him off in a quiet corner setting up a camera on a tripod. He had aimed it in the direction of the young violinist who, despite his air of detachment and devotion to his music, was aware of being a target and had arranged himself in a more aesthetically pleasing posture.

"He's a perfect boor," Daisy pronounced when Maddie joined her and Laurie, "but so picturesque, don't you think? Such soulful eyes!"

"Have you see that fair-haired young man by the window?" Maddie asked. "He seems to be one of the same ilk."

Laurie looked in the direction she indicated, and his eyes brightened. "Oh, yes, very good. Like one of Lautrec's café idlers. I'll do him...candidly, while he still looks like himself, then I'll ask him if he'll pose.''

Laurie moved his tripod and aimed his camera lens at the young man, who moved his head toward the window just then.

''Blast,'' Laurie said and changed the plate.

He focused again and disappeared under the short black cloth attached to the back of the camera, waiting for his subject to turn his head in his direction again.

The young man's conversation with Florence had become more animated, Maddie noticed. In fact, Florence was speaking angrily to him. Maddie could not hear what was being said, but she found herself holding her breath, hoping that Laurie would take the photograph before the boy walked off in a huff.

Then he turned at last...and saw the camera.

What little color there had been in his face drained out of it. He reacted instinctively, throwing the glass in his hand at the camera. It missed, landing noiselessly on an empty sofa behind Laurie, who came out from under the cloth to say, ''What in heaven—?'' Together, Maddie and Daisy moved their heads toward the door.

But the young man had disappeared.

Chapter
Fourteen

NO one but Maddie, Daisy Jervis, and Laurence Fox had been aware of the immediate cause of the mysterious young man's abrupt departure from Florence's salon, and none of them could imagine the real reason behind his aversion to cameras.

Thinking quickly, Maddie asked Laurie if he had snapped the shutter before that glass had been pitched at him, but he had only the spoiled plate he had exposed before that. She asked him to develop it anyway, intending to tell Oliver Drummond as much as she could remember about the young man and to instruct him to find out whatever else he could in case the young man proved to be connected with the anarchist group Teddy had been involved in. Such an association would at least account for his skittishness about being photographed. A photograph, however blurred, could identify someone to the police.

Laurie, as usual, asked no awkward questions, and

when Florence, still looking a little flushed, complained to them that people who left without thanking their hostess had no manners whatsoever, Laurie agreed without enlightening her and diverted Florence's attention from the wet spot on her sofa by asking her to pose for him with Viktor. Maddie smiled at him gratefully. One could not be sure about Viktor, either, and a likeness of him might also come in useful.

"Laurie," she said, when he escorted her and Daisy back across the square to the Ritz, "whatever became of the photographs you took of Florence? I don't remember seeing them anywhere in her suite."

He frowned and said, "They weren't there, although I can't tell you why. Mrs. Wingate received the parcel I sent from London, thanked me profusely, paid me, and said she was going to send them home to her friends. I had assumed she would keep one or two for herself, but it seems not."

"She was dreadfully keen to be in the illustrateds, too," Daisy said. "Only because Mrs. Malcolm was, of course."

"That's the other odd thing," Laurie said. "She changed her mind, saying Mr. Wingate wouldn't like it."

"That seems unlikely," Maddie said. "I'm sure Geoffrey goes along with any whim Florence takes into her head, as you see from this salon nonsense. There must have been some other reason she did not want to tell you."

"Well, of course. She knew she could not hope to compete with *you*," Daisy offered. Maddie smiled at Daisy, grateful for her loyalty but unconvinced that Florence had a hidden jealous streak in her nature.

"Or she simply did not care for the way the pictures turned out," Laurie said. "You know that I would not be insulted to be told that—people see themselves in different ways, after all—but Mrs. Wingate may have thought she was sparing my feelings."

They finally agreed that this was the most logical explanation, but Maddie was left with the suspicion that logic had nothing to do with it.

It was another mystery, but not one that occupied her mind for very long. She was more interested in the partially satisfactory image Laurie's plate turned up of the skittish young man, his facial features blurred, but the rest of his head and clothing quite clear. Oliver had once told her that it was sometimes easier to identify someone by the shape of his ears than anything else, so Maddie hopefully presented him with both that photograph and the better likeness of Viktor Kemeny.

Maddie had little real hope of connecting the young man to Teddy, however. The more she thought about it, the more difficult it was to imagine Teddy succumbing to the kind of desperation Geoffrey Wingate at least considered a common trait among those whose allegiance to anarchism took the form of reckless acts of violence.

Teddy had never been reckless—careless, perhaps, but too fond of his comforts to toss them away because some spellbinder talked him into joining his cause.

Unless he hadn't stayed with it. What if he'd gone to France on his own, rather than to meet someone? Suppose he'd never even come to Paris but had gone on to Rome or Vienna or goodness knew where? Maddie's heart sank at the thought of spending years in a search that might ultimately be fruitless.

And yet . . .

She had not been able to shake that feeling that came to her when she first arrived—that Paris was somehow going to be the end of her search. Here she would find out what had really happened to Teddy.

Now she would have to make Devin Grant show himself.

She searched her mind for a bait that would lure him out of wherever he was hiding, but it came to her only when she glanced into her mirror on the way to breakfast one morning. She stopped to look at herself, wondering how he really saw her. As the American Beauty Rose? She doubted that; he was not taken in by the kind of artifice Laurie had applied to get that look from her. But there were other kinds, and she considered them for a moment, formulating a plan in her mind. Devin Grant had never shown himself to be a knight errant, but he was at least a gentleman and ought to respond automatically to certain situations. It might work. If not . . . well, it was a lovely day and she would still get a pleasant walk out of it.

In any case, it was not too soon to throw Laurie and Daisy together without the dampening presence of Maddie or Lady Jervis playing nursemaid, so when the two young people came to collect her to go and climb the Eiffel Tower, she pretended that she had completely forgotten an appointment at the milliner's for that day and encouraged them to go by themselves. They insisted, however, in dropping her off at her destination, so that Maddie had to quickly invent one, and she found herself, when their cab had departed and she stepped out of the doorway she had hidden in, in the middle of the rue du Faubourg-Saint Honoré, by herself.

"You should have told them it was Worth's," she scolded herself. "At least that's close to the hotel."

But if the direction was wrong, the possibilities remained, so instead of taking another cab, she turned and began walking in the direction of the Seine, conscious of the curious glances of passersby and the raised hat of one gentleman whom she pretended not to see. After a few minutes, however, as she crossed the rue Royale, she forgot to be self-conscious and began to look around her, breathing the air of Paris deep into her lungs and its beauties into her imagination as well as her eyes.

She had been aware of something different about this city since she arrived, something that had not been due solely to her own morbid fancies. Whatever it was seemed to make every feeling more intense, whether happy or unhappy. Parisians probably took it for granted, breathing it in with the sharp, fragrant air. It couldn't be isolated, so for now Maddie too just took deep gulps of it as she walked. By the time she entered the Garden of the Tuileries, where lovers strolled and starched nursemaids played ball with their small charges and where chestnut trees rustled in the light breeze, her mind had cleared and she was thinking quite contentedly about nothing at all. She smiled at the organ grinder playing next to the statue of Atalanta and gave him a coin.

She and Daisy has already taken an orienting tour of the museums, but Daisy had not been eager to spend much time in them, moving quickly from one painting to the next, admiring the bright colors or the way a fold of cloth looked so real she could touch it (and did). Maddie's education in the arts had probably been no more extensive than Daisy's, but the art mistress of the private school Maddie had attended had been so enthusiastic about her subject that Maddie had caught a little of her passion and was interested in seeing the originals of the works Miss Milsom had described.

So she had memorized from Lady Jervis's Baedeker the plan of the Louvre, and now she went directly up the Grand Staircase to the Long Gallery. For a few minutes, she walked slowly past the Titians, content simply to let her eyes fill with them, reserving her guidebook to study later.

She had just passed in front of the *Holy Family* when she became aware of someone standing just behind her. She knew who it was. She had been expecting him.

"Are you following me again, Mr. Grant?" she said, without turning around. The lingering narcotic effect of the Parisian air made her smile, and she did not want him to see that. Not just yet.

"It's easier when you're on foot."

There was silence for a few minutes as Maddie walked to the next painting. But she was more aware of him, even without looking at him, than of the painting in front of her. She was certain that if she turned around, the sight of him would be no less pleasing than the masterpiece in front of her. They did not touch, either, but there was something between them, like static electricity, that bound them. She sensed that he was embarrassed, but this seemed so unlikely that she began to doubt her perceptions.

"I'm relieved that you do sometimes remember that you are a gentleman," she said, deliberately provoking him.

"I'm sorry," he said then, sounding as if he meant it, "about the other night."

She had been right; it made her feel better—and bolder—to know that she was. She wondered which way she would have to move to brush lightly against him, as if by accident. But no, he was apologizing. She would have to say something. It came out more kindly this time.

"What _were_ you doing there, Devin?"

"Those were supposed to be the prince's rooms."

Of course! she realized. How could she have forgotten that? At least the first mystery was easily solved.

"I was experimenting, to see if he would be safe there from . . . break-ins, and so on."

"Has he never stayed at the Ritz before?"

"It's different this time."

She sensed that she was treading on delicate ground now, and she no longer had any desire to punish him by prying into areas he did not want probed and that she did not need to know about anyway.

"I'm sorry, too," she said.

He made no reply, and she moved on to the next painting, waiting until she felt more capable of ordinary, everyday conversation, until she was able to force her attention back to the paintings.

"They say Titian's women are so beautiful," she said then, "but I can't see it."

"It's the hair," he said, after a moment. "You can see it better in his nonreligious work."

She turned around abruptly then, and, as she'd suspected, he wasn't looking at the painting at all, but at her.

"Mine isn't red," she said.

"I'll bet it is in the sunlight." There was a hint of a smile in his voice, as if he were testing her receptiveness. But what did he mean by that? He hadn't ever seen her in the sunlight that she could recall, at least not without her hat and veil.

"Have you seen the impressionists' exhibition at the Luxembourg Museum?" he asked.

"I've seen prints of some of their work."

"And were not impressed, I see. It's different with the originals. Shall I show you?"

She looked up at him. This was absurd. He was asking to escort her to the museum as if he were eighteen years old and they'd just been introduced by their aunts. But she felt just as awkward and didn't know why.

"Thank you," she said, resisting the impulse to curtsey, "I think I'd like that."

They went out the river entrance of the museum and crossed to the Left Bank on foot. Maddie had never ventured to that side of the river before, and she looked around curiously. It was an older part of Paris, with narrow streets leading off the main boulevards and lined by small, sometimes crazily leaning houses. There were shops on the ground level of many of them, selling everything from fresh fish and vegetables to used shoes and clothing. Devin pointed out landmarks, not the usual ones, but the house where Victor Hugo had once lived and a square that still showed scars from the barricades thrown up by the Communardes in 1871. He had an anecdote to go with every café they passed, and soon the constraint eased between them, so that when they entered the Musée de Luxembourg they were actually laughing. But then they walked into the exhibition room, and Maddie drew a sharp breath.

He had been right. Miss Milsom's prints and book reproductions were only a pale imitation of the real thing, as if Laurie had tried to capture them on film. The essence was different.

She looked up to see if there were a skylight in the roof, but there was not. The light came almost entirely from the paintings, large and small, hung closely together around the room. They were all landscapes, and they all seemed at first to be of the sky. Maddie walked up to one, but unlike the Titians, a closer examination told her nothing. She had to back up several steps before the splashes of white and color re-composed themselves into a recognizable image. Falling silent again, she walked around the room and found that many of the paintings were of the same subject: a country garden, taken at different times of day and from slightly different angles of vision. In that way they were like Laurie's photographs, in imitating the human eye and the way it moved from one object to the next, but otherwise they were nothing like those static, black-and-white images. They were like nothing else she had ever seen.

"I've never known a woman who could be silent as long as you can," he said, startling her back to earth.

"What can I say?"

"I take it that means you like them."

"Like them!—" She stopped, at a loss again. "Yes," she said finally, almost reverently.

After another moment, though, she added, motioning toward a brilliant yellow field with a farmhouse in the distance. "But where were they done? No place in the world can really look like this."

"It depends on how you look at the world, of course, but yes, there are places like this."

She had turned back to the painting before he said again, "I'll show you."

And again, he was saying something else that she did not understand but that reached deep into her for something she did not know was there. *What is it?* she asked herself. *Tell me and I'll give it to you.*

For a moment, a vision of spending the day in the country, alone with Devin Grant, forgetting the past and living only in the present, rose to her imagination's eye. That was madness, of course. They couldn't do it, even if they could get away with no one knowing they had done it. No, it wasn't possible.

"I have a car," he said.

She looked up at him, and he was laughing again behind those hard gray eyes.

"An automobile?"

"Not just any automobile—a Daimler."

She thought for a moment, wondering how to make it possible. Then she remembered his offer at Maxim's, to be at her service if she needed an escort. Perhaps that was all he had meant to say earlier. But she did not think so.

"Laurie will be thrilled," she said.

It broke the spell between them, and he laughed aloud. "Bring Laurie, then, and your little protégée, Daisy. But for God's sake, leave Lady Jervis behind!"

"How am I going to do that?" she asked, as they left the building and began walking back to the river along the boulevard Saint-Michel.

"I'm sure you can be very inventive," he said, steering her around a crowd of people fighting for space on a streetcar. He pulled her inside a doorway for a moment to keep her from being jostled, and when he made a move to go on, she put her hand on his sleeve to stop him.

"Devin—" He smiled, and she realized that she had begun to use his Christian name without being aware of it. "Thank you for showing me those paintings."

"My pleasure."

They went on then, their progress slowed somewhat by all the other people in the street. The Latin Quarter was busier and more congested than the Paris that Maddie was getting used to, but it was more exciting, too. All kinds of people thronged the streets, from thin, serious-looking students with satchels full of books to off-duty taxi drivers to the fat, observant concierges of small hotels, who sat in their doorways observing everything that went on in the street. Devin knew this Paris very well, she realized, and she was grateful to him for bringing her there, even though she had no doubt Louise would have palpitations when— if—she heard where Maddie had been.

They passed another café, and he asked if she wanted something to drink. More than that, she wanted to rest her feet, so she agreed, and they went through the front part of the café, which was open to the street and spilled out into it, into a glass-enclosed room that led in turn to a garden and a view of the Sorbonne to the rear. Most of the round, marble-topped tables were already taken, but a waiter appeared, made a little bow, and led them to a table in a corner of the room, where they would not be quite so much on public display. Devin ordered a *café au lait* for Maddie and a calvados for himself, and the waiter scurried away again.

There weren't very many other women in the café. Those who were there glanced furtively at her, except for one, sitting by herself. Maddie recognized the expression on the woman's face and wondered how she had got away from home, and if her husband would beat her if his supper wasn't ready when he got back. But then a man sat down with her and took her hand. Not her husband, Maddie decided. Not a beater, either. Perhaps this woman had found an escape.

"What are you looking at?" Devin asked. Maddie turned to find her coffee in front of her. She picked up the cup, smiled, and tried not to look at the woman again.

"Those two look as if they've been here all day," she said, indicating a pair of elderly gentlemen who never spoke to each other, but who had a pile of newspapers in front of them that they were working their way through.

"They probably have," Devin said. "There are very few social clubs here, as there are in London, so men like that spend their days in their café instead. Everyone has a favorite, and they are as devoted to them as any Englishman to White's or the Reform Club."

"Is this your favorite? That waiter knew you."

"I haven't been here for a long time, but it was one of my haunts once. I was at the Sorbonne for a year, back when Paris was still new and exciting and foreign."

"It still is to me," she said, and when he raised his eyebrows, she added, "foreign, I mean."

He laughed, but she said, "I don't think you're bored with it yet, however familiar it may be."

"No." He frowned and was silent for a moment as he looked around him instead of at her. One of the old gentlemen got up to leave, taking one of the newspapers with him. The waiter wiped off his place at the table with a cloth and pocketed the change left on the top saucer. There was a parcel left on the window ledge next to the table, and the waiter gestured to the second old man as if to ask if it belonged to his friend. The old man shook his head.

Maddie said, "But it's not the same as it was?"

He looked at her and smiled. "Nothing ever is. I still loved it last year. Now I'm afraid something will happen— not to the city, but to my memories of it. Memories should live longer than places, even people, and if they die prematurely, it's as if someone you loved died before you could tell your love."

"I know."

She did know and wished she could tell him about it, but it was not time yet to confide in him. She studied his face for a moment and felt a little pang at seeing the tiredness in the gray eyes. She wished she could ease that a little for him, but did not know how. She realized, too, that she knew very little else about him, either. What memories did he have of Paris? Of anything? What did he do when he was not with her? It was like trying to imagine the dark side of the moon.

"Do you have a valet?"

He laughed, surprised by the question. "No, why?"

"I was just trying to imagine your everyday life. Don't all English gentlemen have manservants?"

"I'm not what society considers a gentleman. I don't have much of a daily routine, either. No servant would stay for long."

"You must have a cook."

"Yes, a cook and a housekeeper. I manage to bathe and dress myself."

"You're laughing at me, but I'm fascinated. Do you live in a house?"

"Not in London. I have rooms there, in the Albany."

She raised her eyebrows. "Now, Mr. Grant, even an ignorant Yankee knows what an exclusive address that is. You must be a man of some influence—"

She stopped, realizing what she'd said, and laughed at herself. "Well, that *was* ignorant of me!"

He smiled. "I'm pleased that you admire me for myself and not for my friends in high places."

She widened her eyes innocently. "Did I say that?"

"Lots of girls would take advantage of it."

"I'm not a girl," she said.

She could see that he hadn't missed the point, but he said only, "*Nice* girls don't display such vulgar curiosity about a gentleman's living arrangements."

"Maybe nice girls have no curiosity of any kind."

He laughed, and she was glad to see his expression relax a little after all; she wondered how much more vulgarly curious she could afford to be without offending him. But she was never able to decide on what to say next, because just then something caught his attention. The second old man scraped back his chair and got up to leave. Devin looked around, and all at once Maddie felt him go rigid. She looked in the same direction, but except for the now empty table next to the window, everything looked exactly the same to her as before.

He turned back to her and said, "Maddie, listen to what I say and do exactly what I tell you."

There was an implacability in his voice that stopped her from asking why.

"What?"

"Get up and walk out the door in back of you into the garden. Go as far as you can on the path and you'll find a gate leading to the next street. Go through it and wait for me there."

She hesitated only an instant, without saying anything else, before she did as he asked. As she reached the door, she caught a glimpse of him reflected in the mirror over the bar. He had got up, quickly but not hurrying, and was reaching for the unclaimed parcel left on the window sill.

Maddie found the back door and went out. She was halfway down the garden before she heard the explosion.

She stopped abruptly, paralyzed with shock for a moment. From the front of the café a woman screamed, and turning, Maddie saw smoke rising from the street.

"Devin!"

Panic seized her. She had a sudden mental picture of the anarchist Emile Henry sitting all morning in the café he blew up, waiting for more people to arrive so that he could kill more. Forgetting what Devin had told her to do in her fear that he had been hurt, she ran back into the café and was almost knocked down by one of the waiters who was trying to prop up a fallen awning. Inside was mass confusion, but no one seemed to have been hurt. Devin wasn't there.

The bomb had exploded in the boulevard Saint-Michel. People were converging on the spot from all directions, shouting and gesturing wildly. She ran out onto the pavement and looked for Devin over their bobbing heads.

For an instant, she was afraid he was lying on the cobblestones, somewhere in the midst of that stampeding throng. But then she saw him.

He was bleeding from his forehead and bending over someone on the ground. But when Maddie pushed her way toward him she found him calmly helping a woman pick up the packages she had dropped. The old man, still clutching his newspaper, was sitting on the edge of the road looking stunned, and a cabdriver was cursing as he tried to quiet his horse, but no one else appeared to be badly hurt.

"Devin! Are you all right?"

He looked up, frowning. "I told you—"

"I know. I did, but when I heard the explosion, I was afraid you'd been hurt. You're bleeding."

He put his hand to his head and wiped off the blood. "It's nothing. A piece of something that flew off the street."

It was then that Maddie saw the hole in the ground that the bomb had gouged out. She looked around to see if any other damage had been done, and suddenly, out of the corner of her eye, she saw someone she recognized. Watching the commotion from behind a tree, as if calculating the extent of the damage, was the mysterious young man from Florence's salon.

"Devin, look over there!" she said, pointing. The young man saw her point and turned to run.

"He did it!" she said. "Go after him!"

Devin watched as the young man disappeared down a side street but made no move to follow him.

"Why don't you go after him?" Maddie shouted above the noise of two women arguing about whose basket of bread had fallen into the gutter. He still didn't move, so she turned to run after the boy herself, but he caught her before she had gone more than a few steps and held her by the arms from behind her as she struggled to get free.

"Maddie, stop it! It's all right."

She could feel him relax a little and tensed her body, as if waiting for a chance to break loose again.

"I'm all right," he whispered into her ear.

She took a deep breath, shocked back into sobriety by his perception. She hadn't known herself that it was sheer terror for him that made her act that way, but the extent of that terror frightened her, too. She pretended not to have heard what he said.

"You're supposed to be looking for anarchists, aren't you? You've just let one get away!"

"How do you know he's an anarchist?"

That stopped her. "Well, I don't. I think he is."

He turned her around, finally releasing his grip to look disbelievingly at her. Calming a little, she told him briefly about seeing the boy at Florence's salon.

"Why didn't you tell me this before?"

It was his turn to be angry now, and he barely held it in check, but Maddie thought he had no business being indignant at her.

"You haven't been around to tell! I told Oliver, but you haven't spoken to him much lately, either!"

He unclenched his fist and, putting his hand on her shoulder instead, guided her up the street, past the scene of the confusion, to where they could hear themselves think. She had to walk quickly to keep up with his long, still angry stride. At the corner of the boulevard Saint-Germain he hailed a fiacre and, opening the door for her, pushed her inside.

"Hotel Ritz," he told the driver, but Maddie held the door open for a moment longer.

"What are you going to do?"

He looked at her for a moment, and she saw that the

anger had gone again, as quickly as it had flared. He squeezed her hand, then closed the door on her.

"I'll tell you tomorrow," he said through the window.

He didn't leave her any choice but to trust him. As long as she could look back and see him, he stood in the same spot in the street, so she wouldn't know which way he went.

Chapter
Fifteen

RUNNING into Paul Bertaude was his first real bit of luck, Oliver Drummond thought, and it came none too soon. He did not want to see Mrs. Malcolm involve herself personally in this business any more than Devin Grant did; but unlike Grant, Oliver understood just how capable she was of getting involved, and very likely doing a good job of it. She could be foolhardy at times, but she was no coward, and it was no small task to keep her from knowing that he was concerned for her safety. Oliver was too precise in his habits to be accused of anything approaching recklessness himself, but his opinion of Madeleine Malcolm had little to do with the kind of logic and orderliness he applied to his work. He would, if the circumstances demanded, take any risk to keep her out of danger.

It wasn't just the way she had treated Louise that commanded his loyalty. She had been kind to Louise, not only respecting her opinions and taking her advice, but helping to build up those last reserves of love that Louise had in her and fanning them like a flame until the fire was no longer in danger of going out.

But there was something else about Madeleine Malcolm that brought out the knight errant in a man. It probably had something to do with her willingness—eagerness, even— to give of herself to anyone she loved, even when she knew she would be hurt by it. Devin Grant had probably discovered that by now, too, and although there were reasons that Grant couldn't yet be open with her, Oliver was certain now that he would be as careful as he could not to hurt her. And if they hadn't become lovers yet, that couldn't come too soon, either.

She deserved someone like Grant, someone at least as strong as she was and infinitely more generous than Edward Malcolm could ever have been. Oliver didn't suppose she had ever fully realized how selfish Malcolm really was. Louise had, but was wise enough to confide her observations only to her husband. Oliver himself had made that judgment when he accidentally heard the end of a quarrel between the Malcolms. It must have been only the last in a long line of rows about her devotion to the women's residency, because after it, she never went there again; and she gave up everything else but the directorship of the trust she had set up to keep the residency running. She could manage that from her home, and Oliver was glad to see that she hadn't let her husband defeat her entirely.

Oliver doubted that Malcolm even knew what she had given up. She hadn't flung her sacrifice in his face or tried to make a martyr of herself, the way some other woman might have done. Of course he may have known and kept quiet about it, realizing that he'd pushed her too far. She was at home all day again, and he had no more reason to accuse her of neglecting him. Not that he'd ever said that outright. He'd had no modesty about what he said in anyone's hearing, and Oliver had heard the kind of blandishments he practiced all too frequently.

"Of course it's important work, sweetheart," he'd said, when his wife came in late, discouraged, and in need of a little cuddle. "It's just that, well, I wish I could see a little more of you, that's all."

And she had believed that. Well, even Louise conceded Teddy Malcolm's charm, but she couldn't expect Oliver to see him quite the same way.

"I brag about you to all the fellows," he'd had the cheek to tell her. "They say they wish they could get their wives out of the house occasionally, but they can't love them the way I love you."

Oliver, in fact, considered that Edward Malcolm's charm was simply a more insidious kind of cruelty than that inflicted by their brutal mates on the women whose bruised bodies Mrs. Malcolm patched up. Malcolm's claiming all her attention at the same time that he relegated her to an insignificant corner of his own life must have been torment for her. She really wanted nothing more than something wholly her own.

Oliver guessed that it was Devin Grant's job that had kept him and Madeleine apart this long, and not because he suspected her of some complicity in whatever her husband had been up to with those anarchists. He must have given up that idea by now. It was more likely that he couldn't give as much of himself to her as he wanted because the job consumed too much of him. Or at least, this case did.

Which was why Oliver Drummond was attempting to overcome his own professional scruples to help him get it done.

When Oliver had given up his job with the Pinkerton agency to go to work for Madeleine Malcolm, he had kept up all his old contacts, on the chance that one of them might come in handy some day. So when he spotted Paul Bertaude, whom he had last seen at a Chicago political rally, in a Montmartre café, he sat down in the one across the street and thought that day might have come. He waited, not wanting to intrude if Paul were working on a case, but within five minutes Paul had seen him and had come across the street to talk.

Paul was about Oliver's age, but he was unmarried and therefore available to travel in the course of his work. His French mother had handed down her slim, dark good looks to her son, and Paul had always looked more at home in Berlin or Rome or Paris than in St. Louis. He was based in Paris now, he told Oliver, and was waiting now for some information he needed for his current case to arrive. Oliver ordered an absinthe for him, and the two men spent half an hour catching up with each other's activities since they last met. Finally Oliver showed him the photographs taken at

Florence Wingate's salon. Paul did not recognize Viktor Kemeny, but he did know the other man.

"It looks like Aristide Dalou," he said immediately, then looked more closely at the photograph. "Yes, I'm sure it is. He's one of those bored young aristocrats always out looking for excitement. He used to wear an earring, and you see, there's a mark on his earlobe that might be a hole. Where was this taken?"

Oliver told him. "Yes, he'd fit in at an affair like that, if he was in the mood for it. It's the sort of thing that would have bored him five years ago, but if he were there pretending to be someone else, he'd have thought it good fun. Not much here," Paul said, tapping his forehead, "but he knows people, and he can be bribed."

"Where can I find him?"

"His favorite café, more than likely. It's the Black Dog, in the Latin Quarter. He pretends to be a student at the Sorbonne, and loiters around there trying to look like a man with important matters on his mind. How's your French, by the way?"

"*Comme ci, comme ça.*"

Paul winced at the accent. "So I see. Well, Drummond, come with me. I will find this Dalou for you."

This turned out to be not so simple a task as Paul had envisioned, however. They did indeed spot Dalou in his café, but he saw them first, got up, and disappeared through the back door of the building into the shadowed walks and guarded doors of the Sorbonne.

"What scared him off?" Oliver said.

"God knows. Maybe he owes somebody money and thought we came to collect."

They split up to make a circle around the university grounds, but met again at the other side without either of them having seen their man.

It was then that they heard the explosion from the boulevard Saint-Michel. They didn't even look at each other before they ran off together in that direction, and when they came around the corner, Oliver saw Devin Grant in the middle of the street and came to an abrupt halt. He thought Grant saw him, too, but when Mrs. Malcolm suddenly came out of a café, ashen-faced and terrified, Grant turned to her. She clutched his arm, and he seemed to be reassuring her that he was unhurt. Then she and Paul spotted Dalou at almost the same instant.

"There he is!" Paul shouted in English and lit out after the boy. Mrs. Malcolm cried out, too, and when Grant didn't move, she made as if to go after him herself. Oliver, trusting Grant to take care of her, ran off after Paul.

They chased Dalou down to the river, where he suddenly dodged between two horse buses, and by the time Paul and Oliver had gone around the back of the second, Dalou had disappeared again. Oliver cursed his luck and his middle-aged legs in equal measure.

"Well, at least I know what he really looks like now," he said, stopping to catch his breath. "Thanks, Paul."

"Don't thank me yet," Paul said, grinning as if he enjoyed chasing petty criminals through alleyways. "I'm not going to let that *vaurien* get away from me so easily. Come on."

So Oliver went, following Paul through Montmartre and most of the rest of the city, in and out of places that seemed so foreign to Oliver he thought they must have crossed a frontier somewhere. Late that afternoon they finally drove their quarry to earth, almost literally, in the cemetery of Père-Lachaise. The sun was low on the horizon by then and cast long, eerie shadows on the tombs and monuments. Oliver held back for a moment at the gate. He hated cemeteries.

But Paul was relentless, almost triumphant, Oliver thought with astonishment. "Come on, then."

Dalou had gone in by the northwest gate, and they found him sitting on a bench near the tomb of the victims of the Commune—maybe he found it inspiring, Oliver thought grimly—smoking a cigarette, confident that he had given them the slip. Paul and Oliver came up behind him, glanced at each other and, on Paul's signal, came around either side of the bench and sat down. Dalou moved to get up, but a firm hand on either side pulled him down again.

"Who are you?" Dalou asked, his pale eyes darting nervously from one of them to the other. He reminded Oliver of a cat trying to decide which of two large dogs would do him the most damage. "If you're the police, you've got nothing on me. I didn't do it."

Paul raised an eyebrow. "What, didn't throw that bomb? Of course you didn't. Who would be stupid enough to believe you capable of something like that?" His contempt was evident; Dalou's face went red.

"Who are you, then?"

"Friends of Teddy Malcolm," Paul said. Oliver caught

the flash of recognition in those feline eyes before Dalou blanked it out. Paul pulled a fifty-franc note out of his pocket and waved it in front of Dalou. Paul had told Oliver that Dalou's family had disinherited him, and his ideals weren't holding up well under his new poverty. Sure enough, Dalou's eyes lit up.

"Where is he?" Oliver asked, in English. Dalou understood but replied in French.

"Dead."

"How?"

Dalou shrugged. "How else? They shot him, the dogs. Threw his body in the Seine."

"Who did?"

"Another foreigner. Who cares."

"Did you see this?"

"No, heard about it later."

"How do you know it's true?"

"A friend told me," Dalou said, offended that anyone would think his friends capable of an untruth. Paul laughed and gave him the note, which Dalou quickly pocketed. Then Paul brought out a hundred-franc note. Dalou grabbed at it, but Paul pulled it back.

"Everything you know about Malcolm—*vite!*"

Dalou wasted no time complying with this demand. Oliver thought he would happily betray all of his so-called friends for a hundred francs. Malcolm had arrived in Paris in the autumn, Dalou said, in the company of a couple of foreign anarchists—English, or maybe American. They'd gotten in touch with *Chiens Noirs*, the Black Dogs, an anarchist group that met at the café of the same name.

Dalou had belonged for a while, but they were all too serious, always talking about whom they were going to assassinate next, not that they had killed anyone, yet. They were all talk. Foreigners always were.

"Who was the leader of the group?" Paul asked.

Dalou shrugged. "No one ever knew. One of the English took charge, but he wasn't the leader. That one never came to the café."

"Who else belonged?"

"No one. Everyone. Every day rumor said this one or that was the new leader. A man might put out the rumor that such a one—someone he disliked—belonged, just to get the man arrested and out of the way for a while."

Dalou laughed. "Me, I think the gang put about all the rumors just to keep the police busy."

"When was the last time you heard anything of them?"

"Not for months. They've gone under cover. But the new rumor is they really are going to assassinate someone this time."

"Who?"

Dalou looked at Paul with the contempt of one who could not be bothered with such trivial affairs. Oliver couldn't help being fascinated by the twisted morals of this youth, who was just stupid enough to be dangerous. Paul, however, did not seem to think him worth further effort. He gave Dalou the banknote and promised him more if he could report anything more useful.

"How do I find you?"

"I'll find you," Paul said.

He glanced at Oliver, and the two men rose and walked

away down the path. Dalou lit another cigarette and stayed where he was.

They heard the bell then that signalled the closing of the gates. Paul and Oliver stopped just outside the main gate, next to a sign that offered a private burial place of two square meters for 1,000 francs. Oliver wondered if perhaps Teddy Malcolm—or the body thought to be his—was buried here somewhere, in the *fosse commune*. He had never thought to find out about that.

It was dark by the wall, where tree branches hung over from the cemetery. Oliver shivered and moved toward a streetlight that had just been turned on. "Do you think it's true?" he asked Paul, "about the assassination plot?"

Paul shrugged. "It could be, though. One hears the same rumor at least once a week."

"But who's the target?"

"Probably some minor government functionary. Just high up enough to draw attention to the gang's demands—whatever they may be this time—or maybe just to make a noise. They like to do that."

"You don't think it might be . . . some foreigner?"

Paul shook his head. "I doubt it. We don't know enough yet, but there's been nothing like that since the Empress Elisabeth was shot last year. It was a single assassin, however, who did that. As a rule, the bigger the gang, the smaller the target."

"Will you report all this to the police?"

"Yes, I'll have to do that. But don't worry, my friend; I'll keep my ears out for you."

Oliver thanked him, and they parted at the corner of the

avenue Gambetta, where Paul caught a tram home, declining Oliver's offer of a cab. They made a date to meet again; and as Oliver settled back in his cab, he tried to decide what he was going to report to Devin Grant. He couldn't wait any longer for Grant to make the first move. Oliver was convinced that the Prince of Wales was really in danger.

As he watched the streets broaden, then narrow again, as the cab approached the Place Vendôme, he remembered the look on Mrs. Malcolm's face when she thought Grant had got in the way of that bomb. This time, he would not go to her first with his suspicions. In fact, he didn't think he'd tell her about them at all.

Chapter
Sixteen

THE next morning brought splendid motoring weather, or so said Laurie, who had no more experience with motoring than Maddie did. Daisy had earlier confided in Maddie that her father had taught her to operate a Panhard motor, but she begged Maddie not to mention this skill to Laurie, so Maddie only smiled at him and said she was sure he must be right and they depended on him to explain how the motor worked.

Laurie and Daisy, unable to sit still in the lobby of the Ritz to wait for Devin to arrive with the Daimler, dashed out to the square every five minutes to see if he was coming, then came back in again to ask if she thought he had had a breakdown already?

Maddie preferred to wait in the cool, quiet lobby, leafing through *l'Illustration* and pretending that she was looking forward to the same light-hearted little adventure that her young friends expected. In a way, she was, but her eagerness was mixed with apprehension.

Something was going to happen, she thought, not like what had happened in the Latin Quarter, perhaps, but being alone with Devin Grant could be dangerous in more than one way. She ought to have refused this excursion, she supposed, but instead she had involved Laurie and Daisy in it, too. How did things get out of her control like this? Why was she just sitting there waiting for the inevitable?

She kept her hands busy with the magazine, but her restless foot tapped impatiently on the carpet, and she had to remind herself to unclench her teeth in order to speak. Her voice, she thought, sounded decidedly strained, but Daisy did not seem to think it out of the ordinary.

Daisy had brought special motoring clothes that, she said, were all the thing in London, even providing extras for Maddie so that they were both now swathed in loose-fitting, pearl-gray cotton dust-coats buttoned up over their day dresses and provided with capacious pockets for the goggles Laurie insisted they wear to protect their eyes. Louise had done up both ladies' hair with extra pins and attached gauze motoring veils to their hats, which could be wrapped firmly around their faces should the wind prove too brisk. Daisy had looked in the mirror and declared that she looked like a gray mushroom, but Laurie later told her she looked splendid. His opinion fortunately carried enough weight with Daisy that she willingly posed, glowing, for Laurie's camera and he for her Kodak.

At two minutes past nine, a hooting noise from the

square caught Laurie and Daisy unawares, and they bounded out again, leaving Maddie to follow along on her own. Outside, Devin was getting down from the driver's seat of a silver-painted 12-horsepower Daimler, whose motor he left running as he helped Daisy up. When he took Maddie's hand, he squeezed it a little harder than necessary and smiled. It was a warm, open smile, and it put her a little more at ease, or a little more off her guard. She reminded herself of that possibility as she took her place in the car, staring straight ahead of her as she waited to start.

A large portion of the Ritz staff appeared at the door of the hotel to avail themselves of this novel form of entertainment, maintaining their dignified expressions only with difficulty when Daisy leaned over the side of the contraption to wave her parasol at an urchin who tried to climb onto the boot for a ride. Devin tipped the doorman generously to ensure his equally attentive welcome on their return, climbed back into the Daimler, and let out the clutch.

Maddie was surprised at how high up the seat was, and because it was not enclosed like a carriage or a hansom cab, she felt not only as if she might fall off, but that she would do so before the whole world, which seemed to be watching them as they drove out of the Place Vendôme. Seated behind her and Devin, however, Daisy and Laurie felt no such giddiness in the even less spacious rear seat, which consisted only of a cushion and metal back and armrests. Devin glanced at Maddie, who was clutching the armrest as he maneuvered through the rue de Rivoli and turned west toward the Neuilly Road.

''You'll get used to it,'' he said.

Maddie shot him a doubting look, but by the time they had reached the Porte Maillot, she found that he was right. As they picked up speed on the far side of the river, she was able to balance herself even when taking her hands from the side of the motorcar to arrange her veil around her neck. After a time, she was even confident enough to wave back to the people along the road who waved their hats and shouted after them.

Maddie had been in fast carriages before, but the Daimler was speeding along at twenty miles an hour. Even so, the motor was quiet enough for her to hear Laurie and Daisy's lively chatter from behind her, although she made no attempt to speak to Devin while he was steering around startled horses and indignant carriage drivers.

In less than an hour they had arrived at a place called Cormeilles-en-Parisis and stopped to stretch their limbs. Laurie, their designated navigator, had detoured them through this village so that he could see the bust in front of the church of the pioneer photographer Daguerre, who was a native of Cormeilles. Maddie and Devin, meanwhile, sat on a bench at the edge of a little square, and he poured her a cup of tea from an insulated jug he had brought along.

"Are you comfortable? We can go into that café over there instead."

"This is fine, thank you. I also see a *patisserie* on the corner and trust Laurie to spot it and bring us back a little something."

They lapsed into silence for a few minutes, as they watched the townspeople go about their business. There were no sounds but footsteps and the occasional song of a bird in the square's lime trees. It seemed to sing out more clearly than usual now that the drone of the car's motor no longer addled her ears. This place could not have been more different, Maddie couldn't help thinking, from the bustling café they had stopped in yesterday.

Devin must have sensed the direction of her thoughts and said, "The police arrested your young anarchist last night." Then, when she looked questioningly at him, he added, "And they let him go again this morning. He said he'd been on his way to a lecture at the Sorbonne, and he was in fact registered there as a student. There was also no evidence that he had planted the bomb."

Maddie sighed. "I suppose it shouldn't matter. He has no connection to . . . to our business, does he?"

When he hesitated, she said again, "Does he?"

"I talked to Oliver Drummond last night," he said instead.

Maddie had to laugh. "You have a wonderful way of not answering questions," she said. But when he didn't respond to the hint, she asked another question. "Have you two made up again, then?"

He smiled. "If you mean, are we working together again, yes. We're not friends yet. Your Oliver is very loyal, you know. He accused me of using him—and you—to further some ulterior purpose of my own."

"Are you doing that?"

He hesitated, then turned a little on the bench to take her hands in his and look into her eyes.

"Maddie, you know that I also work for the Prince of Wales?"

"Yes."

"That work is very important to me, and right now, I'm afraid, it's vital to a lot of other people, as well. What I do for him is apart from what I am trying to do for you, but the cases overlap in ways I hadn't entirely expected."

She could feel the warmth of his strong hands through her gloves and had to concentrate to comprehend what he was saying.

"Sometimes I may be using one case to solve the other, but I'm not using *you* in any way—at least not deliberately— and I will find out what happened to your husband. I promise you that. But I can't promise any more, and I can't tell you any more. Do you understand?"

She didn't, but somehow she knew he was being as truthful as he could, or as he was allowed to be by his own conscience as well as by forces he could not control. She didn't know why she trusted him, either, but she did now. Perhaps she always had, and that was why she had been afraid of what he would say. Whatever it was would be the truth.

"I understand."

"Good," he said, letting her go as if he had been holding his breath as well as her hands. He looked around. "Where have Daisy and Laurence got to? We ought to be getting on."

"Where, by the way, are we going?" she asked.

"I thought we could get as far as Cocheret comfortably. You may see your impressionist landscapes there. We can lunch at the inn and return to the city in good time for dinner."

"Hullo," Daisy said just then, from behind them, and when they turned she snapped their picture with her Kodak. Maddie laughed, but Devin shook his head and said he hoped they had brought a limited supply of film.

"Oh, no," Laurie assured him, "we are well supplied." This he demonstrated by taking a number of views of the Daimler, with and without passengers, until at last Devin ordered him to get in or they would never go any farther. So Laurie tucked his equipment into the blanket at his and Daisy's feet, and they were off again.

They had left the last paved roads when they drove out of Argenteuil, but there must have been a rain the night before—or perhaps they were high enough off the ground— for the dust did not rise enough to be annoying, and they passed only the occasional farm cart. Maddie took off her veil and breathed deeply of the clean, fresh air.

The road led for a time straight as a die through an avenue of poplars, then began to climb and wind through more rolling country where they rode either along a ridge with long views on either side, across rich fields dotted with fat cows, or through low roads like leafy tunnels with high hedges on either side, where Devin blew the horn whenever they neared a curve that might conceal a vehicle on the other side. The only populated places they passed were villages with a single main street and almost identical brick houses lining it behind walls they could only just see over. At last they stopped in one of these villages, which at first appeared no larger or more likely than any other. But Devin seemed to know where he was going. He turned onto a narrow lane and pulled up before a large building with a blue slate roof and flower boxes at the windows. An elegantly scripted sign over the open door revealed that it was the River Inn.

"What river?" Maddie asked.

Devin smiled. "You'll see."

The landlord emerged from the inn just at that moment, bobbing up and down in numerous bows seemingly triggered by the honor of entertaining such a distinguished—and hungry-looking—party. Still bowing, he led them through the dark interior of the building to the garden in the rear, and it was there that Maddie realized they were expected, for a table had been set with white linen and green-and-white Limoges china for four people.

"Oh, how jolly!" Daisy exclaimed, when she saw the table. "A picnic lunch!"

The second thing Maddie saw was the view. From the road, there had been no hint of the sweep of countryside beyond. From the profusion of wild roses, nasturtiums, and marigolds that made up the inn's garden, yellow-green grassy fields dotted with red poppies swept down to the sun-bedazzled Eure River in the distance, where pale green willows rose along the banks as if placed there by an artist choosing the most pleasing composition. Maddie stared speechlessly for several minutes, then finally turned to Devin.

"It's beautiful."

"I thought you'd like it."

He came up behind her to help remove her dust coat, and, light as his touch was, she made an involuntary movement away from it and removed her hat by herself.

Laurie set up his camera, but Daisy for once was more interested in the menu and attacked a buttered roll as soon as the landlord brought it out. When broiled fresh trout and asparagus followed, even Laurie's attention was caught, and they all set to with large appetites, which Devin blandly assured them was the major hazard of motor travel.

By the time they arrived at cheese and coffee, Maddie was growing drowsy in the sun and would have been content to spend the whole afternoon sitting on the garden terrace and looking at the view. Daisy and Laurie, on the other hand, seemed to have been revived by their meal. They looked at each other, Daisy nodded encouragement, and Laurie spoke up.

"Excuse me, sir—"

"Please don't call me sir," Devin interrupted. "It makes me feel like your grandfather."

"I beg your pardon, sir—er, Mr. Grant. I wondered, if you prefer to stay here at the inn for a little, Daisy and I might take the motorcar for a spin?"

Devin eyed Laurie appraisingly. "Now I do feel like your grandfather. Are you to be trusted, young man? Do you know how to operate the thing?"

"Oh, yes, sir. I was taught in London . . . not on a Daimler, but I'm quite a good driver."

Maddie glanced at Daisy, who had obviously put Laurie up to this little fib, but she said nothing. She thought that Devin meant to play it safe and refuse, but then he looked at her. She didn't think she had made any signal of her preference one way or another, but he must have seen something that made up his mind for him, for he took the ignition key out of his pocket and held it out to Laurie. "Half an hour," he said.

"Oh, thank you, Mr. Grant!" Daisy said, jumping up to hug his neck, then blushing at her own temerity. Laurie promised to be careful, and taking Daisy by the elbow, he led her outside before Devin could change his mind.

"You are very rash," Maddie said.

"I'm sure the Daimler will survive. At least it will be quiet here for the next hour or two, and we needn't be on constant alert to be photographed."

"Hour or *two*?"

He smiled. "You don't really expect to see them back in half an hour, do you?"

She hadn't thought otherwise, and now, unaccountably, thinking of it made her heart lurch oddly. The fantasies she had guarded so closely were suddenly coming to light, and she was afraid of what they might turn out to be.

"Where *did* you get the car?" she asked, wondering if she could fill an hour or two with small talk.

"It belongs to a friend of the prince."

"Oh, dear."

"A very rich friend who has already bashed up two other motorcars by exceeding both his skill and the speed limit. A little scraped paint, which I'm sure is the most Laurie can do to it, won't trouble him."

"He must be a good friend of yours as well."

But he only smiled and offered her another cup of coffee, which she accepted, reluctant to waste the afternoon napping, even if her imagination shied away from the alternatives. They fell silent again, and Maddie was a little surprised at how restful he could be when he wanted; he did not expect her to make small talk after all, or to listen to him talk. Or to make a move toward him before she was ready to. But she would have liked to know what he was thinking. She looked his way.

He was looking at her; he had been for some time, she guessed. His eyes captured hers, and now she did know what he was thinking. A little shiver of excitement passed over her; for a moment she thought it was just a breeze from the river, and she looked in that direction instead.

"Shall we take a walk in the garden?" she said.

He stood up and pulled her chair back for her, then offered his arm. She disregarded it—she could not touch him, not yet—and instead swept a large straw hat from a wall peg, put it on, and walked down the shallow steps to the garden ahead of him. Away from the shade of the terrace trees, the midday sun was hot and white, and she put up her hand to shade her eyes until they became more accustomed to the glare. It was so intense it seemed to make its own noise, until Maddie realized that what she heard was the hum of bees among the enormous marigolds and hollyhocks in the garden.

All the while she was aware from the edge of her vision that Devin had scarcely moved, and was watching her again. She put up her chin and her defenses and sat down on a white-painted iron bench, pushing her skirts to one side of her so that, when he joined her, he would not be too close.

Chapter Seventeen

"DO you still want to find him?"

Maddie did not pretend to misunderstand the question. A month ago, she knew, she would have flared up at it, protested angrily that she had hired him for the express purpose of finding her husband, and who was he to question her sincerity? But now she felt a deep desire to be honest with him, except that she was not quite sure she could be honest with herself yet.

Devin hadn't wanted to bring it up; that much was obvious. What surprised her was that she was sorry he had. She would much rather have gone on as they had for the last few days, talking about anything but Teddy. They had been having so much fun.

"I must," she said, but then went on quickly, so he would not back off too far, "I've been thinking that . . . that Teddy may not have stayed with the anarchists. He may have gone away somewhere on his own, to another city or even another country.''

''Why do you say that?''

''Because I don't think he had anything in common with those people. He may have found them exciting for a while, but he isn't the kind of man who would give up everything for a cause.''

''I thought he was such an idealist.''

Had she really said that? The words seemed to mock her, even if Devin didn't. She didn't know what to say.

He did. ''I'm sorry, Maddie. I shouldn't have—''

He had put his hand over hers, but she shook it off. ''It's all right. I deserved that. Nevertheless''—she had to force the words out now—''even if Teddy has found a new life for himself and does not want to come back, I must see him—or at least talk to him—once more. I need to say certain things to him.''

He was silent again for a time, during which she did not dare to look at him, before he said, ''Shall we walk down to the river?''

He held his hand out for her and they were on the path before she remembered, ''What about Laurie and Daisy?''

''They can find their own river.''

The path petered out not much past the edge of the garden, and they began walking across the sloping field. The willows near the distant water seemed to come no closer; and although the grass grew taller and thicker, making walking difficult, neither of them suggested going back. Devin went ahead of her to push the grass aside, disturbing the bees at work in it and startling a wild canary into flight. Impulsively, Maddie pulled off the hat and tossed it over a clump of marigolds. Devin heard the faint noise and turned around, then stopped.

"Your hair's coming loose," he said and reached out to push a pin back in. His hand must have been cold, for it made her shiver when he touched her cheek lightly. She took the hairpin from him and stepped around him, smoothing her hair with an automatic gesture as she walked. But in another moment, he caught her arm and said, "Sit down for a while."

There was a patch of flattened grass near a mound of pale yellow hay. Obediently she sat down, tucking her legs under her the way she used to do when she was a girl.

"What is it you want to say to your husband?" he asked.

She didn't answer at once but looked down at her hands folded in her lap, as if searching for the right words. "I wasn't—I haven't been all that good to Teddy. I want to make it up to him. Or at least, to tell him I'm sorry."

"What could you possibly have to be sorry for?"

She supposed she should not be telling him these things, but she had never been able to say them to anyone before; and somehow, today, if she did not think too much about the implications of confiding in him, she wanted to tell him.

"When we were first married, I adored Teddy. I wanted to do everything for him, to be kind and understanding and interested in anything that interested him. But I was never any of those things. Instead, I went out and did things he could take no part in . . . and blamed him for not joining

241

me anyway. I was never home when he was, and then I accused him of—of being useless."

Now that she had begun, the litany seemed to pour out of her. "He was always so good to me, never angry, even when I behaved stupidly. And I was senselessly jealous. The night—the last time I saw him, I even said he took more interest in his silly horses than he did in me. It was a ridiculous thing to say, but I can't forget that it was the last thing he heard from me. If only—"

"Stop."

He was sitting with his knees bent slightly and his hands on them, playing absently with a piece of straw. The word came out softly but forcefully, cutting her off like a knife into soft bread.

"Never say *if only*! You can't change the past, and unless his character has greatly changed, nothing else would be likely to change either. What would be the point of telling him all this? Just to make *you* feel better?"

"You don't understand. I want to tell him that it was *my* fault. I was stubborn and selfish and proud, and I made no effort to understand or sympathize."

"Damn it, Maddie!"

He stood up then and paced angrily in front of her, flattening the grass even more. "How can an intelligent woman be so unintelligent about a man who isn't worth two minutes out of her life? Stand up!"

Flabbergasted, she did, and he took her by the elbows and shook her. "Maddie, nothing was your fault! He was the selfish one. He wasn't worth your time, much less your love and loyalty."

She shook herself free. "But I *didn't* love him! I mean, I didn't love him enough. Oh, God."

Had she really said that? He had surprised it out of her, but she knew now that it had been there all the time. She hadn't cried in front of anyone for years, but suddenly the tears flowed, astonishing her as much as him. "I didn't know how to love him," she said, between sobs. "I don't think I know what love means."

She turned away from him, covering her face with her arms and trying ineffectually, like a little girl, to dry her tears with her sleeve.

"You're a fool, Maddie." He turned her toward him and before it registered on her what he was doing, he covered her mouth with his own. She tried to pull away, but he moved his arms around her, imprisoning her within them, and suddenly all the heat of the day concentrated itself in his mouth, the liquid fire pouring into her from him and heating her insides unbearably. Her arms went up around his neck and her fingers met the thick hair at the nape and twined into it.

"No—" she protested, not because she wanted him to stop but because she had to tear her mouth away from the source of heat before it melted her. But he would not let her go, and then it was too late, and when he released his grip to pull her down on the grass, she moaned only to protest that he had stopped. Leaning over her, he put one hand under her back to keep her away from the ground and took her head in the other hand, drawing it up gently to kiss her again, less violently, and again.

"There isn't a cold or unloving bone in your body," he

said, moving his hands down her back as if to prove it. "You just haven't been loved as you should be . . . as I can love you.

"I want to love you," he said in a low voice that she would not even have heard if she had not known what he was saying without having to hear it.

"No, Devin." It was a feeble denial, for she did not want him to stop kissing her. "I'm afraid. . . ."

He pulled back to look into her eyes but did not let her go. "Of what?"

"I'm not . . ." She didn't know how to say it. "I'm afraid I'll disappoint you."

He chuckled softly, and as if he had put a brake on himself, his urgency slowed. She could feel his breathing change, too, as he began to kiss her face, her neck, her hair, each light touch another sweet reassurance, until he reached her mouth again and entered, a little deeper, a little more forcefully, but never quite hard enough to satisfy the desire that was growing instead of cooling inside her. When would it stop? she wondered. How far would it go before she no longer felt anything?

"What did he do wrong, darling?" he whispered. "Did he kiss you like this?"

"No . . ."

Why did he say that? What could it matter that another man had tried and failed?

But then she began to understand that there was something different in what he did, in what she was feeling, in the way she responded involuntarily to his touch. The realization made her gasp and want to test herself a little more, but she was still fearful.

"Not here," she said, although she had thought, "not now," and did not know what she really meant.

He lifted his head, and there was a dizzying mix of laughter and desire in his eyes. "Shall we go back to the inn and rent a room?"

"No!"

"Here, then."

His mouth closed on hers again, and she felt something else unlike anything she had ever felt before, something that dispelled her fear of disappointment just long enough to make her reckless. She knew she ought to stop him while there was still time, before she reached that last peak she had never been able to scale. But instead she arched her back so that her body touched his along its full length and she could feel his skin hot against her even through all their clothing. Where she could touch it directly, his skin was surprisingly smooth and smelled of sun and poppies and tasted lightly of salt. She wanted to taste more, and the idea of what he would feel like without that cloth barrier between them made her tremble. He lifted his head, and she saw the passion blazing alone and naked in his eyes—had she really thought them cold?—and heard his breathing come faster.

He began unbuttoning her bodice with expert fingers, and she giggled crazily. "We forgot Louise."

"Do you think I can't button them up again?"

"I shouldn't like to think you an expert on ladies' intricacies."

"Necessity makes experts of us all. Stand up."

Fascinated, she obeyed and stood still, moving her arms or lifting a foot as he instructed. She watched him pull her bodice and the blouse off from underneath her and lay them gently on a patch of dry grass. Her skirt and petticoat and silk drawers followed, and decorated the haystack. He took his time, pausing to kiss the newly exposed flesh of her arms and neck and above the top of her chemise.

She was wearing the kind of stays that fastened up the front, and it took him only a moment to release the metal tags. She felt the sudden coolness on her waist and breasts, reminding her of the night he had burst into her hotel room, when she had had to hold a gun between him and her trembling, barely clad body to keep him from doing what he was doing now, and what she had not known she wanted then. He ran his hand down her side, closer to the skin now than before, then removed his own clothes and disposed of them carelessly in a heap beside him. In those few seconds when he was out of reach, she didn't know what to do with her hands, but when she covered her breasts with them, he took them away again and laid her gently back on the grass.

"Didn't your nanny tell you that no nice-minded girl wears beautiful underwear?" he said as he caressed her lacy muslin chemise. He didn't take it off at once, reaching instead beneath it to release the garters that held up her pale pink stockings, then rolled the stockings slowly down each leg. As each tiny patch of nakedness was revealed, he kissed it, moving his mouth slowly down the insides of her legs. She reached toward him, sitting up a little, the center of her more eager than any other part, but holding back, waiting to be touched first, for his gentle hands to warm that part of her too and make it tremble.

When he raised his head again and held himself a whisper away from the length of her to look into her eyes, she held her breath, waiting . . . no longer sure for what. And still he lingered over her lacy chemise, and she wondered if she really had been wicked to buy such a garment that no one else had ever seen. But it seemed right that it should be him, that he should see it in the way he did.

Then he ran his hands back up her legs, taking the chemise with them. He took hold of her waist, lifting her slightly to take the garment all the way off over her head, and she gasped when she realized they were both naked now. Hurrying, breathing audibly, he held her up long enough to slip the chemise between her and the ground and lay her gently back on it. Then his mouth took hers again, and his hands covered her breasts. She returned his kiss, eager to discover what it was in him that drew her so strongly. But when she reached up for him, she found her arms too weak, her will gone, overtaken by sensation. His body pressed hers down, and her weakness did not matter, for he had strength for both of them.

His mouth was all over her now, hotly, desperately, and her flesh became hot and desperate wherever he touched it, until she begged him to end it. But he knew it was too soon, and he parted her legs only to slide his body down hers to kiss the insides of her thighs, sending a tremor of pleasure through her. She moaned and reached for him, to pull him closer to where she wanted him most. But he approached the end with agonizing slowness, while the rest of her melted away under his touch, her flesh turning to ashes, leaving only that central place untouched, unmoved, as it had always been.

Then he moved over her again, and his core touched hers. Suddenly, instead of being snuffed out, the flame inside her roared up, as if she had been dry tinder all along, just waiting for him to set her ablaze.

"Oh, Devin!"

"Tell me."

"Please . . . I don't know. . . ."

"I love you."

"Yes!"

He entered her then, and the final searing flame shot through her, and she cried out with the delicious agony of every inch that he made her climb with him, higher and higher, beyond that impossible peak and into the heavens, until she fell, shuddering, gliding gently down again, away from the heat into sudden, cool release—and she knew that she had not been destroyed, but healed. She was whole again because he was what had been missing in her.

It seemed hours before her breathing returned to normal and she opened her eyes to see a single red poppy at a curious angle above her, as if it had been watching through the grass all this time. She laughed softly, and he moved a little, lifting his arm from across her breasts.

"Don't go," she said, shivering with the sudden touch of cool air. He kissed her ear and whispered, "Awake now?"

"Did I sleep?"

"Only for a few minutes."

She took a deep breath. She ought to get up, but it was so comfortable there, so soothing.

"I had no idea," she whispered. "It's never been like that."

"I know."

She looked at him fully for the first time, admiring the dark smooth skin of his arms, and the taut muscles beneath it, his strong thighs and the film of light hair that covered his chest. There was a scar on his shoulder; she touched it, gently, as if it might still pain him.

"What is this?" she said.

"A mistake."

She kissed it. "There. It's forgiven."

He smiled and moved his hand along her arm. She shivered, and he thought she was cold and drew his shirt over her. It was hot and dry from the sun, and the crisp fabric absorbed the heaviness out of her, leaving her feeling weightless and free. She moved her head to kiss him, to tell him she wasn't cold any more, but then he reminded her, "It's getting late."

"What time is it?"

He reached into the pocket of his coat for his watch, looked at it and smiled, but said only, "Late."

She sighed and looked up at the sky. He was right; she could no longer see the sun, which beat at them at a deep angle through the grass. He reached for her clothing and dressed her again, gently moving her limbs into the clothes, as if she were a child. She felt drunk and smiled giddily at him as he stood in front of her to button her blouse. He laughed at her unexpressed invitation and kissed her breast through the chemise, leaving a deliciously warm, moist spot on it. She sighed.

"Hussy."

"Yes."

A dark flash of desire came back into his gray eyes. "I told you."

"Yes."

He took her head between his hands and kissed her mouth. She opened it willingly, wanting more, but he drew a deep breath and let her go, then bent down to find some loose hairpins in the grass for her to use. He found a comb in another pocket and smoothed the hair off her neck for her to fasten in a practiced knot at the back of her head.

"They'll be wondering where we've got to," he said, handing her back her jacket.

Maddie's eyes widened. Daisy and Laurie! She had forgotten them completely. For the first time all afternoon, she blushed.

"I'll think of something," he said, understanding the reason behind her suddenly heightened color. Quickly, she buttoned up her collar and looked for her hat. He found it and replaced it for her.

"You look respectable."

"I doubt that, but I suppose I'll have to do."

As it turned out, however, they were not the ones who had to make explanations. When they arrived back at the inn, the Daimler had not yet returned. Maddie looked to Devin. "Where can they be?"

"I'll go look for them. There must be a horse to be borrowed in the village."

He went to find the landlord and asked for a room where Maddie could wait in privacy while he went out, and she went gratefully upstairs to make herself more presentable. She smoothed her skirt and shook bits of hay off her shoulders and brushed them out the window. She could hear Devin at the stables in back talking to a groom, but before he could leave, she heard another sound and leaned her head out the window.

He heard it too and looked up at her. "That must be they."

She nodded, checked her face in the mirror again, and went back downstairs to find an abashed Laurie apologizing profusely to Devin.

"I'm ever so sorry, sir, but it broke down—not five miles down the road, I swear, but I couldn't ask Daisy to walk back here, so I managed to fix it myself."

Maddie looked toward Daisy, who was still sitting in the car. She rolled her eyes expressively at Maddie, who laughed. Laurie took offense.

"Well, I did fix it, didn't I?" he said, glaring accusingly at Daisy and, belatedly, holding his hand up to help her down from her perch. Maddie noticed that she had acquired a light sunburn, but otherwise looked ridiculously happy. Still, it wouldn't hurt to tease Laurie a little.

"Come along, dear," Maddie said, putting her arm solicitously around Daisy's shoulder. "There's a little parlor upstairs where you can rest for a moment." She shot a smiling glance at Devin, who took the hint and dragged a protesting Laurie around the inn to the stable pump to clean off his dust.

Upstairs, Daisy gave way to giggles and an urge to tell Maddie every detail of how she, and not Laurie, had been driving, because only she knew how, and how he had begged her to teach him.

"So I started to, but the first thing he did was to run the car into a ditch, so he had to go fetch a farmer with an ox to pull it out again, which took an age. I sat under a tree the whole time and tried not to laugh, and I must say Laurie was very good about it. He never lost his temper, and he forgot all about taking photographs!"

Maddie let her talk, injecting a comment only when Daisy paused for breath. She was glad the two young people had come to no harm and had even enjoyed their day, but at the same time she was grateful that she would not have to talk about how she had spent the time, at least not until she could invent something convincing to say about it. She wanted to hug the truth to herself a little longer, for it was too precious to share.

Chapter Eighteen

THEY returned to a golden Paris, and not simply because the sun was setting over the city and casting gilt over the old stone of the buildings. For Maddie the whole world seemed golden that afternoon. She wished it did not have to end.

But it ended abruptly. Laurie was the first to notice the discreet but palpable excitement buzzing through the Ritz when they arrived. The lobby was even more tranquil than usual, but there was a sense of important things happening behind doors.

"What's going on?" he said, reaching automatically for his camera before Daisy reminded him that he had run out of film long ago. Devin frowned and looked around. Half a dozen plainclothes Paris policemen trying to mingle with the crowd around the entrance intruded on his professional notice, and he let out a muttered curse.

"Devin?" Maddie asked. "What is it?"

"The prince is here." He handed the key for the Daimler to Laurie with instructions to drive it around to the carriage entrance and leave the key with Henri at the door. Then he jumped out and ran up the steps into the hotel without so much as a good-night to any of them.

He hadn't meant to be rude, but he was halfway across the lobby before he thought what Maddie might think. He came to a halt, cursed again, and was about to turn around when a familiar voice called his name.

"Grant, my dear fellow!"

Devin fixed a civil smile on his face and made a bow as the imposing bulk of the Prince of Wales emerged from the private salon that had been set aside for his use on the ground floor; he wore a white flower in his buttonhole and a warm smile on his round face. His usual cigar was in one hand, and the other was placed on Florence Wingate's waist. Devin's apology stuck in his throat as he took in this unexpected development.

"I hear you have been out cavorting in Rothschild's motor," the prince said. "Are you exhausted? You should be after all that fresh air."

"Not at all, sir. I am at your service."

"In that case, you must meet another who, although she does not, regrettably, share our nationality, claims the same devotion. My dear, allow me to introduce you to my most ardent protector—"

"Mr. Grant and I have met, sir," Florence said, at her most Southern and with a smile that became an impish grin when she turned it on Devin while holding her hand out to him.

He shook it absently. "Mrs. Wingate. Sir, I must apologize for not being here to meet you. No one told me—that is, I neglected to check with the hotel on your arrival time when I left this morning."

"Really, dear boy, you must rid yourself of this unfortunate habit you have of assuming blame that does not exist. It was simply that we stopped at Rouen for luncheon. Rouen bored me within the hour, so I made up our minds that we would travel directly on to Paris. And a fortunate thing it was that I did so, for I walked into the hotel at the same moment that Mrs. Wingate here was leaving it—a happy accident, indeed. We're going to the Epatant tonight. Will you join us?"

"Yes, of course."

"You needn't make it sound like a chore, dear boy. You always have the damndest luck at baccarat."

"If Mr. Grant wins at cards," Florence said, "ah'm sure it is entirely through his skill. He does not look to be a man who leaves anythin' to luck."

The prince laughed at that and told Devin he must take care around clever American ladies who did not hesitate to speak their minds. They agreed on a meeting place later that afternoon, and the prince went off still holding on to Florence, who gave Devin a knowing look over her shoulder.

Devin waited until the prince had kissed Florence's hand and got into the lift without her before he turned on his heel and went to make up for what he considered to be his lapse in duty. Nothing apparently was amiss in the security arrangements, the Ritz having become accustomed long since to the prince's whims, but Devin could not help feeling that something was going to go wrong. He recognized that his concern probably stemmed from his dereliction of duty that afternoon, but that did not mean that something might not go amiss just the same. He was glad he had not been at Rouen when the prince's other escorts were discommoded by his change of plan.

And so he erased from his mind, if not from his senses, the memory of Maddie's lovely body, warm with sun and passion, and of the unexpectedly intense feelings she had evoked in him, and he focused his energy instead on looking after the prince. He had a word with the police detectives assigned to follow the prince's carriage everywhere it went and satisfied himself that they were reliable. He took a cab to the Union Artistique, the exclusive club known to its habitués as l'Epatant, to have a private word with the owner about the honor his establishment was about to enjoy.

Then he returned to the hotel to make a nuisance of himself with the prince's equerry, who finally told him, "Look, Grant, I have no more control over the great man's caprices than you do. Furthermore, although I shall deny it if you mention it to a living soul, I have no idea where else he plans to go today. He does *not* tell me everything. God forbid that he should."

Devin had to laugh at that. "Sorry, Fritz, I suppose I'm just jumpy, what with all this talk of plots. Does he still insist on going to Baden, by the way?"

"He is convinced he ought to make a gesture of good will toward his cousin Emperor Wilhelm, although personally I think mere gestures are lost on that stone wall."

"I suppose we can be grateful to the kaiser for closing the casinos," Grant said, "so that there isn't a great deal to do at any of the German spas. If this visit is cut short for lack of amusement, we will both be spared a lot of trouble."

Frederick Ponsonby looked up at him sympathetically. Ponsonby was a good-looking man about Devin's age, a former guards officer who currently served as an assistant private secretary to the queen. But the prince liked him and had spirited him away from the gloom of Windsor for this trip. Devin knew Ponsonby had jumped at the assignment as a welcome change from dealing with an imperious old lady's crotchets, but service to the Prince of Wales had its perils, too, as Ponsonby was fast finding out.

"I'm more than happy to leave you to attempt to instill some sense of dynastic responsibility in him," Ponsonby said. "I have only to keep his lady friends from meeting one another."

"Better you than me," Devin retorted, making Ponsonby laugh.

"Do you know what I've already had to deal with?" he asked, relaxing for a moment and ticking the items off on his fingers. "One social-climbing German tourist who wants the prince to officially open his carpet factory in Berlin. An ex-army officer who claims he served the prince's father and was promised a pension he never got. And an opera dancer who wants a copy of the key to the royal suite so that she can give him a private performance!"

"What did Mrs. Wingate want with him?"

"Who?"

Devin explained, and Ponsonby rolled his eyes.

Devin grinned. "Yes, I can see that taking care of him out of doors, in the sight of thousands, is infinitely easier than minding his business behind closed doors. But don't worry about the Wingate. I doubt she's clever enough to hold his attention for long, and in the meantime I can keep an eye on her."

"Thank you," Ponsonby said, restored now to his usual even temper. As Devin went out, he promised to let him know at once about any changes in the prince's social calendar of which His Royal Highness might see fit to inform his humble servant.

That very day proved the impossibility of keeping up with that calendar, for the prince told his staff no more than that he was in Paris to enjoy himself and that the best way to do so was to remain open to any amusing novelty that came along. The prince was an ardent Francophile; he spoke the French language and understood the French style better than any other Englishman. He crossed the channel several times a year for no more reason than that he felt an inclination to stroll along the boulevards, looking into shop windows and purchasing, perhaps, a dozen shirts at Charvet, a hat at Genot, and a diamond necklace—presumably for the Princess Alexandra, but no one was so indiscreet as to ask—at Cartier. He registered at the Ritz as the "Duke of Lancaster," deceiving no one but maintaining the fiction that he was no different from any other tourist.

The "duke" wasted no time getting on with his pleasures, and that very afternoon Devin found himself accompanying him on a promenade up the Champs-Elysées to the Café des Ambassadeurs, after which it was time to go to dinner at Léon's and then to the gaming room at l'Epatant, where Devin sat opposite the prince, watching Florence Wingate whisper advice to him from her vantage point just behind his ear. Fortunately, Geoffrey Wingate soon joined them, and when the prince's party went on to finish the evening at 2:00 A.M. at the cabaret at the Lion d'Or, Florence was no longer with them, relieving Devin of that worry, at least. He even allowed himself to sit down and order the first wine he'd considered all evening.

He sat there in the semidarkness watching the prince and his Jockey Club friends only a few tables away, loudly applauding a new, very young and pretty *chanteuse*, who was well aware of her audience and played to him shamelessly. The contingent of French policemen, appropriately disguised as patrons of the café, was still doggedly in attendance and holding up better than Devin was. He hoped this would be their last stop. He would need his sleep, for tomorrow promised more of the same, starting with a drive in the Bois de Boulogne and ending with a visit to the theater where, if Grant was lucky, the prince would *not* join the cast as he had been known to do in the past.

It was noisy in the café, but the part of the noise that was directed at the prince was within normal limits—Grant could always hear when a sour note struck—and none of it mattered to him personally, so he blocked it out and for a few moments indulged in conjuring up images of Madeleine Malcolm, of her soft skin and the perfume that came from her hair—he'd have to find out what scent she used and send her some—and her smile. It pleased him that she smiled so much, not just at him, but because she found beauty in the world. That was more important to him than if she smiled like some coquette, only to please him. She smiled at life, and that had the effect of dissipating some of the tension that had been building in him lately and of softening the hardness he had developed as both a professional and a personal defense.

But how was he going to tell her the truth that would make that smile die in her? He hadn't lied to her thus far, but he hadn't told her every truth either. He should have told her at the beginning, but they hadn't trusted each other enough for that. Now...

It had been just too coincidental that she should have come to him just when she did, when he was frustrated in his own search for a simple answer to Lamont's murder. Every lead he had followed had turned up new questions and no answers, so it was not surprising that he had looked to her for one. It was also too much of a coincidence that her husband's body had been fished out of the Seine just when it had, even if she didn't believe it was really his.

It hadn't taken him long to realize that she had no real idea of what her husband had been involved in. But she had no idea, either, of being in any danger herself simply through her association with him. Or perhaps she really was in no danger. If he told her that, he wouldn't be able to keep her out of the way of accidents; but if he made her go home—and he could do that only by killing her happiness—he would lose her forever.

His imagination could not take in the idea of waking up

without her somewhere nearby—in the same city, if not in the same bed. How had she come to occupy such a large space in his life so quickly, so easily?

The empty chair at Devin's table scraped against the floor just then. He jumped, nearly knocking over the wine bottle. A hand reached out to catch it, and a voice whispered, "Take care, my friend. It is only I."

"Claude! Good God, man, don't sneak up on me like that."

"*Imbécile*. You might have seen me coming across half the club floor."

"Well, I didn't. What do you want, Claude?"

"I have information for you," Claude hissed, "but if you don't want it—"

"Of course I want it. But did you have to come here with it? I told you not to meet me in public."

"You should be grateful I see you at all, never mind in a room full of *flics*. You lied to me, Devin."

"What about?" Devin said, knowing the answer already.

"About this Malcolm," Claude said, not yet angry enough to raise his voice above a whisper. "You know perfectly well he is dead."

Grant took a deep breath. Claude had more right to be angry than he did, and it was unfair to take his edginess out on him. "That doesn't mean his name might not still mean something to someone," he said.

Claude sat back, making an effort to look as if he were just another patron of the café, enjoying a night out. "Well, you may be right. Here."

He wrote a name on a napkin and passed it to Devin, who read "Frank Hartwell." He looked up sharply.

"You know the name?" Claude said.

"If you know about Malcolm, you know I do. Do you also know where he is?"

"Unlike your Malcolm, he floated up again. Marius saw him last night in the rue Saint-Roch."

Devin raised an eyebrow. He knew the street well, having used it as a back way into the Bristol when the prince used to stay there. "Hardly his usual neighborhood."

"No. They say he is the leader of this new group, these Black Dogs. Others say he is only the real leader's dog."

"That seems more likely."

Devin fell silent, considering all this for a few minutes. On the round platform that passed for a stage, a comedian was impersonating an elderly foreign visitor unexpectedly confronted with a nubile young can-can dancer in his hotel room. The sound of laughter came from the prince's table, as if from a long distance away.

"Look at them," Claude said with disgust, "stuffing themselves and swilling wine. How stupidly the upper classes behave themselves."

"You've no respect for anything successful, have you, Claude?"

Fournier's black eyes glittered in the dim light, but he did not pick up this unexpected gauntlet. Instead he asked in the voice he adopted with his journalist's guise, "What do you see in him, anyway?"

"Unlike some," Devin said, with no particular emphasis but a steeliness in his voice that he did not often feel called upon to use, especially with his friends, "he is not all talk. It is talk and the slogans so easily coined by idle talkers that cause trouble, not money or the spending of it. He may lack imagination, but there is nothing wrong with his mind, and he uses it. He has contacts that may seem stupid and useless to those who don't have them and see only the trappings, but he makes use of them, too, and of his predilection for amusing companions and his access to both heads of state and high-born women. He has used his whole life to gain the kind of knowledge of the world that he will need when he becomes king."

There was a pause before Claude said, "If he ever becomes king."

Devin looked into Fournier's eyes. "When was the last time you were out of Paris, Claude?"

Fournier did not respond, conceding defeat. He picked up the napkin he had written on, concealing it in his pocket, then stood up to leave, but Devin reached up to grasp his arm.

"Merci, mon ami."

Claude shrugged. "Oh, by the way..."

"Yes?"

"There is someone else asking questions. A Pinkerton."

Devin stood up himself at that and kept his hold on Claude's arm as he escorted him out the back door of the club. "Name of Drummond?" he asked, as he closed the door behind them.

"No, Bertaude. Paul Bertaude. You know him?"

Devin scowled. "No, but I'll find him. Leave him alone, Claude. I don't want him to know he's being watched, and your friends are writers, not policemen. They wouldn't know how to hide themselves.''

Claude smiled. "Do you think we haven't been on intimate terms with the police and their methods?''

"Yes, but you've hardly been inconspicuous about it.''

Claude shrugged. "Whatever you say. Marius and Jean-Pierre, they have writing to do now, in any case.''

Devin took the hint; he also took his billfold out of his pocket, counting out a generous sum and handing it to Fournier.

"I'm sorry I was angry before, Claude. Thank you.''

"You do not have to pay for your anger, my friend. But I will take your money. I will also try to help you again. I think you are worried about more than your job now, *c'est vrai*?''

"Possibly.''

"Bah, you English!'' Claude spat into the alley. "You apologize for your anger, and you do not even admit you have other emotions.''

"Possibly,'' Devin said again, but smiled and embraced Claude, who shrugged it off and walked away down the alley.

Damn, Devin thought irrelevantly, as he peered into the black street after Claude. He'd have to buy a new pair of shoes. He'd wear these out before he left Paris if this kept up.

Chapter Nineteen

IT was sweet—too sweet, too deliciously soothing—to simply lie back and remember how he had loved her. Maddie had never felt like that before; she had never been able to respond like that to Teddy, and she had loved Teddy, or thought she had.

"I love you, Teddy," she had said, constantly it seemed, when they were first married. Perhaps she had only been trying to convince herself by saying the words over and over. She had never been able to connect them with the act of love, or the act with the emotion, which at least in the beginning, Teddy really had stirred in her.

With Devin it all seemed to be the same thing. The feelings became the act, and the act was pure feeling.

Maddie got up and rummaged in her travel desk for the photograph of Teddy that Laurie had taken on the boat. She sat down with it for a moment and tried to make the image come alive, to remember that she had been happy with Teddy, too . . . at least in the beginning. But the image stayed fixed to the paper and did not move. She had looked at it so often now that it was as if the image were all, that there was no flesh-and-blood man behind it.

And for the first time she really believed that Teddy was dead.

She stood up and began pacing the carpet. Was she telling herself that now only to justify her feelings for Devin Grant? When had she stopped being so sure that she would find Teddy? Was it only after she fell in love with Devin? But when was that? She hadn't seen it coming, but all at once it was there.

She hadn't seen him since that day in the country, but he had sent several messages, and with the last one, one of those lovely little English enameled pillboxes. It had a poppy on the lid. She found it now on her bedside table and turned it over in her hand, smiling at the memories it conjured up.

All of his messages had been tinged with regret that he could not come to her now because of his duty to the prince. The short, hastily scrawled notes on backs of envelopes or whatever was at hand where he wrote them were very like him. She could see him writing them, so that when he begged her to be patient and never believe he was not thinking about her, she believed him.

Nevertheless, she had to do _something_ to give her impatience an outlet. She went to her window to look down at the Place Vendôme. The view was not quite so good as the one she had given up to the prince's entourage three days earlier, but she could see the base of the column, around which there seemed to be more traffic than usual this morning, as if something were going on in the square. Perhaps the prince was leaving the hotel for some reason, for even when traveling privately, he attracted a following wherever he went.

That gave Maddie an idea, and her growing restlessness made her snatch at it. *Anything Florence Wingate can do*, she told herself, *so can the American Beauty rose*.

"Louise!"

Her maid answered the summons almost instantly. "Oh, good, you're here. Louise, be a dear and see if you can find out what the Prince of Wales will be doing today . . . and where. Try the concierge's desk first. . . . If Monsieur Pontcarre is there, he will tell you."

Having long ago learned to gauge the determination behind Mrs. Malcolm's impulses, Louise did not hesitate in taking herself off on this errand with no delaying questions or arguments. Maddie, meanwhile, began shedding her morning dress and was standing before an open wardrobe in a loose wrapper, surveying her newest and most fashionable promenade gowns, when Louise returned to say the prince was about to leave for a drive in the Bois de Boulogne.

"Perfect. Here, help me with this dress, please, Louise."

Half an hour later, Maddie was also on her way to the Bois. She secured Laurence Fox's escort, if not Daisy Jervis's company. Because Lady Jervis insisted she needed new clothes for their next stop, Baden-Baden, Daisy was dragged off by her mother to a dressmaking establishment, the unfashionable location of which, Laurie said, Daisy intended not to reveal to a living soul.

They were in luck. Laurie guessed that the prince would make for the Longchamp racecourse, where it would be more difficult to catch up with him. But on entering the Bois from l'Etoile they learned from the gatekeeper that although there was no race that afternoon, the prince's party had just set off up the allée de Longchamp anyway.

They passed through the gate into Paris's most popular park. Since the second empire, when Baron Haussmann had transformed this overgrown haunt of footpads into an open, green paradise, it attracted on any sunny summer's day a gleaming array of carriages full of fashionable Parisians, and foreigners wanting to be Parisians. The broad, tree-lined avenues, immense sweeping lawns, lakes, and flower beds made lovely views—for those who might even prefer them to viewing one another.

The prince's carriage was making leisurely progress, giving the royal tourist plenty of opportunity to ogle the ladies in other vehicles, and Laurence soon spotted it just ahead of them.

"What shall we do?" Maddie asked. "We can't very well overtake him."

"Look, he's turning down the other avenue."

Laurie tapped their driver on the back and held a whispered conference with him. Then they too made a turn, onto a narrower lane skirting the Pré Catalan, the open-air restaurant in the center of the park. Not ten minutes later, they were driving along the avenue de

Saint-Cloud when they saw the royal party coming at them from the other direction.

"Oh, well done, Laurie!"

Mr. Fox grinned and wasted no time in unfolding his new pocket camera in anticipation of passing the prince at close range.

But Maddie had no intention of merely passing by, and when she spotted Devin Grant riding alongside the prince's carriage, she hesitated only briefly to catch her breath at the handsome picture he made on horseback, then thrust to the back of her mind the other images the sight of him conjured up. She called out to him.

She thought he might be angry at her temerity, but instead he smiled, almost in admiration, she thought, and signaled the prince's driver to stop.

"Good afternoon, Mrs. Malcolm," he said, lifting his hat politely. "You are looking very well."

His eyes left her in no doubt of precisely how well she looked, and she was able to suppress a blush only through sheer happiness at his reaction to her. She had hoped he would be glad that she had taken the initiative in seeking him out, but she had not expected that caress in his eyes. She felt it almost physically and was possessed with the idea of returning it—and not in kind.

But he was more in control of himself and said, "My lord duke, I should like to present Mrs. Edward Malcolm, an American lady who is an ardent admirer of yours."

Maddie suspected that she was only one of at least a score of women who had been thus introduced to the "Duke of Lancaster," but he was as delighted to acknowledge her as if she were the first. He tipped his hat; she bowed her head, thankful for Devin's reminder that she was not to address him by his real title.

"Happy to meet you, Mrs. Malcolm!" he said. "I had no idea Grant kept such lovely company, but it seems I underestimated him. Is this your first visit to Paris, ma'am?"

"It is, sir, but not, I trust, the last."

"No, indeed! One must always live with the expectation of seeing Paris again. It keeps one young—not that you need consider that, for you will be young for a very long time yet." He hesitated and leaned a little closer toward Maddie to study her out of his round blue eyes. "Do you know—forgive me, ma'am—but have we not met before?"

"You may have seen Mrs. Malcolm's photograph in the *Illustrated News*, sir," Devin offered, with what Maddie was sure was some mischief-making motive. "Mr. Fox here is making quite a name for himself photographing beautiful ladies."

"That's it!" the prince exclaimed, slapping his knee in delight. "The American Beauty Rose! I am indeed honored to make your acquaintance, my dear, and to see that you are as much the beauty in person."

Maddie did blush at that, but the prince transferred his attention to Laurie just then. "Is that a new Kodak you have there, my boy? My wife is quite the aficionada, you know. Would you like to take my picture, so that I may take a copy back to her?"

"Yes, sir. Thank you!" Laurie said, not so overwhelmed by the honor bestowed on him that he was not quick to take advantage of it. Maddie was sure that he would not have been so amateurish as to forget to load the camera with fresh film either.

Laurie jumped down from the carriage, made his bow, and aimed his camera. The prince, who was already well practiced in the ways of cameramen, assumed just the right posture and looked off to the right of Laurie's ear just at the moment he snapped the picture. Laurie wasted no time in taking several shots but did not press his advantage.

"Thank you very much, sir," he said, to indicate he had finished. "I am much obliged."

After exchanging a few more words establishing that Mrs. Malcolm was also stopping at the Ritz and that Mr. Fox would send up a print of the photograph the next day, the prince asked Maddie if she were going to the theater the following night to see the divine Sarah Bernhardt.

"I intend to, sir," she said and saw Devin grin. She hoped his good will would extend to getting her tickets, for up to this moment Maddie had not even thought of going to the theater.

"Splendid! I look forward to seeing you there, Mrs. Malcolm. Good day to you."

He tipped his hat again, and his driver, obviously accustomed to these royal attentions to female admirers and the subsequent brusque royal dismissals, started up the horses again. A moment later the party, including Devin, was gone.

Maddie tried to tell herself it would be a mistake to hope for too much, but she allowed herself to be happy about the meeting in the Bois and to look forward to the evening. But when four theater tickets duly arrived, accompanied only by Devin's note that he would try to see her in the interval, she had to steel herself against the possibility of not seeing him at all. Ridding her imagination of the dream of his making love to her again that night was harder.

Laurence Fox and Daisy Jervis were more than excited enough when they set off for the Théâtre de la Renaissance to mask any apprehension on her part, however, and Lady Jervis acknowledged it only unwittingly, by treating Maddie like a contemporary and complaining good-naturedly about the high spirits and lack of discipline of the young.

It had been long enough since Maddie was last inside a theater to make her curious about it. Most of the ladies were in the dress circle, while below them, a more gregarious group of people milled about the orchestra pit. The old-fashioned decoration reminded Maddie of the theaters in New Orleans, which was where she first went to a play with Teddy. He had liked the theater, but like most of the patrons tonight, he liked it most for the company. Sometimes he even slept through the acts in order to be awake during the intermission, when he would go off and visit his friends.

She remembered that once, in St. Louis, she had watched him over the balcony as he made his way through the crowds below. It had been that period when he worked for Richard Brokmeyer, and Maddie thought he was particularly good at being friendly to people who might be of use to his employer. But then she had seen him deliberately cut someone—an old friend who looked after him in astonishment.

"Didn't you see George Lasker waving to you?" she had asked him when he came back to the box.

"I saw him."

He'd looked at her then, as if at a child who could not be expected to understand, and explained that George had voted against Richard at the last council meeting.

"Well, why shouldn't he? He belongs to another party and must vote his own way," she had replied.

"But his was the deciding vote. We lost because of it."

She'd asked him then if he'd still be talking to George if he'd been in the majority, which set off a quarrel—they were happening more frequently then—between them. Maddie had been left with the uncomfortable feeling that her husband was an opportunist, and worse—one to whom honesty came naturally only when it came in handy.

She had managed to block that little incident out of her mind until now, and now she wondered if there had been more of them that she simply refused to recall.

Looking across the auditorium now, she could see Devin standing up in a box by himself. Presumably it was the prince's, and Devin was making sure that everything was in order. He cast a critical eye over the rest of the theater, passing over Maddie's box as if he didn't see her in it. But then he did; his glance came back, and she saw that it was different for a moment. He smiled, but then continued his scrutiny with that same searching look.

It was only when the lights were beginning to dim for the start of the performance that the "Duke of Lancaster" entered his box. But he was instantly recognized, and a cheer went up from the pit. He waved in acknowledgment, then sat down as a signal that the play could begin.

The performance was only of mild interest. It was a palid revival of a Rostand drama Madame Bernhardt had played before, and most of the audience was far too interested in what was going on in the Duke of Lancaster's box, which was directly opposite Maddie's, to watch the stage. The prince was an ardent admirer of Bernhardt, however; so the actress was not ignored entirely, although Maddie for one thought her style rather stiff and stylized.

When the lights went up again for the intermission, Maddie could see Devin at the rear of the prince's box, apparently performing as gatekeeper, letting in only the select few he knew the prince wished to see. That meant he would not be coming to her.

"Shall we try to gain entrance?" Laurie asked, having spotted Devin, too.

"No," Maddie said, unwilling to go begging, especially if she were to be rebuffed.

"Perhaps you're right. I don't have the finished print for him yet, in any case, since a person who shall remain nameless spilled my last bottle of fixitive."

Daisy sniffed. Laurie's exclusive meeting with the prince still rankled with her, and it was only partly compensated by this visit to the theater where Daisy was obliged to gaze at the prince through her opera glasses as everyone else was doing. She raised them now and observed that Mrs. Wingate had just sat down next to the prince.

This, obscurely, doubled Maddie's determination not to join the throng; but when by the end of the second interval

Devin had still not come to see her, she began to realize that her pride would not warm her in bed that night. Besides, she could no longer even catch glimpses of him at the back of the royal box.

Only when the lights had dimmed for the last act did she became aware of the door opening at the rear of her own box. There was no further sound for a moment, so she leaned toward Lady Jervis to say she had a headache and was going to the ladies' withdrawing room for a moment. Then she rose quietly, so as not to draw the attention of Daisy and Laurie sitting in front of her, turned, and walked into Devin Grant's arms.

He had waited for her on the other side of the curtain that separated the box from the door to the corridor, and when she parted the curtain, he reached out for her and, before she could say anything, covered her mouth with his. She could not resist—this had been too much on her own mind not to welcome it—and she melted into his long, almost desperate embrace.

"Oh, God, I've been wanting to do that all day," he whispered, when he finally let her breathe again.

She smiled up at him and stroked his cheek with her hand. "Couldn't you wait another hour?"

He looked down at her, and despite having tried to prepare herself, the confirmation that he would not be coming to her after all still came as a shock. "I'm sorry," he said. "I can't."

She had been so noble that morning, so secure in her confidence that she would be able to wait for him. Yet now she had to resist the impulse to berate him like an angry wife, to accuse him of breaking promises he had never made. She said nothing, but she could not help pushing away from him, her desire suddenly cooled, and he understood.

"I'm sorry, Maddie. I can't come to you tonight, and I can't tell you why I can't. You must see that it will always be like that, whatever my private desires, and however strong they may be."

"Of course."

Even Maddie could hear the ice in her own voice. She didn't mean it like that, but she couldn't help it. Suddenly he pulled her to him again and kissed her, harder, with passion but without the gentleness he had shown up until now. His body was hard and rough against hers, his mouth cold and hurting, tearing at the tender places he had caressed before, forcing her to submit to his deliberate assault.

"Don't be that way!" he said, when finally he let her go and thrust her against the opposite wall. "Don't be ordinary! I don't want to be apart from you any more than you—"

He stopped, apparently aware that his anger added to hers was twice as wasteful as one alone. He looked at her once more, in sorrow rather than anger, which made her long to take it all back, to beg his forgiveness.

But he was gone before she had even thought it.

Louise had fallen asleep on the sofa where she had been waiting for Maddie long before her mistress came in at almost three o'clock in the morning. Maddie looked at her, her heart, despite its own bruises, going out to her loyal Louise, and she tiptoed softly past her so she would not wake her from the rather awkward position she had fallen asleep in and would doubtless awaken stiffly from in the morning. She began to undo her own buttons, but gave it up finally and lay down on the bed without removing her clothes.

But sleep would not come. As soon as Maddie's head touched the pillow, her mind came awake again. Staring at the white-painted ceiling, she saw the sun-dappled whiteness of that pond off in the distance behind the River Inn—but then the clouds seemed to cover the sun and the water turned dark and angry. Turning her head, she saw in the hotel's window curtains the curtains of that little upstairs parlor in the inn waving gently in the afternoon breeze—and then the heavy red velvet curtain closing over the theater door after Devin left her.

She knew she would not sleep tonight. She got up again to close the drapes over the window. But then she stopped to look down into the Place Vendôme, where the kind of night light that is just preparing for morning dusted the cobblestones with silver. No one moved in the square, but it seemed alive, or at least, more alive than Maddie felt just then.

Quietly, she took up the opera cloak she had discarded on the sofa and let herself out of the room without waking Louise. A drowsy night concierge came to life when she reached the lobby and went out to signal a cab for her from the rank at the corner.

"Pont Sully," she told the driver.

That was the bridge where Teddy's body had been found and, presumably, where he had died. Maddie had never gone there before, but then, she had not up until now admitted to herself that Teddy really was dead.

She asked the cabbie to wait at the end of the bridge while she walked out onto it. No one else was there; even the Île Saint-Louis was deserted. Downstream, Notre Dame Cathedral loomed up blackly in the night. The gas lamps at either end of the bridge did little to illuminate the river below, which Maddie could hear more clearly than she could see, swishing softly against the stone supports of the bridge. She stared down into the darkness, willing her eyes to penetrate it, to reveal its secrets to her.

Perhaps Devin had been right, so long ago in London. Perhaps she had not wanted to face the truth of Teddy's death because it meant she must let him go without being able to tell him good-bye or that she was sorry for not really having loved him. She could admit now that she had not loved him—now that she understood only too clearly what loving meant. But if she could only have ended it more finally with Teddy, she would feel freer now to love Devin.

Devin had said, too, that she might have embarked on this search with no real hope of success because she felt responsible for Teddy's leaving.

She picked up her head, frowning. The only time they had talked about that at all had been that afternoon in the country, yet he had been remarkably perceptive all along. How could he have known so much about her, even at their first meeting?

Maddie shivered a little in the damp air. She could not resolve these things tonight, so she sighed and turned to signal the cabbie to come for her. But just at that moment, she saw someone standing under the lamp at the end of the bridge. A man. She took a step forward, gasped, and suddenly the man darted down the steps leading to the street, then down an alleyway.

Maddie ran to her cab, her heels clicking loudly on the deserted bridge, and pulled the door open. When she called to the driver to follow the man, he shrugged but turned the cab around anyway while Maddie drummed her fists impatiently on the rolled-down window. But when they were facing the other way again, the streets were still. There was no sign of the man. Maddie looked out the window and saw that the chase was hopeless; wearily she told the driver to take her back to the hotel.

The man she had seen was Teddy.

She was almost positive it was. His height and hair and clothing and the way he stood there under the lamp—she was certain it was Teddy.

But why had he run from her?

And why, when she ought to feel renewed hope at finding him alive after all, did she feel such a crushing sense of loss?

Chapter
Twenty

DAWN was breaking when Maddie returned to the hotel. Before she allowed herself time to think about it, she went up to Devin Grant's room and knocked. And knocked again, but there was no one there.

She returned to her own suite and picked up the telephone, but he did not answer her ring either.

Then Louise woke up and began to fuss. Had Maddie just come in? Why had she not wakened her sooner? "You look pale," Louise continued. "What's the matter?" Maddie listened to one last ring and gave up, replaced the receiver, and submitted to Louise's ministrations. She crawled into bed half an hour later, and the last thing she saw was Louise pulling the heavy drapes across her windows to shut out the morning.

She slept soundly and dreamlessly until noon, when Florence arrived and swept aside both the drapes and Louise's ineffectual protests. Maddie came groggily awake and recognized Florence only a moment before she sat down on her bed and scrutinized her face.

"My dear, you are looking positively peaked."

Certain that she must indeed have dark circles under her tired eyes, Maddie put her hand over them and said, "I'm sorry, Florence. I suppose I do have the tiniest little headache."

Louise harrumphed but did not contradict her. "I'll send for some breakfast, Mrs. Malcolm."

Florence watched Louise's stiff back until the door closed on it, then giggled. "What a gorgon! She reminds me of a governess I had once. Why do you keep her on, Maddie? She would depress me no end."

"She loves me," Maddie said, having no appetite for sophisticated evasions before breakfast.

"Oh." Florence studied her even more closely, as if Maddie might be sicker than she thought. Then she got up and opened Maddie's wardrobe.

"Well, I'm sure she's right about breakfast . . . and pots of coffee to go with it. It will do you a world of good to eat something nourishing, and I'll help you finish the coffee. Where are you off to today? Shall I help you choose something to wear?"

Maddie got out of bed and reached for her dressing gown. "Oh, I don't know." The delightful notion of going back to bed and not getting up until dinner time occurred only to be discarded. She would be the American Beauty Rose in front of Florence if it killed her.

"I think Laurie and Daisy wanted to go to Père-Lachaise today."

She frowned then. Had she got that right? Or was her tired mind confusing something Oliver Drummond had told her with Laurie's plans for today? Well, it hardly mattered, although Florence gave her an odd look.

"To a *graveyard*? Well, of all things. Really, Maddie, you are too good—chaperoning those youngsters all around, but graveyards are the limit! Let the dragon—Lady Jervis, I mean—take them. You should do something for yourself today. Better still, I'll do something. We'll have lunch together, just us girls . . . what do you say?"

"Thank you, Florence, but—"

"Now, but me no buts. That's from Shakespeare, did you know? Someone told me so at my salon, so you see I am becoming literary after all. Anyway, we'll have lunch at the Café Riche or Henry's—just *entre nous*—and then we'll go shopping for something—anything—that we don't need and that's outrageously expensive. I haven't given Geoffrey a good shock in at least two days.

"Anyway," she added, taking a dark blue afternoon dress out of the wardrobe and holding it up to herself to see how it blended with the pale green one she was wearing, "I shall need some new things for Baden. What is one expected to wear at a spa, do you know?"

"Why are you going there?"

It was just the opening Florence was fishing for. She plopped herself down next to Maddie on the sofa and said, "Bertie—I mean, the Prince of Wales—invited us! At any rate, he said he would be charmed to see us there. Isn't that just too sweet of him? He told me all about Baden— on the map, it says Baden-Baden, goodness knows why—

at tea the day we met, and yesterday he said Geoffrey and I should come along. Of course, we can't travel in the royal carriage, more's the pity, but I'll find a way to get together with him; you see if I don't.''

Maddie had no doubt of it. The prince had not only taken tea with Florence the day he arrived, but he had promised to bring some of his French friends to her next salon. Florence was over the moon with delight over her success, and for the next half hour did little but tell Maddie what the prince had said and what he would be doing and where he would be going that night. Maddie was tempted to crow a little about her own meeting with the prince in the Bois de Boulogne.

"Well, my dear," Florence said, coming to the end of her news and reaching one soft, fragrant arm around Maddie's shoulder. "You just stay here and rest for another hour, so that you can come to my salon this afternoon. I'm almost certain Bertie will be there, and you wouldn't want to miss meeting him, would you?''

Louise came in with breakfast just then, and Florence promptly took the tray out of her hands.

"That will do, Louise. I'll serve Mrs. Malcolm while we continue our little chat.''

"Yes, madam," Louise said, sniffing. "I'll be outside, Mrs. Malcolm.''

Maddie smiled warmly at her to make up for Florence's summary dismissal. "Thank you, Louise.''

Florence wrinkled her nose, but when Louise had gone, she said, "I do beg your pardon, my dear. I'll be as sweet as pie to her later, I promise. Have some coffee.''

Maddie was relieved to find she had some appetite, and after she had swallowed a cup of coffee and some fruit, she felt much better.

"I tell you what," Florence said, apparently not concurring with this diagnosis. "You must come to Baden, too, and take the waters. It'll be far better for you and more relaxing than all this excitement here in Paris. Anyway," she added slyly, "your terribly handsome gentleman friend will be there. He's left already, in fact. I saw him from my window earlier this morning."

"What?"

"Now, don't be coy with me, darling. I know you spent the other day in the country with Mr. Grant."

"*And* Mr. Fox and Miss Jervis."

"Oh, pooh. You may have been chaperoning them, but who was looking after *you*, pray tell? I know that if I had a chance like that—"

"Florence, I don't want to talk about it."

Maddie got up and put her hands over her ears, convinced that if she let Florence reduce her relationship with Devin Grant to a juicy bit of gossip, it would vanish into the darkness, as Teddy had from the Pont Sully last night.

Oh, God. Teddy.

Her stricken look registered even on Florence, who pulled her down on the sofa again, apologizing profusely.

"Oh, my dear, I didn't mean to pry, I swear! I was just teasing. Here, have another of these delicious little rolls, and I won't say another word about it."

Maddie gave up and submitted to Florence's chatter. She

supposed she was not very good company just then, and she felt a little guilty, too, for not being more grateful to Florence for her friendship. She could scarcely condemn Teddy for dropping his friends if she did just the same, even if more politely. So she tried to look interested in what Florence was saying, and whatever she could do by smiling and being agreeable she did.

Florence did not, to her credit, bring up the subject of Devin Grant again; and she did her considerable best to lighten Maddie's mood, so that by the time Louise interrupted to say that Oliver wanted a word, Maddie almost thought she could be friends again with the voluble but good-hearted Florence. She finished helping Maddie button up her dress, and they made plans to meet for tea later, since lunchtime was already well past. At last, Florence removed herself, being gracious to Louise on the way out and even stopping to greet Oliver, who, however, limited his conversation with Mrs. Wingate to a terse good-morning. Florence shrugged lightly at Maddie, as if to say she'd done her best, and floated out, leaving her pervasive jasmine scent behind her.

The look on Oliver's face told Maddie at once that he had something important to tell her, so she wasted no time in inviting him into her room, where Louise was busy closing the bed curtains and whisking Maddie's night things out of sight. But Oliver took no notice of any of this.

"Mrs. Malcolm, do you know where Mr. Grant is?"

"As a matter of fact, Mrs. Wingate has just told me he left for Germany last night."

"Yes, that would account for my not being able to reach him by telephone."

"I had no idea Mr. Grant was in such demand," Maddie said.

"I beg your pardon?"

"I'm sorry, Ollie, I was just being unladylike. What did you want to see him about?"

When he hesitated, Maddie looked at him more seriously. He had never been reluctant to confide in her before.

"What is it, Ollie?"

"I am sorry to confess, Mrs. Malcolm, that there is something I have been reluctant to discuss with you—not wishing to concern you unduly—but I now think you should know that in the course of my other inquiries, I seem to have uncovered a plot . . . against the Prince of Wales."

Maddie raised her eyebrows. "What sort of plot?"

Oliver hesitated but said, "An assassination plot."

"Oh, dear." Maddie sat down on the sofa. "Does Mr. Grant know about this?"

"Yes, I went to him as soon as I had the first indication of it. Even then he was aware of it. It seems rumors have been afoot for months, but only recently has any definite plan been hinted at. In any case, he expressed his gratitude at my coming to him with this information, and we agreed to work in concert, letting as few other people into our confidence as possible."

"Including me."

"Yes, ma'am. I'm sorry."

"It's all right, Ollie. I understand the need for secrecy,

and you need not give me any details. But have you discovered something new that you need to tell Mr. Grant?''

''A colleague of mine, whom I ran into unexpectedly and who has been assisting me, overheard a conversation last night that led him to believe that this attempt will indeed take place in Germany. The assassin was not one of the men Paul overheard, unfortunately; but it seems this man has said he is determined to succeed this time, even if he has to—to kill everyone around the prince to get at him.''

Maddie could almost feel her heart stop for a moment as she closed her eyes and a flash of picture—Devin leaning over to say something to the prince—came into her mind. She opened her eyes again.

''I see.''

''Precisely. You will see also my need to reach Mr. Grant, then. Have you also, Mrs. Malcolm, any idea of when the royal party will leave for Baden?''

''That is something else that Mrs. Wingate is doubtless privy to,'' Maddie said, ''but unfortunately it was the one thing she neglected to mention to me. I can find out for you, I expect, when we meet later today.''

She glanced inquiringly at Oliver, who nodded. ''Thank you,'' he said. ''That will be helpful. I think, also, I should go myself to Baden as soon as possible.''

''Shall I attempt to drop a hint to the prince?'' she asked. ''I'm sure I could get close enough to him to do so.''

Oliver considered this but shook his head. ''I understand that the prince puts no credence in such tales and would only be annoyed if such a warning came from such an unusual source. Also, if the plan is indeed to—to dispose of him in Baden, he will probably be quite safe at least until he leaves Paris. I will make the arrangements for your journey at once and also send a telegram to Mr. Grant on the off chance that he would inquire at the Hotel Stephanie for you, which is one of the largest hotels in the town. If that meets with your approval, of course.''

''Yes, thank you, Ollie. When will you leave, then?''

''Tonight, if possible. I shall report back to you before that, of course.''

''And Louise will begin packing for me as soon as she has said good-bye to you.''

Oliver opened his mouth to say something, but the protest was never voiced. Instead, he bowed and went off to make his arrangements, leaving Maddie to consider the implications of what he had told her.

It was obvious to her, if not to Oliver, that Devin's sudden departure meant he, too, had discovered more about this plot against the prince—perhaps even the details of when the assassination attempt would take place—and where. If he had any hint of danger to himself for being close to the prince, Maddie was sure he would dismiss it as unimportant. He certainly would not have mentioned it to her.

But had he also discovered that Teddy was alive? She was unsure why she had not been able to bring herself to tell Oliver about that, unless because saying it confirmed it; and there was still a certain unreality about that whole predawn encounter on the bridge. It had, in any case, nothing to do with the assassination plot, and there was no point just now in adding to Oliver's worries.

On the other hand, perhaps Devin did know that Teddy was still alive and thought he was also still involved with the anarchists, even with this new plot? *There have been rumors afoot for months*, Oliver had told her, which meant Devin may have been looking for Teddy all along. Could he possibly have been the man Oliver's friend heard discussed, the man who made such cold-blooded threats? She had told Devin that Teddy was incapable of such things, but it had been a long time since she had seen him. Perhaps he had changed. Perhaps that was why he had run from her at the bridge—left Paris, even, for fear that if he stayed, she would, sooner or later, find him again.

Maddie was no longer surprised to find herself thinking of Teddy as a stranger. Seeing him under that lamp in the Paris dawn had made her realize that she had not really wanted to find him alive for some time.

Poor Teddy. Even if nothing had been her fault, he had still not been treated fairly by fate. She wished she had been able to see behind the happiness he always seemed to wear like the latest fashion, but which, it now seemed, had not changed whatever driving unhappiness lay beneath the façade.

The realization that Teddy was no longer a part of her did not prevent Maddie from feeling disloyal to him. She had been so insistent on her devotion to him that it had even begun to sound false to her. No wonder Devin had not believed her, even from the start.

My motives, Mr. Grant, are none of your concern.

If only she had confessed her doubts to Devin sooner, surely that would have helped to tear Teddy's memory out of her mind? He would have understood, just as he had understood what she needed when he made love to her. But for too long she had thought that saying aloud how much she loved Teddy would make it true again, just as telling Oliver now that he was alive would make that true.

I know that if he were dead, I should feel it.

What nonsense that was. She had felt as she wanted to feel. She had wanted Teddy to be alive, but she could not prove he was; then, when he had at last slipped out of her heart, if not from her mind, and she wanted to know that he was dead, he had appeared out of the darkness again.

But even now, she did not hate him. She felt nothing toward Teddy beyond pity, certainly not any wish to hurt him by starting divorce proceedings without making one more effort to talk to him, to try to explain that they had not drifted apart—they had never really been together.

Now she loved Devin Grant, and that overshadowed everything else. And she knew that she would do anything in her power to keep him out of danger.

Chapter
Twenty-one

BADEN-Baden was tucked into a corner of the Black Forest like an enchanted village in a Grimm brothers fairy tale. The winding, cobblestoned streets and old timbered houses and steepled churches added to the charm of the setting, but it was the thermal baths, discovered by the Romans twenty centuries before, that had attracted royal, titled, or merely rich visitors to the town year in and year out.

Only Devin Grant had no eye for the beauties of Germany's most popular spa, and no time to spare for its medicinal waters. He was blind to the lushness of the trees lining almost every street and to the magnificent views of the surrounding forest that appeared around every corner. All he wanted to do was sleep.

But not yet. He had been able to snatch a little sleep on the train from Paris, though he had spent most of the journey mulling over what he had learned from Paul

Bertaude when he finally caught up with him. The plot against the prince was real. Devin believed that, however little sense he could make of the scattered information he had unearthed. He also had to believe that the attempt really would be made in Baden—for if it were not, he would be helpless to do anything to stop it. That consideration had almost kept him from leaving Paris. If he were not even on the scene to at least make an attempt to stop the assassin, he would never forgive himself.

Baden made sense of a sort. The assassin, or his controller, more than likely believed that the hostility, due to mutual distrust, between the prince and his nephew the German kaiser would afford them a better chance of escape than they might have had in France—or least of leniency if they were captured.

Grant wouldn't have been surprised to learn the kaiser himself had a hand in the plot—if only in the sense Henry II was said to have had in the murder of Thomas a Becket when he voiced a wish, within hearing of his knights, for someone to "rid me of this meddlesome priest." The kaiser, of course, would deny any involvement afterward—and he'd believe his own lie, too. Grant held a low opinion of Wilhelm, who he thought ruled like a medieval baron, lording it over everyone but leaving the dirty work to others while he wandered around Europe on his private train visiting relatives who would rather he visited someone else.

"His notion of being a good administrator," Ponsonby had once confided, "is to write notes in the margins of state papers—useful stuff like *Schwein*! and *unmöglich*!"

But Ponsonby was able to stifle his feelings, smile graciously, and speak politely to the emperor on his visits to his uncle at Cowes or Windsor. Grant kept out of the way on those occasions and had succeeded in keeping out of Germany, too, since his first visit with the prince several years before. He had to admire the prince's continuous attempts to make peace with his nephew despite the differences in their temperaments and opinions, but he thought it a losing cause, if not exactly a waste of time. Ignoring the protocol-conscious emperor might be courting disaster some time in the future, he conceded, even if attempts to mollify him now might simply be pushing the inevitable only a little further into that uncertain future.

The prince would be staying at the Hotel Stephanie, as usual, and as usual nothing would persuade him to do otherwise. But that did not stop Devin from mentioning as loudly as possible to anyone within earshot that the prince would be staying at the Hotel D'Angleterre this time and persuading both grand hotels to go along with this deception and to suffer his peremptory installation of discreetly plainclothed police guards in the one and more obviously uniformed officers in the other. Why he imagined an assassin clever enough to elude identification would be deceived by such amateurish precautions, he did not know. But he had to do something.

He also familiarized himself as quickly as he could with the town, spending his first twenty-four hours there walk-

ing around it, from the railway station where the prince
would arrive, to the Pump Room and the Friedrichs-Bad,
the ruined castle just outside the town, and the nearby
Black Forest resort of Freudenstadt. He was tempted to
stop at one of the baths, if only to soak the tension out of
his aching muscles, or at one of the wine cellars in the
Gernbacher-Strasse, to slow his racing mind. He compromised
by doing his reconnaissance on foot instead of renting one
of the cabs lined up in front of the railway station. At least
the fresh air would keep him awake.

He stopped in at the local police station to identify
himself and was offered one of the younger, brighter-
looking members of the force to assist him in interpreting
the local dialect and introducing him to those cafés and
places of entertainment that stayed open late at night and
to which the prince would doubtless find his way in his
relentless pursuit of novel amusements.

Sergeant Guntar Brenner was an eager recruit, and even
if his eagerness proved quickly exhausting—to Devin—his
youth meant he had enough energy and sheer good health
to add miles to Devin's own resources. He also seemed to
know every shopkeeper and café owner in town; he had
grown up there, he told Devin, and his father had been a
policeman before him. So Devin gave him Edward Malcolm's
photograph and sent him off to make that face known in all
those shops and cafés, then finally persuaded himself that
he could safely go to sleep for a few hours. But his
exhaustion stretched his nap through the entire afternoon,
so that he woke to the muted glow of the forest-shrouded
sunset gilding the windowpanes in his hotel room. Turning

his head slightly, he saw a figure seated at his desk, a figure too small—and too quiet—to be Brenner's.

"Drummond?"

Oliver turned around. "Good. I thought I'd have to wake you up."

"What the devil time is it?"

"About half past seven."

"Damn."

Grant swung his legs over the side of the bed and reached for his shirt and jacket. He glared at Oliver as he put them on, waiting for him to say something, but when he did not, Devin had to ask, "Is she here?"

"Not yet."

"I should have known it was too much to ask of her that she stay in Paris." Oliver smiled at that but said nothing, so Devin went on. "Why didn't you at least stay with her?"

"Why didn't you tell me about Frank Hartwell?" Oliver countered.

If he was trying to catch him off-balance, Grant thought, he had done it. He sat down on the edge of a sofa to put on his boots. "What about him?"

"That he's a dead ringer for Edward Malcolm, to start with. That would have explained a good deal . . . if I'd known."

"How did you find that out?"

"A friend—a colleague of mine—got a good description of Hartwell from one of his sources. It sounded familiar somehow, so I showed him a photograph of Malcolm. They were as alike as brothers."

"This friendly colleague, I presume, is Paul Bertaude—to whom, may I remind you, you never saw fit to introduce me."

Oliver smiled in what Grant chose to interpret as a patronizing way. He hadn't moved from the desk where he had been making notes on the hotel's stationery, except to turn the chair slightly toward Devin and cross his legs with a movement that was precise without being fussy. He was dressed even more carefully than usual, in a neat black wool suit with creased trousers and a watch chain and fob in his waistcoat. He looked like a haberdashery salesman, Devin thought; nevertheless he felt somewhat at a disadvantage, half-dressed as he was, so he buttoned his cuffs and waistcoat and brushed his hair. Even then, he felt rumpled by comparison.

"Mr. Grant—" Oliver began, as if he were going to sell him something after all. But then he surprised him.

"—I would prefer to stop this sparring between us, which is helping neither of us. Mr. Grant, I know that Edward Malcolm is dead."

Devin raised his eyebrows. "Do you know how?"

"I don't care. At least, not at the moment, and I'm sure you'll tell me about it later, when you have less on your mind. Until such time"—*he's beginning to sound like a schoolmaster now*, Grant thought—"I am willing to assist you."

"With what?"

"Preserving your sovereign to gain his throne."

That stopped Devin in his pacing of the carpet. Damn.

298

Drummond was right. He no longer had the luxury of choosing his allies. He needed any help he could get.

"Shall we begin again?" Oliver asked, as if he could read Devin's mind.

"Tell me what you've heard."

So Oliver told him of his meetings with Paul Bertaude in Paris and their encounter with Aristide Dalou. Oliver had a good memory and could repeat everything he had heard, word by word. For once, Devin did not interrupt with questions but let the conversations Oliver resurrected for him flow through his mind, where the extraneous information was filtered out and the new details attached to the picture he had already formed. It was, thank God, actually beginning to look like something now.

Oliver consulted the notes he had been making to finish his story and explained Paul's conviction that the assassination attempt would indeed take place in Baden.

"Here, in the town?" Devin asked, as a new thought came to him. "Or just in Germany?"

Oliver considered that for a moment. "I suppose we must consider that it could occur outside the city limits."

"On a train, for instance?"

"Which one is your man on?"

Devin studied him for a moment and finally made the last concession, telling him the prince's itinerary and when he was due to arrive in Baden.

"Not the train Mrs. Malcolm is on, then," was all Oliver said, taking state secrets in his stride. The relief in his face was evident, and for a moment Devin felt a kind of kinship with this man, whose loyalty to his mistress was only another form of the love Devin had for her.

"How much have you told her?" he asked.

"The generalities about the plot. Nothing about Hartwell . . . or about her husband."

Devin frowned and stared out the window for a moment. Oliver waited in silence until he'd made up his mind. Devin turned around and said, "I'll tell her about that. . . . I have to be the one."

Oliver folded his notes and put them in his pocket, then picked up his hat and started for the door. On his way out, he paused, looked at his watch, and said with a slight smile, "Her train got in twenty minutes ago."

Ten minutes later, Devin was halfway up the stairs to the second floor of the Hotel Stephanie; in another minute he was beating on Maddie's door. Louise opened it, saw who it was, and planted herself firmly in the crack between the door and the wall.

"I'm sorry, sir. Mrs. Malcolm is resting. She has only just arrived, and it was a tiring journey."

"I won't keep her long," Devin said, gently but firmly pushing Louise aside and entering the room. Maddie was standing by the window, swathed in a dressing gown that he couldn't help noticing let through the last golden light from the window, outlining those wonderful legs of hers. She looked as if she did not know how to greet him but finally didn't care and smiled anyway. She moved a step toward him, then remembered her maid.

"That will be all for now, Louise. Go and lie down for a while. I'll ring when I'm ready to dress for dinner."

Louise hesitated, but Maddie's smiling yet determined look seemed to convince her that her dismissal was not negotiable. Louise went out the hall door, closing it reluctantly behind her.

"There wasn't a large enough suite available for all of us," Maddie explained, coming to Devin and reaching her arms up to circle his neck. "She and Oliver have to sleep in the servants' wing upstairs."

She looked up at him in open invitation to take advantage of this fortuitous arrangement, and he was tempted enough to bend his head to kiss her. Her lips opened to let him enter the warm chamber of her mouth, and for a moment he forgot why he had come in the welcome of her desire for him. Then he tore himself away.

"Why did you come? I asked you to stay in Paris. It isn't safe here for you."

He was surprised to see the smile fade not just from her lips, but from her eyes; her whole body seemed to change, from eager welcome to despairing rejection. She turned back to the window.

"What is it?" he asked, concerned, moving involuntarily toward her again.

Very softly, she said, "You didn't ask me not to come. You didn't come to see me at all."

"I sent you a note asking you to stay in Paris, saying

that I'd be back as soon as I could. When did you leave? It must not have been delivered in time.''

She turned back to him. ''*Would* you have come back?''

''Of course. Maddie, I—''

Something about the look in her face then stopped him for a moment in wonder. He looked again, but it really was joy he saw—a joy as radiant as if she had just heard a report of a death refuted and could come alive again herself. Had she really still doubted him? He had been so sure of his love for her that he must have thought it needed no expressing. He took her in his arms again and kissed her again. She tasted like mountain air, like the Black Forest, like all the other natural wonders he hadn't had time to look at in his hurried tour of the town, but that he now breathed in through her kiss.

She wanted more, leaning into him as if trying to come even closer. He responded by plunging even deeper into her mouth, as though he could reach her heart that way. She moaned in the back of her throat, and he felt it echo in every nerve and muscle.

When he finally pulled himself away he had to gasp for breath to reassure her, to say, ''I love you, Maddie. How can you think I wanted to leave you, that I wouldn't have come back? I love you. I want you with me all the time, forever, to sleep with, to love . . .''

He found the fastening of her dressing gown and opened it, searching for the ripe breasts he could feel straining toward him, tantalizingly close under the fabric. But she stopped his hand and moved back a step.

''What is it?''

She looked at him, searching his eyes for something. He thought she was trying not to tell him something, so he waited until she had decided. Then she said, so softly he barely heard it, "I've seen Teddy."

It didn't register immediately. *Drummond said nothing about this* was his first thought. *She must not have told him.* But he knew it couldn't be true and said so. "That's impossible."

"No." She looked up at him. "I did see him. In Paris, late one night when I. . . . Devin, I wasn't looking for him anymore, I didn't *want* to find him—then there in the dark, there he was."

"Where?"

She told him, not telling him why she had gone to the bridge at that hour of the morning, but going into great detail about what the bridge looked like, what Teddy looked like, her voice rising toward the end until he realized that she was becoming hysterical, and he reached out to pull her to him, gripping her arms hard enough to hurt, so that she snapped out of her frenzy.

"It wasn't he," Devin said.

"What do you mean?"

He looked down into her puzzled eyes. "You saw a slenderly built man of your husband's height and coloring. Did you speak to him?"

"No."

"Did he say anything to you? Did he seem to recognize you?"

"No. I did wonder about that, about why he should have run away again. All I could think of was. . . . Devin,

303

was Teddy really involved in this plot? Have you known it all along and only wanted to spare me?''

''In a way. No, he wasn't, but yes, I have.''

Bewildered, she looked at him again in that searching way, as if seeking an answer to a question she was afraid to voice. He looked over her shoulder, not wanting to meet her eyes, not wanting to tell her the truth. So she had to ask him again.

''Devin, why did you say it's impossible that it could have been Teddy?''

She spoke very low, almost as if she hoped he wouldn't hear, and when he took her closer into his arms, kissing her neck, breathing in the sweet scent of her freshly brushed hair, he could feel her bewilderment as palpably as he could her scantily clothed body.

''Do you love me, Maddie?'' he whispered.

''Yes.'' She said it quickly, as if she didn't want to think about it. But he wanted her to.

''Will you always love me, whatever happens?''

''Yes!''

She believed it, but he could not, knowing what he did. He wanted to take her, to love her so violently that she would never forget it, because after he told her what he had to tell her, she would never let him do it again.

But he could not bring himself to do that to her even once, so at last he told her the whole truth.

''It's impossible—because I killed him.''

He could feel the shock go through her, like a bolt of electricity, but she didn't immediately try to push him away. He wished he could see her eyes, know what she was thinking. But when he moved his head to look at her, her eyes were dead, the passion shocked out of them, and she said, very calmly, "Get out."

He'd expected that, but now he didn't want to give in to it. He wanted to explain. He gripped her shoulders to hold her still in case she tried to bolt.

"Maddie, I didn't know who he was. I certainly didn't mean to kill him. I didn't mean to kill anyone, but he got in the way."

It was coming out muddled, so he started again. "He was pretending to be someone else—another anarchist—and he threatened Claude, so because I thought he was the other man, I shot him—"

"No!"

She twisted violently to free herself from him. "I don't want to hear any more! Get out!"

She was like a wild thing in his hands, and all he could think to do to stop her was to kiss her again, clamping his mouth on hers like a vise. She stopped moving then, so he moved his hands to pick her up and carry her to the bed. But as soon as he loosened his grip just enough, she tore herself away. She lost her balance and fell on the carpet, but when he reached to help her up, she lashed out at him, beating at him with her fists. He stepped out of her range and stared down at her, his fists clenched helplessly at his sides, hoping the storm would pass quickly.

But it wasn't going to. There were too many old sins—and not just his—surging to the surface for either of them to control.

"You murdered him! Get out of my sight. Get out!"

She turned her face away from him then, crossing her arms over it, and sobbing. Her anger seemed to leave her, only to transfer itself to him.

"You just said you didn't want to find him!" he shouted, even though he was standing directly over her. "He wasn't worth looking for, Maddie.... He was no good. He was weak and easily led, and he didn't care what he put you through. I'm sorry it had to be me, but it would have happened sooner or later. He would have stepped into some other situation he didn't belong in and didn't know how to handle."

She curled up into an anguished knot in the corner of the sofa and put her arms over her head, not wanting to listen to him.

"Maddie—"

Their shared anger cooled as quickly as it had flared, and he reached down to her. She shivered pathetically as he lifted her up, and he wanted to comfort her, hold her in his arms and tell her everything would be all right. But he knew she wouldn't let him. Not now. And it wouldn't be all right. Not until she had forgiven herself.

He laid her gently on the bed and left without another word, closing the door on her muffled sobs.

Chapter Twenty-Two

MADDIE did not go down to dinner that night and despite Louise's increasingly anxious questions, refused to say why she had lost her appetite, refused to say anything that would explain the blankness in her eyes and the defeat in her posture. When Louise finally, if reluctantly, left her, she lay down on her bed and for the first time in her life gave way to self-pity.

What had she done? . . . only given in to a dream, another dream of ending what was unhappy to find new happiness. She had dreamed the same thing once before, and it had turned into a nightmare, with no clear awakening to end it.

"Teddy, what would you do if I died before you?" she had asked once, when she was young enough to think of death as still only a theory, not a reality.

"I shall be so old by then," he'd said, "that I guess I'd just die, too."

If only she'd believed at the beginning that Teddy was dead, she might have spared herself this long drawn-out attempt to bury herself with him. If only she had not gone to London chasing that impossible dream, she would not have found another dream, one that had now proved just as elusive.

Why was it that whenever she tried to give her love away, it was flung back in her face? Teddy had not wanted it, or he would not have left her like that. She would have given him a divorce—and all her money if he wanted it—if only she'd been able to say good-bye to him once and for all. She would have been free, then, to give her love again.

She was only now beginning to understand how Teddy's little lies had weighed her down and restricted that freedom he pretended to give her. Just as the little adventures he found in life were not enough to satisfy her need to do something lasting and her own, so the little lies he told to make his life go more smoothly only slowed hers down.

The burden of remorse she carried about with her had made her talk as if she had loved Teddy more than she really had, so that what she shrank from now was the memory of the lies she had told Devin Grant about loving Teddy, lies that she had believed were the truth when she told them, but that he had seen through all along. No wonder he had not wanted to tell her the truth about how Teddy had died. He must have known she would have to find her way through her own lies before she would be ready to face the truth.

But how could she convince Devin now that she could

forget those lies? Could she live with him, without always remembering them—and being reminded of her own failure with Teddy?

But how could she live without him now?

"Will you always love me, whatever happens?" he had asked her, and believing it, she had said yes. Even now, she thought she could believe it, if only—

"Never say if only!" he'd said, too. "You can't change the past. . . ."

Maddie's mind revolved in a dizzy spiral, looking for an answer, any answer. Her emotions went in circles, through self-pity to anger to despair. Finally, she cried herself to sleep and did not wake up until after ten o'clock the next morning.

But then it was as if a storm had passed and the sky was clear of clouds again. She lay awake in bed, looking up at the ceiling and feeling drained. She remembered why she had been so miserable, but she could not remember now how it felt. She could remember Teddy now only as a face in the distant past, someone she had met briefly and not really known, someone who had no connection to her life now. It was as if a war had ended.

All that was left was Devin. She wanted more than anything else to run to him, to tell him she loved him and that she would love him whatever happened, or had happened. But was there still time? Had he believed perhaps that the shock of his confession, which was really just the final painful tearing out of everything that was past, was the end of their love? No, it was a beginning; she had to be sure he understood that!

Despite her desperate need to tell him this, however, she knew there was something else that mattered to him now, something that had to be finished before they could be free to forget the past and the rest of the world in the wonder of each other. And she knew that if she did not help him finish this thing, she could never hope to be allowed to share his life later.

She had wasted so much time fighting to change the past. Would she know how to fight for the future?

She got up and rang for Louise, who entered her room with trepidation, to find Maddie ransacking her closet for something to wear.

"Oh, there you are, Louise," she said, backing out of the wardrobe. "I'm going out. But please bring me a pen and some paper first."

Louise, understandably taken aback, hesitated. Maddie looked up from where she was kneeling on the floor searching for shoes to go with the dress she had chosen.

"What is it, Louise?"

"Nothing, Mrs. Malcolm. That is . . . are you quite well this morning, ma'am?"

"Yes, of course." Maddie began stripping off her robe and nightdress, but when Louise moved to help, she waved her hand dismissively. "Pen and paper, Louise."

"Won't you . . . wouldn't you like some breakfast, ma'am?"

Maddie paused with her hand reaching for a clothes

hanger. "Oh, yes. I'm starved. Order up a nice *big* breakfast, Louise, *after* you've brought the paper. And tell Oliver I want to see him."

An hour later, having eaten her breakfast, sent a message to Devin's room, and had a talk with Oliver from which Louise, who was beginning to feel decidedly put-upon, was excluded, Maddie was dressed and on her way across the Oos River by the nearest bridge. With Louise trailing determinedly behind, she started up the Lichtentaler Allee, trying to look like any other tourist out to take the air.

A glance in the mirror while she was dressing had told Maddie that her long night's sleep had not entirely removed the red from her eyes and that she was looking paler than usual, but she had rouged her cheeks, put some drops in her eyes, and put on her newest, gayest morning dress to go out walking on the broad, tree-lined avenue that was Baden's most fashionable promenade. Here the devotees of the spa's restorative waters drank while they walked, sipping from their cups and glasses whenever they paused to admire the view down across the river to the town itself.

The gentlemen wore dark city clothes, spats, and top hats, but the ladies were dressed to the nines in picture hats and filmy summer dresses. In her robin's-egg blue walking dress, Maddie thought she fit nicely into the elegant picture, but she found she had to deliberately pace her steps more slowly, from a brisk, anxious walk to a stroll, to keep people from looking after her curiously. She made herself stop every few minutes to put up her parasol and admire the view over the stone balustrade above the river.

It was while she was paused at one of these overlooks that Maddie became aware of someone other than Louise standing behind her. She drew a deep breath and prayed it was not too late to make him understand. It was a moment before he spoke, and then he sounded like someone else, like a servant she had sent for.

"You wanted to see me?"

"Yes." She made herself turn around and look up at him, hoping her eyes would tell him what she wanted to say. He studied her for a moment, then seemed to release his breath very slowly. He put one hand out, tentatively, to stroke her cheek, and she caught it in her own hand and held it there. For a moment she wished she had chosen a less public place for this meeting, but she had done it deliberately, after all. She took his hand away from her face, but held on to it just the same.

"I wanted to apologize—"

"Don't," he said. "Just say that you forgive me."

"For killing Teddy?"

He winced at that, pulling away from her a little as if she had struck him. "There is no forgiving that, only that I didn't tell you sooner."

"If you had, I would never have forgiven you."

"I know. I still should have told you."

"Why didn't you, then?"

"At first, because I was afraid you had some connection with the people who caused—the people your husband was involved with. Later . . . because I was afraid. I knew you would be angry, or disappointed, or shocked, and in any case would never want to see me again.''

''That's not true.''

He looked in her eyes, not quite trusting her words.

''It's true that I was all those things,'' she said, ''but they're gone now. I do want to see you. I do want your forgiveness, too.''

She thought something cleared from his face, as if he had felt some of the same storm that had ravished her all through the night. But he still had something left to say, to finish the past.

''May I tell you what happened now?''

She nodded. He put her arm in his, and they walked a little way up the path before he began. Louise trailed behind them, close enough to see them but not to overhear.

''It all started so simply,'' he said. ''There was an accident at one of the prince's shooting parties: a servant of one of the guests was shot. There had to be an inquiry, of course, so the prince asked me to help. That's when it began to get complicated.

''The man had been shot with a pistol, not a hunting rifle. A stranger had been seen in the woods at the same time. I came up against a blank wall when I tried to find out more about the servant. What I now believe happened is that he was paid to assassinate the prince, but that at the last minute he backed out . . . and was shot for his treachery.''

''But by whom?'' Maddie asked.

He smiled wryly. ''That's the one question that would have answered all the rest. I poked around in London for a long time, looking for some information about the stranger who'd been hanging about in the woods. I got tantalizing little clues, but few of them seemed to fit the same puzzle. I also got a vague picture of the man in the woods, but not enough to know what he looked like—until I went to Paris."

"Looking for Teddy?"

"No, before that. I didn't know Edward Malcolm existed before—before that night. In Paris I traced the servant to an anarchist group, whose chief was—or was reported to be—a man named Frank Hartwell, who was an American or a Canadian. He spoke English, but not like an Englishman. Anyway, I pretended to be interested in joining the group, and my friend Claude Fournier acted as go-between with this Hartwell.

"But he didn't believe my story about joining the group. He must have suspected some treachery, in fact, because he went into hiding for a while. Claude finally flushed him out, and although Hartwell wouldn't see me, he agreed to meet Claude . . . at midnight, on one of the Seine bridges."

"Pont Sully."

"Yes."

"What I believe happened then is that your husband took Hartwell's place, whether at Hartwell's instigation or because he thought it something of a lark, I don't know."

"Why should he think that?"

"They looked alike, he and Hartwell, enough at least to be mistaken for each other in the dark. And I think your husband had done that before—stood in for his boss—it's the only way some of those clues I picked up could have been planted, although I saw that only in retrospect and after I went back to find out where your husband had come into the story.''

They paused for a moment at a grove of the exotic trees Baden was famous for, trees that had been brought there from all over the world and that inexplicably thrived in the alien climate. But Maddie glanced only fleetingly at the little explanatory plaques attached to some of them, and Devin did not even trouble to look.

''That was why I was so convinced when we first met that you were hiding something,'' he said. ''It was too much of a coincidence that you should have come to me so soon after I had come back from Paris, where I first found out about your husband.''

''I suppose it would have been like Teddy—to skirt danger for a lark.''

The idea no longer surprised her, but her acceptance of it stopped him for a moment. He said, kindly, ''I don't think it was just that. I think Hartwell had some power over your husband, had caught him at some petty crime, perhaps, and threatened to turn him in.''

''Or to send him back to me.''

''Perhaps.''

They walked on a little farther, and he continued, ''So Claude walked out into the middle of the bridge to talk to the man he thought was Hartwell. Of course, I'd come along, too, and hid in the shadows to watch. He—your husband—got a little carried away with his part and began to threaten Claude. I could hear them arguing. Hartwell must have heard it, too, because just then I saw a movement at the other end of the bridge. It only registered on my mind that there were two Hartwells when the one at the end of the bridge raised a gun. I don't know why exactly; he may have thought his surrogate was getting out of hand, or he may have been aiming for Claude. That's what I thought, anyway, so I aimed at Hartwell. Just then, your— Malcolm—saw Hartwell, too, and ran toward him. He crossed my line of fire just as I pulled the trigger.''

When he had finished his story, they did not speak for a few minutes, walking on together in silence. The path wound into an evergreen wood, and the sunlit views were blotted out temporarily. It was cooler there, too.

''So the man I saw on the bridge was this Hartwell?''

''It must have been. I think he was following you, even in London, perhaps because he thought you knew about him, and he wanted to be sure you were not going to be a threat. Your secretary was a real threat, of course, nosing about the way he was, and that complicated things still more. Hartwell should have disappeared again, but by that time he may have been feeling as frustrated as I was.''

''Do you believe, then, that this man Hartwell is the assassin—the potential assassin?''

He raised an eyebrow at her but didn't answer at once. She thought he was trying to gauge how much to reveal to her, or how much she already knew. She decided to tell him.

''Oliver told me that Florence's young man—that is, the one at her salon who was brought by her Hungarian violinist—said there was a higher authority behind him.

The leader's dog, he called this man who looks like Teddy."

He smiled at that but said only, "Oliver is far too confiding."

"He isn't really. As soon as he learned there was more to this case than my finding Teddy, he stopped telling me anything I didn't drag out of him. He really did want to help you, Devin. He still does."

"I know."

When she looked at him quizzically, he explained about his meeting the day before with Oliver.

"I suppose I might have known. Where is Oliver now?"

"Scouring the lower depths with Sergeant Brenner, I expect. They will make a wonderful team."

"Who's that?"

He explained, and she laughed at the picture he conjured up of an overeager St. Bernard puppy. But then she stopped him again in their walk and said, "Devin, I know I've been a hindrance to you in your work—unintentionally, believe me—and I want to make it up to you."

"Why do you always think you have to atone for your behavior?" he said, echoing the anger of the night before, and for an instant she was frightened again. But then his voice softened.

"You don't have to atone for your imagined sins, my darling. Haven't I said that at least once already?"

"I put that badly, then. Old mistakes don't die easily. What I meant was, I want to help you, Devin."

"With what?" He was going to be deliberately unrevealing, she knew. She would have to convince him that she at least understood the urgency of his task, which he had been no more able than she to disguise by deliberately slowed steps along the Allee, which she could nevertheless barely keep up with. His hands clenched into fists whenever they were not touching her, and he had to make an effort to erase the frown that kept reappearing on his forehead.

"You know what I'm talking about. I—_we_ came here expressly to warn you about it."

"You could have warned the subject of your concern directly, in Paris."

"I don't think so," she said, challenging the statement with her eyes.

"No, you're right. He wouldn't have listened. Ponsonby would have, but you don't know Fritz—or do you?"

He was weakening a little, she could see; she tried not to smile at her victory. "No," she said simply. "I don't know everything. But please, Devin"—she put her hand on his arm—"I _can_ help. Between us—all three of us—we can stop these people."

He looked at her as if he were weighing this, coldly in his detective's mind, deciding if taking a chance on her was a greater risk than going on the way he had begun on his own. Or he may have been simply thinking ahead to what to do next.

"Devin, if you weren't involved, I wouldn't have come here. I _would_ have stayed in Paris."

He raised his eyebrows.

"I mean, I would have done my best to help, but I would have sent Oliver by himself, or telephoned. But because it was _you_, I wanted to be here, to help you." She lowered her eyes and said, so softly she was not certain he heard, "And I missed you."

"I was only gone two days."

"I know."

He looked down at her for a few minutes, and finally she saw in his gray eyes what she was looking for; they lost their sharpness and a welcome warmth came into them—a fire that she knew this time would not go out, would not even flicker. He picked up her hand and kissed it, and his warm breath was unbelievably evocative; all the emotions she had felt when he made love to her seemed to be concentrated in that tiny little kiss. The unbidden thought that he had just put aside all that had happened between them before, and that the next time they would begin again, reaching for new heights, new fires, made her catch her breath at the depth of her desire for him.

He seemed to know what she was feeling, and his voice was low and husky when he said, "I wish this weren't so public."

She smiled. "That's why I chose it. I was afraid I wouldn't be able to be businesslike and impersonal somewhere else."

He smiled. "There is a concert tonight. Would you like to go?"

"Are you attempting to divert me? Or do you expect there to be something more exciting than Wagner going on tonight?"

"My love, I sincerely hope there is nothing more exciting than Wagner to be had in Baden this evening. I am only going to eavesdrop, for as much as I would like to

319

dally with you in the ruins of the *Schloss*, or stroll along some secluded river path, I must go out in public and keep my eyes and ears open. Your being with me will at least make the duty a pleasant one.''

''Well, I suppose that is some concession, however ungracious, to my offer to help.''

''I also do not want you out of my sight.''

''Are you afraid of what I might do? I promise to behave if you promise not to exclude me.''

He smiled faintly but said nothing, and after they had walked a little farther, he stopped her and said, ''It isn't a game, Maddie.''

''I hope you know me better than that.''

''I'm sorry, but I had to be sure you understood. This unknown mastermind behind the plot must keep a close watch on his minions. It is therefore very likely that he is in Baden as well. He could be anywhere. He could be anyone. He could hurt you, too.''

''I understand that.''

He looked into her eyes and seemed to make up his mind. He raised her hand to his lips and kissed it; she closed her eyes, feeling the fear that he held inside himself transmit itself it to her. She welcomed it, for it meant she was really a part of him now, sharing in whatever he was feeling. She turned her fingers a little to squeeze his hand, to tell him that way, too, that she understood.

''I'll pick you up at eight o'clock.''

Chapter
Twenty-three

THE evening was warm and windless; and since the concert hall was not far from the hotel, Maddie suggested to Devin when he came to call for her that they walk there so they would have a few minutes to talk. But he was not very forthcoming—less, she suspected, from reluctance than from his simply having too much on his mind to spare thought for small talk. Maddie wished just the same that he would confide in her, as he had begun to in Paris, that afternoon when they went to see the Impressionists. Surely, Paris was not so far away or so long ago as all that?

They were walking along the modest little river that was as unlike the Seine, admittedly, as this picturesque resort village was from Paris or London. The shallow water shimmered in the pale moonlight filtering through the lime trees, and the air was warm and moist, as if the steam from the hot baths had been let into the air. It wasn't a night for hurrying or for jostling with crowds of other people in a small room, and Maddie walked slowly, prolonging the pleasantly languid sensation of the heated night and waiting for it to ease enough of Devin's tension that he would tell her about it.

Finally, she took the initiative. "Louise and I went to the baths this afternoon," she told him. "After I left you."

He put his hand on her bare neck and stroked it gently, with a warm, circular motion of his palm that she found soothing and stimulating at the same time . . . and much nicer than the baths. "Did it help?" he asked.

"It was Louise's idea. I think she considered me a prime candidate for a restorative boiling. But it was more relaxing than I'd expected. A rather intimidating matron took me in charge, ordering me—not suggesting, mind you, ordering me—to shower, then to be dried not with a towel, but in a hot, dry room, where I turned pink all over."

The suggestion of a smile around his mouth told her he was listening, so she went on. "Then she massaged me and put me in a steam bath. When I was properly pink again, she put me back in the shower . . . and turned on the *cold* water! Well, I rebelled at that, you may be sure. She insisted that alternate hot and cold baths was the proper treatment, but I insisted just as vehemently that I wasn't ill enough for that kind of treatment and held out for another hot bath. Well, she led me to it, but then left me in it for what seemed hours, and I nearly fell asleep. Fortunately, there are always several attendants on hand, expressly, I suspect, to keep people from drowning themselves!"

He laughed at that and gave her a suggestive look. "I should like to have seen you—all pink."

"I don't believe they have mixed baths . . . men and women, I mean, not hot and cold!"

"Pity."

He took his hand away from her neck then, but she caught it and put it back, then drew him to her by his other hand and raised her face to his. He took it between his large, rough hands, kissing her gently but firmly, not stopping until she moaned softly and pressed closer to him.

"Do we have to go to the concert?"

"I wish we didn't."

He kissed her once more and reluctantly let her go. She sighed, and they walked in silence the rest of the way to the Conversationshaus, a huge colonnaded building set against the hillside, where a band was already playing on the promenade in front. A large crowd of stylishly dressed people were milling around the grounds, apparently paying little attention to the music. To join them Maddie and Devin had to cross a bridge and pass through two rows of bazaar stalls selling all manner of wares.

And there, haggling over a lace tablecloth, was Florence Wingate, with her husband waiting patiently nearby. Geoffrey saw them first and waved.

"Good heavens," Devin said under his breath. "Did you know they were here?"

"I knew they were coming," Maddie said, "but I thought not for several days."

"Madeleine, darling!" Florence exclaimed, when Geoffrey

had finally caught her attention. "What a *lovely* surprise. I called your room this morning, but that woman of yours said you were out takin' the waters for your rheumatism or something. Did she give you my message? No, I can see she didn't. But never mind, here we all are. How are you this fine evenin', Mr. Grant?"

Florence gave Devin a gloved hand and a flirtatious glance and asked, none too subtly, if the prince had arrived yet.

"I'm sure you'll be the first to know when he does, Mrs. Wingate."

Florence laughed, taking no offense at his insinuation. "Well, of course I will, dear boy. I was only askin' to be polite, you know."

"Are you going to listen to the concert?" Maddie asked, feeling suddenly possessive of Devin and slipping her hand a little more tightly into his arm.

"Well, darlin', we were on our way there, but then I discovered this delightful little bazaar. Do look at this lace—you know I collect fine lace—handmade, I've no doubt, by some little elves in the Black Forest. It probably has pine cones woven into it."

"Florence would far rather empty my purse than fill her mind," Geoffrey said, despite his wife's kicking his shin for his honesty. "But I can recommend the band to you; I heard them rehearsing earlier today. And there are some chairs set up under the trees, where it is very quiet and you can see the violinist up close."

"Heaven protect us from any more violinists," Florence

said, laying the piece of lace over Geoffrey's shoulder while she picked up another to examine.

Maddie would have liked to invite Geoffrey to join them, for she thought he sounded a little wistful, as if Florence's energy had exhausted him for the day, but it wouldn't do for him to leave his wife alone in this crowd. She compromised by suggesting that they all meet for supper later on and was promptly invited to do so in the Wingates' suite in the Stephanie—for this time they were staying in the same hotel—and they made arrangements to meet.

It was only when she and Devin had at last found a secluded place to sit down and listen to the concert that she realized he had withdrawn into his own thoughts again. She would have liked to leave him to them, but something told her that this time, she should not let him. This time he should let whatever it was out.

The orchestra had followed an attempt to arrive at an end to Shubert's Unfinished Symphony with a selection from Mozart, which, Maddie told Devin, even badly played was better than some of the modern German composers who made far too much noise about everything, in her opinion. Mozart, at least, allowed them to talk.

But he did not take this hint, so she answered herself, "You're perfectly right, Madeleine, as always. Who can listen to Wagner and carry on a civilized conversation at the same time?"

He did not respond to this, either, so she prodded him more gently. "What's wrong, darling?"

He looked at her, and she was surprised to see how

worried he really was; despite his effort to smooth his frown for her, he could not erase the concern in his eyes.

"It's just been borne in on me again," he said, "how little I've really done about securing the prince's safety when he arrives. It's supposed to be tomorrow afternoon, but Florence is probably right; she'll know about it before I do."

"Don't talk like an idiot. You've been exhausting yourself since you arrived, from what Oliver tells me, from overwork."

"But I haven't *found* anything!"

"Your first job is to be sure the prince is safe. You've eliminated ninety percent of the possible perils that could face him in the town. You can't expect to do everything on your own."

"He expects it of me."

Maddie studied the handsome face in which the laugh lines had deepened recently—and not from laughter. It did not trouble her that he was at the moment only barely aware of her existence; what worried him now had nothing to do with her. But she wished she could ease it.

"You are very loyal to him, aren't you?"

"Of course."

Maddie tried to remember the last time she had felt loyalty toward anyone or anything. She had been so eager to give her devotion when she was a child, then went to the opposite extreme later, suspecting everyone's motives and unwilling to give herself at all, much less totally. Her feeling for Teddy had been a kind of loyalty, but a perverted one, a selfish need to have him there to parade before the world and say, "see what a loyal wife I am." They were not very comforting memories.

"What are you going to do?" she asked, when Devin said nothing more.

He thought for a moment. "Find Oliver, I suppose. See if he and Brenner have discovered anything. Sit down and plan the precise route the prince will take to Baden and make sure it is as safe as it can be, for as far out of town as possible."

Scarcely realizing that he had done so, he set his brain in motion again. She was glad that he felt sufficiently at ease with her after all to do his thinking aloud, even if he didn't expect anything from her but to listen.

"Brenner's boss will help, I expect. If I can get fifty policemen to patrol the railroad station and track, and fifty more in plain clothes to—"

He became aware of her again, suddenly, and stopped. "I'm sorry, Maddie. I'm being a bore. But I'm afraid I can't stay here with you any longer; I'd be miserable company anyway, and it's important that I get to work."

"I know." She looked into his tired eyes; the circles under them were more pronounced in the dim light, but he'd stay awake all night if she let him.

"Come up to my room," she said, but when he raised an eyebrow at her, added, "No, I mean only to sleep a little. An hour or two will do you good. I'll go to the Wingates' supper in the meanwhile and make some excuse for you. And I'll send for Oliver to come to you. He'll help, but you must get some rest before you set out, or you'll fall asleep on your feet somewhere, perhaps when it's vital that you be alert.''

He looked as if he would object, but she knew she made too much sense for him to reject her suggestion. He smiled and kissed her hand. ''Thank you.''

It was such a little thing to be grateful for, but it meant he trusted her completely now. Nothing could have made her happier.

They walked back the way they had come, in silence but in perfect accord with each other, and for the first time in her life, Maddie felt at peace, despite the anxiety she felt for Devin and, by extension, for herself. He was in physical danger, too, after all, although he never talked about that. If some madman pointed a gun at his prince, Devin would step between them and get himself killed without even thinking about it. But Maddie was just as determined to help the man she had given her love to as Devin was to protect the man to whom he owed his loyalty.

Louise had for once obeyed her instructions not to wait up for her and had gone to bed in the Drummonds' little room under the eaves, so they had the suite to themselves. With only the most fleeting regret for the use they might have made of this delicious, unexpected privacy, Maddie showed Devin where everything was and waited until he had lain down on the bed and dropped off to sleep before she pressed a cold towel to her face to freshen her cheeks, ran a brush gently over her hair, and went out again.

"There you are, darlin'," Florence said, opening her own door to Maddie. "Do come in. We've had the most delicious-looking little supper sent up—cold smoked trout, vegetables in some sort of interesting cream sauce, strawberries, *and* champagne. But where is your handsome cavalier? Doesn't he ever eat? I've never seen him do so, you know, so I was determined to help fatten him up."

"He received a telegram," Maddie said, shaking Geoffrey's hand and joining him at a linen-covered, candlelit table just inside their open balcony doors. "Oh, this looks lovely. The hotel chef is so clever about arranging these little dishes, isn't he? Have you had a meal in the hotel restaurant yet?"

"What sort of telegram?" Florence said, sitting down with them and holding her glass out to Geoffrey to fill with wine. "Mr. Grant's, I mean. I trust it was nothin' in an emergency nature?"

"Oh, no, I don't think so. I didn't read it, of course, but I gather it was from Frederick Ponsonby to let Devin know that the prince will be arriving slightly earlier than expected."

"Well, I'm glad you mentioned it, dear, for now I will have to go back to that sweet little dressmaker in the Augusta Platz to urge her to finish my new gown. I daresay if the prince arrives early enough, he will be sufficiently rested from his journey to hold some sort of *do* in the evening. I don't suppose you've heard anything about the hour he's expected? No, naturally you didn't

329

read the telegram. Well, I shall send my card to his suite first thing in the morning.''

Florence rattled on a little longer, trying—Maddie suspected—to regain her advantage of being more intimate with the prince than anyone else, despite Maddie's being privy to telegrams from the royal party. Not that there had been such a telegram, but it had seemed to Maddie a clever way both to account for Devin's absence and to gently depress Florence's pretensions. At the same time she provided herself with an excuse not to accompany Florence on her shopping the next day—not that Florence had asked her to come, but she was likely to do so.

Even considering Florence's chattiness, Maddie noticed that Geoffrey had even less to say than usual tonight; indeed she thought he looked tired and hoped he was not unwell, but she did not remark on it since he listened attentively to the conversation and, furthermore, seemed to understand Maddie's little subterfuge. He even winked companionably at her when Florence's attention was elsewhere.

Maddie stayed for a last liqueur and a display of Florence's trophies from the bazaar, then began to yawn discreetly and presently made her excuses, promising to telephone Florence the next day. Geoffrey insisted on escorting her back to her room, and they walked down the hall in a silence that Maddie concluded was natural to Geoffrey and not a constraint imposed on him by Florence's unusual volubility this evening. At her door, however, he made a little bow and kissed her gloved hand lightly, saying, "Thank you for staying friends with Florence."

Maddie had in fact been conscious again of her distaste for that supposed friendship, and Geoffrey's words made her feel even more ashamed of her pettiness, but she said lightly, "Well, why should I not?"

Geoffrey smiled. "Florence is a little . . . overwhelming. And most people tire quickly of her conversation when they realize it is always about herself. But she does not mean it maliciously; she can be kindness itself to one who is simply willing to listen."

"I know. Good night, Geoffrey."

"Good-bye, my dear."

Maddie let herself into her room as quietly as she could and went to see if Devin was still sleeping. He lay unmoving on the bed, his features barely distinguishable in the pale moonlight. She sat down on the side of the bed and looked at him, wondering what was different about him.

Then she realized that unlike Teddy, he did not look younger in his sleep. Even the moonlight did not erase those faint lines around his eyes or smooth the rough skin on his hands. Only his hair seemed younger, tousled on the pillow; she reached out to touch it, then let her hand travel down to his mouth and was surprised yet again by the softness of his mustache.

He opened his eyes, but she stayed where she was, suspended for the moment by the unexpectedness of his waking so completely and silently; he didn't even stretch. Her heart began to beat violently.

"Were you awake all along?"

"Only since you came in."

"I tried not to make any noise."

He smiled, and the mustache moved; she took her hand away. "It was the stealthiness that woke me," he said.

"Must you leave now?"

"Do you want me to?"

"No."

He did move then, reaching his hand up to pull her face down to his and kiss her. Then he moved one leg to pull her across the bed beneath him and deepened the kiss. She welcomed him, feeling the warmth spread from where they met all through her, but then, when the warmth became heat, she shivered suddenly, as if to throw it off. All the while his hand caressed her neck, then her breast beneath the silk, and the curve of her hip. When his mouth followed his hand, she moaned and arched against him, inviting him to come yet closer.

Instead he raised his head to look at her. "You are so beautiful," he said, wonderingly. He lowered his head only a little to kiss her lightly, his tongue flickering in and out of her mouth, tantalizing her at first, then making her eager for him to enter her there, to show her how he would claim her wholly. But he was in no hurry to fulfill his promises tonight.

She reached her arms up to stroke his back, and it registered on her that sometime in the night he had gotten up and taken off his clothes. She touched smooth, taut skin, and the contact stirred something deep inside her. She wanted to get closer still; she could never be close enough.

"Devin," she breathed, "love me."

It was only her clothing that was in the way now. Keeping his mouth close to hers, he raised his body enough to pull off her dress, then kissed her again and sat her up to remove the rest of her clothing, not so carefully or slowly as that time in the poppy field. She helped him, for she was in a hurry, too, eager for that closeness. He pulled off her stockings last, and his hands rode back up her legs, stopping at her revealed core to impress her with the heat of his touch there, pressing her with passionate force under the palm of his hand until she began to writhe under it and call out to him.

"What?" he said in a deeper, thicker voice than she remembered. She could not answer. "Tell me, darling."

"Oh, Devin . . ." He lowered his mouth to the sensitive area between her breasts, and pleasure rippled through her, meeting the sensation that spread more slowly, more hotly, from between her legs, melting her with desire. "Please, Devin. Now . . ."

She was rewarded with yet another bolt of sheer sensation as he moved his weight more exactly over hers, and she moved her long legs to hold him there before his first sweet thrust made her rise instinctively to meet it. Then he thrust deeper, sweeter, and again and again until she cried out, unable to bear any more but wanting it to go on forever—as if that sudden burst of fire within her had not been so clearly the peak she had wanted to scale. And he had led her to it, only he. It was the one thing neither could do alone. But together they could do more than the whole world.

He drew a deep breath and lifted himself off her, leaving

the cool, indifferent air to bring her back to reality. She sighed and turned a little to hug some of the warmth to her a little longer. Then she lay her head on his warm, moist chest and closed her eyes.

"I love you," she said and fell asleep.

The light had scarcely changed outside the window when Maddie felt Devin wake up even before she did. Her body shifted slightly when he left the bed, and she reached for the covers that were still warm from him. She did not want to wake up, but a few minutes later he brought her a dressing gown and held it out to her.

"I want to talk to you."

"Can't we talk in bed?" she said, provocatively.

He laughed. "No. Too many distractions."

He turned so that he would not see her as she stood up and wrapped the gown around her. Then she followed him into the sitting room, where he had lighted a fire. She shivered a little as she sank down on the carpet in front of it, disregarding the chairs he had put out. He joined her, wrapping his arms around her from behind. That was better; soon she was warm again.

"What do you want to talk about?"

"Where did you tell Florence I was last night?"

"I said you'd got a telegram that the prince would be arriving earlier than expected. I wanted to make her think that you had to go off and make some official arrangement or other."

He turned her head toward him, and she saw admiration in his eyes. "Well, isn't that my clever Maddie," he said.

"Why, what did I do?"

"It occurred to me after you left that we should have coordinated our stories, but I couldn't have thought of a better one myself."

"Thank you, I suppose."

"What else did you talk about last night?" he said before she could puzzle out what was so clever about the first excuse that had come to her.

"Over supper? Florence's shopping, mostly."

"Can you remember exactly?"

To her own surprise, Maddie found she did remember almost everything that was said, even though she had listened with only half her attention at the time. She repeated it all back to Devin, thinking at the same time that heightened physical sensitivity must also sharpen one's other senses, a phenomenon she had never observed before. She wanted to ask Devin if he had noticed it, but when she finished her recital and looked at him, he was staring into the fire, almost unaware of her again. She waited patiently for him to come back to her, knowing he would. But before he did, she suddenly solved another puzzle.

"Devin!"

He looked at her, still only half-aware.

"Do you suspect the Wingates of complicity in this affair?"

He shrugged, but his admiration for her intelligence was there in his eyes again. "I'm not sure. I have no proof of it, but then again, I know nothing that would disprove it. They always seem to be in the right place at the right time, and now Florence even has access to the prince. Not that I can see her shooting him with her own little pistol and making a public martyr of herself, when with a little forethought she could get away scott-free.''

Maddie clutched his arm, suddenly remembering other things. "But it makes sense! Florence knew, in Paris, when you left for Baden. How did she know so quickly if she—or someone in her employ—wasn't watching you?"

He looked at her intently. "What else do you remember? When did the Wingates arrive in London?"

"They were there when I arrived. Florence said they had come over on the—the *Britannia*—yes, the week before I did. Oliver can find out the date, but why is that important?"

"To trace their movements . . . and their contacts. Which port did they sail from?"

"New York."

"And before that?"

Maddie frowned. "I think . . . yes, they came from Pittsburgh. I remember thinking at the time that was odd, Florence being from South Carolina." She saw that that meant something to him. "Why? What about Pittsburgh?"

"There was a meeting of American anarchists in Pittsburgh last spring. Didn't you say your husband had been there . . . and went to New York later?"

"Why, yes . . . could they have met?"

"It doesn't matter now, but they might have, yes."

"Devin, there's another thing"—memories and impressions flooded her mind faster than she could sort them out—"I wondered why they stayed at the Bristol in Paris instead of the Ritz . . . but it's right across the square from the Ritz. I could wave to Florence when I was in that suite the prince took later."

She remembered, too, the night he had burst in on that supposedly empty suite, and she turned away to hide her smile so it would not distract him.

"But why," she asked, "if it is the Wingates, have they let so many opportunities go by?"

Devin shrugged. "Who knows? There may have been some unexpected hitch in plans. There may have been too many people around. The gunman may have forgotten to buy bullets. This plot has been too hard to pin down all along, a sure sign that the planning was careful, and the planners careful not to let any of it show on the surface. But if Florence is the famous missing head of the dog— and it's too late now for me to look for anyone else—then she would have provided herself, if not with an unassailable alibi, then with a clear escape route. Germany is much safer than France, but she still needs time to get away from Baden."

"So she was biding her time until she learned to predict the prince's movements to the minute." Maddie looked into the fire; it was low now, but she was no longer cold. "To think we were supposed to be friends, and here I am talking about her as if she—Devin!"

"Yes?"

"When Geoffrey brought me back here after supper, I said good-night to him—but he said good-bye. Oh,

Devin, . . . could he have known? Could he be part of it? Somehow I can't believe that of Geoffrey."

"I don't know. He may be innocent; he may never have suspected anything. On the other hand, he may be the cleverest of the lot."

He looked up at the clock over the fireplace and stood up, pulling Maddie up with him. "I must go, darling. I'm meeting Oliver at six o'clock. Stay here, and I'll send word as soon as I can."

The sky was much lighter outside the window now, although it was still not much past dawn. She put her arms around his neck. "How can I help?"

"You already have—immensely. With luck, they'll make a move sooner than they intended, thinking the prince will arrive earlier, and we'll have them. Just stay here now, Maddie, where I won't have to worry about you." He bent his head to kiss her and added, "And so I'll have something to look forward to when I get back."

She returned his kiss eagerly—to give him something to look forward to—and said good-bye.

When he was gone, she picked up the telephone to summon Louise.

Chapter
Twenty-four

"**S**ERGEANT Brenner..."
"Sir!"
Brenner saluted smartly. Oliver sighed. The boy was either standing stiffly at attention or he was fawning all over Oliver like a large dog begging to go for a walk—or worse, looking for a way to prove his devotion to his master, for Brenner had conceived an admiration for Oliver that he expressed in a protective attitude that Oliver could neither discourage nor diminish without hurting poor Brenner's feelings. It was obvious now why Grant had foisted the young policeman off on him, and Oliver had to remind himself at frequent intervals of his need of a translator, if not a watchdog.

"Sergeant Brenner, I assume there is a criminal element in this otherwise delightful town, or you and your colleagues would be out of a job. Where is one most likely to encounter it?"

"Well, sir—there was a pickpocket apprehended in the garden of the Schloss last week."

"Surely he didn't live there?"

"Why, no, sir. He lived in the Küfer-Strasse."

"Fine. Let us go there and talk to his neighbors."

Brenner looked dubious but, ever willing, he led Oliver through the narrow winding streets of the old town to boarding houses named for their owners rather than for the stepdaughter of Napoleon, as was the considerably more luxurious Stephanie, and to workingmen's cafés, which reminded Oliver of the ones Paul had led him through in Paris. For that matter, they weren't much different from the ones he'd frequented himself as a young man in Chicago, except that here the patrons were considerably less open to conversing with a stranger, either because they knew who Brenner was, or because Teutonic reticence closed their mouths.

Brenner made up for his neighbors by keeping up a running commentary on the landmarks they passed. At least, they were landmarks to Brenner, who had grown up on that street and attended the *gymnasium* on that square. This was where his father, long dead, was born, and that other the church where his sister, with whom he now lived in a more genteel part of town, had been married.

Despite Brenner's efforts, however, they learned nothing useful from this pub crawl, and Oliver called a halt after two hours and too many beers downed in an effort to evoke a little *Gemütlichkeit*. He sat down in an outdoor café facing the now-deserted Markt-Platz, ordered another beer for Brenner and a glass of mineral water for himself, and fell to considering his next move.

But his mind began wandering in unexpected directions, and Oliver found himself thinking about Chicago again. It was the sign—in English, oddly enough—over a modest little shop across the square that did it. The place appeared to be a wholesale linen merchant's, but it was the association of the word with what he was looking for, Oliver supposed, that made him think of Chicago. The shop was called Haymarket Hall.

There'd been a Haymarket Square in Chicago, too, but its associations were different now than they'd been when he was a boy and the Haymarket had no blood on it. But in 1886, a workers' meeting there had been broken up by the police; a bomb was thrown into the crowd and several of the policemen were killed. Eight alleged anarchists were convicted of the crime, seven of them sentenced to hang.

Maybe things didn't change all that much, Oliver thought. Bombs. Anarchists. Policemen. Even haymarkets. They'd always be there in some form or other.

Maybe he had drunk too many beers, after all.

Four of the convicted men were hanged, despite the lack of evidence that any of them had actually thrown the bomb, and despite a petition campaign started by the friends and families of the convicted men. It was finally conceded that the jury had been packed, the judge biased, and the convictions unjust. There were still people in Chicago who hated the police and the courts—and the whole world, some of them—for what had happened in the Haymarket.

Oliver frowned. Why did that raise another association—not clearly enough to put a name to it, but enough to nag at the back of his mind? *It could be anyone*, Devin Grant had told Oliver when he asked who he was looking for, who was behind this Frank Hartwell, who seemed to come from nowhere and belong to no one. But everyone belonged somewhere, even if he didn't admit to it. Oliver wondered if Frank Hartwell was even the man's real name. He'd have to ask Grant when he saw him the next morning. He glanced at his watch. . . . No, this morning. It was already past midnight, and even Brenner had fallen asleep over his *stein*.

"Time to go home, Sergeant," Oliver said, shaking the solid shoulder in its cheap corduroy jacket—his plain clothes, Brenner had called them, showing off his English vernacular. "Your sister will be wondering what's become of you, Guntar," he said, a little louder.

Brenner grunted and shook himself awake. He stood up but was too sleepy to salute as Oliver rose, dug some money out of his pocket to pay their bill, and went off across the square. Brenner shuffled along behind, yawning and rubbing his eyes—and collided with Oliver, who had suddenly come to a halt.

Could it be—?

Oliver scarcely felt the sergeant's bulk hitting him, and he automatically adjusted his footing to keep from being knocked over.

Why not? It could be anyone, after all.

"Which way is the post office, Brenner?"

342

"*Ist geschlossen*," the sergeant mumbled, forgetting his English.

"That's why you're a policeman, Brenner," Oliver told him cheerfully, "so you can wake up postmasters in the middle of the night. Come on. I have to send a telegram."

Maybe this was it—the final piece in the puzzle he'd worried over for so long. He couldn't wait to tell Grant.

Maddie had no intention of staying in her hotel room all day, biting her fingernails and pacing the carpet, but if Devin thought she was there he wouldn't worry about her, which was the important thing. She had let him go away the night before thinking she would stay, but she allowed herself only a few hours' sleep before getting up, bathing herself as best she could from the china jug and bowl set out on the washstand, then waking Louise to help her dress. She scarcely noticed her maid's almost comically perplexed look on finding Maddie's clothes strewn all over the bedroom floor, and half an hour later she was wolfing down a breakfast she scarcely tasted while Louise delivered a note to Florence's maid, asking if Florence would join her for coffee.

It was still hard to believe. Maddie supposed it only proved what she ought to have learned from Peter Kropotkin—that anarchists came in all sorts of unexpected forms, and taking the "popular press" view of them only prevented one from seeing them as they really were.

But why had Florence done it? Maddie tried to imagine

what could have moved her to an act so seemingly out of character, to a deception so complete that she had taken in—Maddie hoped—her own husband. She tried to put herself in Florence's shoes but could only imagine that she must have acted on behalf of someone she loved strongly enough to change her life for him. But if it was not Geoffrey, Maddie could not guess who that someone might be.

She should not have been surprised when Louise came back to report that not only was Florence's maid gone, but—she had taken it on herself to investigate—the Wingates had checked out several hours ago.

"Oh . . . *curses!*" Maddie said, resorting to her father's favorite euphemism more to chastise herself than her bad luck. Had she really expected Florence to wait for them to catch her in the act?

She threw her linen napkin down on the breakfast tray. "Louise, where is that pistol Ollie keeps urging me to carry? I gave it back to him after . . . in Paris."

"Are you going out?" Louise asked, disregarding this question and planting herself firmly in Maddie's path to the door.

"That's why I have my hat on," Maddie said, jabbing another pin in to secure it.

"I don't think Mr. Drummond would wish you to leave the hotel," Louise said, unsure why her husband would wish this but absolutely convinced that he did.

"Louise, I'm bigger and stronger than you are, or Oliver is, for that matter. Step aside." Maddie moved forward to tower over her faithful maid, who recognized her determination, if not her only half-sincere threat. "And find me that gun."

"I shall tell Mr. Drummond!" Louise called after Maddie as she disappeared down the hall a moment later.

"Do," Maddie said, knowing Oliver was long gone. Then she stopped, turned, and came back to give Louise a little hug. "Please try not to worry, Louise," she said fondly. "Everything will be all right."

She was not as sure as she sounded, however, especially when she went around to the stables to see if the Wingates had left by the carriage Florence said they had hired for their stay in Baden. Devin wouldn't have time to see about that, unless his appointment with Oliver was in the hotel stables, which seemed unlikely. He would not be able to be everywhere at once, even with the help of Oliver and the redoubtable Sergeant Brenner, so he would be grateful in the end for her help. She breathed a little prayer that that would turn out to be true.

The pistol in her pocket thumped against Maddie's leg as she walked, so she slowed to a more respectable pace as she approached the stables and looked in.

"May I help you, madam?"

A young groom, the only staff member in evidence, got up from the bench where he was polishing a harness and gave her an admiring glance before remembering to bow to her.

"Good morning!" Maddie said with a cheerful smile. "I wonder if you could tell me something? You see, I didn't want to wake my friend Mrs. Wingate—in room 308—before I went out for my morning walk, so I thought I'd just make sure she hasn't gone out herself before I go up to her suite. Do you know her carriage?''

"Yes, madam. It was taken out early this morning, but by a young man, not by Mrs. Wingate."

That startled her. "A _young_ man?''

"Yes, madam. About thirty years of age, I would say. He was slender and blond and wore a small mustache. An American, I believe."

"Oh, yes, of course," Maddie said, pretending she knew who this mysterious young American was. He did sound somehow familiar, but she could not think why. She smiled charmingly at the groom. "In that case, I will leave a message for Mrs. Wingate at the desk and hope to see her later. Thank you so much. Good-bye!''

Trying not to hurry, Maddie went back into the hotel through the lobby. The guests were beginning to wake up now, and there were people standing about waiting for cabs or breakfast; Maddie nodded to those she recognized and stopped to say good morning to the hall porter, who asked if she were going to the baths this morning and spent ten minutes, which Maddie endured as patiently as she could, extolling the distinctive virtues of the various bathhouses in town. Then Maddie remembered that there were more than twenty of them, so she made her excuses when he reached the fourth and went out the entrance that faced the street to ask the doorman to fetch her a cab.

"_Zum Bahnhof, bitte!_" he told the driver on her instructions, then shrugged as the cabbie looked around for her nonexistent maid and her baggage. When he looked Maddie up and down, she realized her error and smiled shyly at him, even managing to summon up a blush as she stepped closer to the carriage.

"You see," she said, standing on her tiptoes to whisper to the driver high on his perch, "I am meeting someone *very* important on the train. . . . At least, I *hope* he is on the next train."

As she intended, the cabbie immediately assumed she was on her way to meet her lover, and smiling and doffing his hat to her, he scarcely waited until she had got in and the door had closed before cracking his whip over his horse's ear. The cab shot forward smartly.

Maddie had no clear idea of what she intended to do, but Devin had said that he was going up the railway line to see that everything was in order, presumably to examine any likely hiding places for the assassin. Since the prince was not yet in Baden itself, the railway line seemed the logical place to be concerned with now, and Maddie hoped that an extra pair of eyes would prove useful. She would simply get on the next train north and use those eyes.

At the station, however, a barrier across the carriageway prevented her cab from entering, and Maddie's heart sank. A large, curious crowd was already gathering around the station, drawn by what seemed to be dozens of town officials in cocked hats and a band of honor adjusting their instruments in readiness. Maddie put her head out the window of the cab, and a train guard gave her a suspicious look.

"Do you have a ticket, madam?" he asked, approaching the cab.

"No, I'm not traveling," Maddie said with her most

devastating smile, trying to think of a way to avoid this crowd. She could scarcely tell them they were all too early and might as well go home and wait. But then she thought of something else.

"I only stopped for a timetable," she told the guard, "not realizing, of course, that I would encounter such a long queue! May one acquire such a thing without waiting for all this to disperse?"

"Where to, madam?" the guard asked, relaxing his stiff backbone a fraction.

"To Strassburg," Maddie said, remembering the last large city they had passed on the way to Baden.

"One moment, please, madam."

The guard went away to fetch the timetable, giving Maddie another chance to look around. Suddenly she saw Oliver Drummond on the other side of the barrier; she pulled her head back into the cab and drew the veil of her hat down over her face—not that such a subterfuge would deceive Oliver, should he see her, but it seemed to have an unexpected effect on the guard, who held a conference with her driver to discover where his passenger was going. Beaming broadly now, he knocked on her window and handed in the timetable.

"Thank you," Maddie said, keeping her face hidden.

"My pleasure, madam," said the guard, looking up at the cabbie and apparently joining his league. "Where would madam wish to go now, please?" he asked, in a conspiratorial whisper.

"What is the next station north of here?"

"Oos, madam."

"Would you ask the driver to take me to Oos, please," Maddie said, reaching a coin out the window to him. "And thank you."

The guard bowed, gave the driver her instructions, and stepped back. In a few minutes, the driver had cleared the crowd, and his horse was trotting cheerfully past the scattered houses at the edge of the town.

Maddie tried to think what Oliver may have been doing at the station but could only conclude that he and Devin had decided to give out Maddie's fortuitous fabrication about the prince's earlier arrival, so that the station would be thronged with people by the time the prince actually did arrive. It was taking a terrible chance, Maddie thought, if no threat was made on the prince before that; an assassin could easily get lost in a crowd of frightened people at a railway station. On the other hand, if he were counting on a clear shot from a distance, he—or she—might be discouraged from attempting it in such a crowd.

Before very long, her cab was passing through pure country, and for the first time Maddie was able to hear the sound of the bells on the horse's harness. It was such a cheerful sound; she could not think why it seemed so sinister today.

Chapter
Twenty-five

DEVIN had sent a telegram up the line to Heidelberg and left Oliver to do his part at the Baden railway station. Then he took the next train north, got the reply to his telegram at Karlsruhe, and continued on to Kirchheim, where he just caught the prince's train as it pulled into the tiny station. Fritz Ponsonby leaned out the window as the train slowed, and as soon as he saw Devin jump on, he signaled the engineer not to stop, so that within five minutes they were up to speed again.

"Good catch," Ponsonby said, clapping Devin on the shoulder. "You should have been a yachtsman. You'd keep your footing nicely."

"I'd have to," Devin said. "I can't swim."

Ponsonby laughed and said he'd go on ahead to the royal carriage to see if the prince would see him. Devin was grateful once again for Ponsonby's tact in not asking

351

the reason for his precipitous entrance. In fact, Devin was going to try to persuade the prince to leave the train and enter Baden by some other means of transportation, an effort he knew to be hopeless but which he felt duty-bound to attempt.

"My dear fellow," his highness said, as expected, when Devin was shown into his smoking room five minutes later. The prince was dressed with his usual exacting care, as if he were going to receive important visitors instead of only a member of his staff. Devin became conscious again of his own no doubt disreputable appearance. But if he did not meet his employer's sartorial standards, the prince seemed to understand that it was a result of circumstance, not disrespect, and he made no comment on it.

"I quite understand that you feel obliged to warn me of my peril, Grant," he said, "but I have no intention of making any change in my itinerary, or of having my cure interrupted by these absurd threats, of which nothing ever comes."

But he narrowed his eyes at Devin just the same and added, "Does it?"

"There is always a first time, sir."

The prince leaned his portly frame toward Devin, who maintained a passive expression, and said kindly, "Well, possibly, possibly. But never mind. You have done your duty, my boy. Yes, I know you think that I am underestimating the threat this time, but I assure you, these things must be faced up to. I cannot run away every time some fool shouts an antimonarchist slogan at me. That is why I hired you. I have every confidence that you will keep me safe."

"I hope I may live up to your good opinion, sir."

"And so do I," the prince said with a wink to take the sting out of the observation. "Do have a glass of wine, Grant. Ponsonby tells me you have come all the way from Baden this morning to leap aboard like one of those Wild West desperadoes one reads about. Have something to take the starch out of your backbone."

Devin could scarcely refuse, particularly since the prince's servant had poured out a whiskey-and-soda even before his master finished speaking and was now holding it out to Devin. He took it and raised the glass to the prince's health before taking a swallow. It felt good, despite his best intentions; but he would have to nurse the one drink, or he'd be offered another, and that would take more than starch out of him.

The prince quizzed him for a few minutes about how he found Baden, before Ponsonby came in with a question. Devin rose to leave, but the prince, seeing that his glass was not yet empty, motioned him to stay. In order to maintain a discreet distance from the conversation, therefore, Devin got up and walked around the carriage.

This was a new one, but Devin was familiar with the prince's style of travel—well-upholstered chairs and thick carpets, a fully equipped bathroom and luxuriously appointed bedroom off the smoking room they now occupied. Because the prince was traveling incognito—maintaining the fiction of being an ordinary tourist as a way of signaling to anyone who might misinterpret his intentions that this was not a state visit—he had only his valet, two footmen, and another equerry with him, besides Ponsonby. The only unusual aspect of this particular supposed pleasure jaunt was the presence of a larger than usual number of policemen who came aboard at each border crossing and large city, a presence that Devin kept as unobtrusive as possible, knowing how much the prince disliked being under continual observation.

There were some new family photographs on the desk, Devin noticed, and went to look at them. The portrait of Victoria, seated at a table signing a document, always traveled with her son, but the newcomers to the collection included one of the prince and his son on the royal yacht. Devin remembered that one, because Princess Alexandra had taken it with her Kodak. He would have to tell Daisy Jervis about it when he saw her again. In fact, there was even Laurie's snapshot from the Bois de Boulogne; he would be glad to hear it had a place of honor, at least temporarily. The latest trophy picture, of the prince standing over the stag he had shot at last year's hunt, dominated a series of informal snaps of royal daughters and nieces in straw hats, probably also taken by Alexandra, who was getting better at them.

Then a sporty image of Prince George caught Devin's eye. Standing next to him was his cousin, Nicholas of Russia, and the resemblance was remarkable. They weren't all that closely related, yet they might have been twin brothers. He picked up the photograph and studied it thoughtfully. Odd how these resemblances worked.

Then the idea struck him. "Of course!"

"Did you say something?" Ponsonby asked, coming up behind him just then.

"I think I've just hit on who it is I'm looking for."

"Well, that's nice, I'm sure," Ponsonby said in the tone of a grandmother confronted with a small child's chemistry experiment. "Who?"

Devin looked over Ponsonby's shoulder and saw that the prince was occupied with lighting his cigar, but he said just the same, "It's a long story, which I'll tell you next time I have time for a cigar with you. Right now I'd best be about my job."

Ponsonby grasped his sleeve and in a low voice asked, "Is he safe on the train?"

"I think so. I'll make certain and report back before we get to Baden. That's a good hour and a half yet, so just keep him occupied in here, if you can."

He went to take his leave of the prince, who shook his hand and said, "No need to look so gloomy, dear boy. When are you going to take that knighthood I've been offering you, by the way? It might cheer you up—impress the ladies, anyway—and that would cheer *me* up!"

Devin smiled and wondered if Maddie would be impressed by a title; he doubted it, and if he wouldn't take it for himself, he knew she wouldn't expect him to do it for her. "Thank you, sir. I've no doubt it would, but it might also go to my head, and how would I get anything done?"

The prince laughed. "Always have an answer, don't you. Well, my boy, I'll keep trying. Be off with you now."

Devin bowed and let himself out of the carriage and into the main part of the train. There was an empty salon car between the prince's private carriage and the first sleeping car, then the bar car, the dining car, and another half-dozen salon cars, all first class. He walked through all of these in turn, checking with the attendants as to the whereabouts of the occupants of the sleeping compartments to be sure no one was out of his seat. He wanted to see everyone who was aboard now and to be sure that no one would get on before Oos, the connecting station for Baden, without his knowledge. At Oos, he would have the royal carriage detached and taken to Baden first. The rest of the passengers could wait safely at Oos. But for now every one of them represented a potential danger.

In the third salon car, he found a trio of familiar faces. Daisy Jervis and Laurence Fox were playing cards. Daisy was looking especially pretty in a new pink-and-white summer dress that emphasized her assets while cunningly concealing her defects of figure. She was also, Devin could see over her shoulder, cheating at cards. Lady Jervis sat in the window corner, knitting.

"Mr. Grant!" Laurie saw him first and stood up. "What a jolly surprise! We didn't know you were on the train, sir."

"I just got on," Devin said, shaking his hand. Daisy looked up at him oddly. "At the last stop, that is to say. How are you, Lady Jervis? Good morning, Daisy."

"It's afternoon," Daisy informed him, "but I daresay the prince keeps you so busy that you lose track of time."

"Don't be rude, Elfreda," her mother said, recognizing the tone if not the provocation.

Devin smiled. "If your daughter imagines she will provoke me into telling her what I have been doing, Lady Jervis, she should know better. May I join you?"

"Yes, certainly, sir," Laurie said, moving over to let him sit down. Daisy gave Laurie a look that made clear what she thought of his fawning attentions to Devin.

"She cheats at cards, you know," he told Laurie, getting his revenge.

"Yes, I know," Laurie said with an exaggerated sigh. "It will no doubt be the ultimate cause of our divorce."

Devin looked from Laurie to Daisy and back again, waiting for an explanation of this remarkable statement. Finally Daisy, giving up her pretended indignation, giggled, and Lady Jervis informed him with a creaky, but nevertheless satisfied smile, that the young couple had become engaged to be married.

Devin extended his congratulations, admitted candidly that he could not say which of them was getting the better bargain, and offered to toast them in champagne when they reached Baden. This naturally enough reminded Daisy of Maddie, who was asked after, so that it was several minutes before Devin was able to ask Laurie if he might have a word with him in private.

They walked into the next car and found an empty compartment before saying anything, but then Devin sat down, glanced at his watch, and came directly to the point.

"Laurence, do you remember that photograph of Mrs. Malcolm's husband that you took on the channel packet?"

"I certainly do! I even brought a copy with me. What's more—"

"Have you by any chance seen anyone on the train who resembles the man in the photograph?"

"Not on the train, no—but look, sir, this is what I started to tell you." He reached into his pocket and brought out his leather photographic case. He pulled a print out and showed it to Devin. It showed a young man, very like Edward Malcolm, with his arm around Florence Wingate on a ferry in New York harbor; the Statue of Liberty loomed over them in the background.

"Where did you get this?"

"It's a copy. I noticed it at one of Mrs. Wingate's salons and was struck by the resemblance, so I . . . well, I borrowed it to make a copy. I brought it back the same afternoon, and I'm sure she never missed it."

Devin scowled. He could not be so sure. "How is it that Mrs. Malcolm never noticed it there? She is not unobservant and would surely have taken notice of it had it been displayed with other family likenesses."

"But that was the odd thing, you see, sir. I had been curious—and a little piqued, I suppose—as to why Mrs. Wingate displayed none of the photographs I took of her. Then I saw that she had no personal photographs at all on display in her suite. Most people have a few, even when they are traveling, of the people closest to them. Their absence puzzled me, so while the violinist was playing one afternoon, I slipped into the bedroom and had a look around. This photograph was on the dressing table, concealed in back of a picture of Mr. Wingate—the only one in the room. I noticed it because the edges showed around the other photograph, which had been cut badly."

"Quite the little sneak thief, aren't you," Devin said, not without some admiration.

"Yes, sir. I don't know what came over me."

Devin laughed. "Who do you suppose this is?"

"Well," Laurie began, eagerly, leaning forward as if to press his case, "it is *not* Mr. Malcolm, however close the resemblance. I compared the two photographs under a magnifying glass, and the differences became clear—the shape of the nose and forehead, and so on. I would guess it to be some relation of Mrs. Wingate's—possibly even of Mr. Wingate's, except that he mentioned once that his wife has a brother—something of a black sheep, one gathers, since she never speaks of him."

Devin sat back to study the photograph for a moment, but he was satisfied now, and his intuition in the prince's carriage was confirmed. He knew what he was looking for and almost, he thought, where and when it would happen. He looked at his watch again and said to Laurence, "I will tell you the same thing I told the prince's secretary not long ago: I thank you, and I owe you an explanation, but it is a long story that will have to wait until a more propitious time."

"I quite understand, sir."

"Good. But speaking of explanations, I think I can guess how you won Daisy, but do tell me how you converted her mother. Mrs. Malcolm told me she was on the hunt for a title for the girl."

"I think I—we—convinced her that I was as likely as anyone to come into a title. She was impressed with my 'connections,' you see, for all of which I have photographic evidence, remember. I even offered to present her to the Prince of Wales."

359

Devin raised an eyebrow. "Don't be too rash in your promises, boy. You're not married yet."

"Well, you see, sir, I rather hoped you would . . ."

"Did you, indeed."

There was a pause while Devin admired the young man's cheek, and Laurie tried to gauge how far he could push his luck. But then Devin laughed.

"All right, I'll see what I can do. But you will have to do me one further favor."

"Certainly."

"Take that photograph of Mrs. Wingate's friend and show it to all the train attendants and advise them to be on the lookout for the man—no, for both of them. I'll show the one of Malcolm, since the resemblance is that close, to the prince's attendants. If anyone has seen any of these people, or anyone resembling either man, come and tell me at once. If you don't see me in your end of the train, make yourself known to Sir Frederick Ponsonby in the prince's compartments, and he will take you to me.

"Meanwhile," he said, standing up, "we have less than an hour before we reach Oos. To work, young Sherlock Holmes!"

Chapter
Twenty-six

IT was so peaceful in the little village street, where the
taxi had stopped under the lime trees, that Maddie's
mind showed a distracting tendency to wander. When
she had arrived in Oos, eight miles from Baden, she had
made firm friends with the cabbie by asking his advice
about a *Konditorei* where she might buy coffee and a sand-
wich to eat while she waited, and about a shop where
she might buy a valise. The cabbie, who had relations in
the town, was more than happy to show her around, then
to wait patiently—with Maddie in the cab and he on top
eating the lunch she bought him—across the cobbled street
from the train station until the next train arrived.

Maddie had seen no reason to disabuse the man of the
notion that she was waiting to meet her lover, particularly
if that made him more willing to tolerate spending most of
the day in her service. Fortunately, he was not a loquacious
sort of person and showed no desire to talk other than to

answer her questions courteously, and he ventured no more than the occasional unsolicited comment on the virtues of Oos, particularly when it had to do with his relations or the leather shop he took her to, which was not only the best in the district but belonged to his uncle, to whom of course he was obliged to speak in order to introduce his so-distinguished American lady visitor.

Neither the cabbie nor his uncle questioned her desire not to have the valise wrapped and, further, to have the shavings which maintained its shape for display purposes left in it, the latter doubtless depending on the former to come back later and explain why the American lady made such odd requests. In fact, Maddie had decided to play the part of a departing passenger when the train came in, so as not to draw attention to herself, and had therefore purchased the valise to look as if she were leaving on a journey. Getting further into the role, she asked the cabbie to park across the street from the station until the train came in, as if to discreetly hide herself from prying eyes, but also so that she could observe the people entering the station without being seen by them.

But traffic in Oos was sparse at best, and Maddie was hard put not to lose herself in daydreams while gazing through the greenery at the little park down the street, where some children were playing, or at the little café across the greensward, where a pair of old men were smoking and playing cards. None of the noises accompanying these activities reached Maddie in the cab through the occasional jingle of the horse's harness and the song of birds in the trees alongside. Every now and then Maddie would offer the driver some of her coffee, or he would ask permission to exercise the horse by walking him up the street and back again, remaining in sight of the station the while.

An hour passed thus uneventfully, while Maddie found herself growing strangely calmer rather than apprehensive or alarmed over what might happen when the train arrived. Even earlier that morning, she had been exhilarated rather than frightened when she set out from the hotel determined to do something to help Devin.

Yes, that was it. She was *doing* something, even if for the moment it was only sitting in a cab staring at the scenery. She had not only not been afraid to act, she had not even thought twice about doing it, and now that she had time to reflect on it, she wondered if it was indeed more natural to her to take action to solve her dilemmas, or those of people she loved. Perhaps that too had been trained out of her when she was too young to mourn its loss.

"What on earth are you doing, child?" her mother had said when Maddie, aged eight, had climbed half-way up a tree to rescue a strange kitten, then got stranded there. The kitten had already scampered away by the time Maddie tried to explain her unusual position to a disbelieving Constance.

"Don't worry your head about that, sweetheart," her father would say when Maddie, aged eighteen, asked if she might have a checking account and pay her own bills. "I'll take care of all that sort of thing for you."

"But lover, it's just a race meeting," Teddy said when

Maddie, newly married and bored at home, asked to go along. "You wouldn't like it at all. I'll bring you back a souvenir and tell you all about it."

And so she had simply accepted everyone else's actions, having been assured—and believing it, because they all loved her—that it was all for her benefit. So she had condoned anything Teddy did, because she did not want to seem ungrateful, or to be a nagging wife, even though she had never been quite blind enough to say to him, "Whatever you want, darling, is all right with me."

Now she knew, without having thought about it, much less agonized over whether she ought to feel grateful for it, that whatever Devin Grant was doing would be something she could be proud of. And even if she were disobeying him in taking a part, she knew he would feel the same pride about her.

And somehow, she could not imagine Devin Grant being content with a complacent wife.

A new noise, faint and rumbling in the distance, woke her from her reverie. She looked out the window on the station side and thought she saw smoke over the trees beyond it. She got out of the cab on the side of the trees and looked around. No one she had not already observed before had appeared. She asked the driver to wait, but paid him just the same, in case she could not for some reason return to Baden with him.

"Thank you, *gnädige Fräulein*," he said, tipping his hat and adding in a conspiratorial whisper, "Good luck!"

Maddie smiled and thanked him, then lowered her hat veil, picked up her valise, and went into the station. She looked around the small, white-painted waiting room, but it was empty. Outside she saw only the platform attendant, so she sat down on a bench, the valise on the ground next to her, to wait.

The distant rumble grew louder, and Maddie could feel the faint vibration of the platform as the train drew closer. She did not look toward the train but kept her eyes on the entrance to the station, where passengers and friends seeing them off were beginning to disembark from cabs and private carriages and to arrive on foot. Another cab pulled up outside, and an elderly gentleman with a shiny new malacca cane and an old, battered portmanteau came in and sat down on the bench at the other side of the doorway. A starchily erect woman in black holding the hand of a cowed-looking girl emerged from the waiting room, followed by two nuns with their hands hidden in their voluminous habits.

And then, just as the train came into view, a hired carriage pulled up outside and seemed to hesitate briefly before deciding to stop. Maddie stood up for a better look at it over the iron fence. At the same time, with a hiss of brakes, the train slowed for a stop. The engine went on by, past the station house. Out of the corner of her eye, Maddie saw a familiar figure swing off the still-moving step of one of the train carriages. Devin.

Then everything seemed to happen at once. The carriage with the unmarked maroon doors came to halt directly in front of Maddie. On her other side, another masculine figure, almost—teasingly—as familiar as Devin's, caught her eye, entering the station not by the main doorway but vaulting over a gate in the fence. Devin caught himself as he touched the ground and turned around, seeing Maddie. Then, at the same instant that she did, he saw the other figure halt in the middle of the platform and raise his arm toward the half-opened window of the unmarked carriage.

But Maddie was one step ahead of him. She raised her own arm, with her pistol in her hand, and said not loudly, but distinctly, "Stop!"

Startled, the other man turned toward her, and for an instant Maddie looked into a face she knew.

Teddy!

The shock was just enough to make her hesitate, to lower her pistol a fraction before she realized, *It isn't Teddy. It can't be. Teddy's dead.*

She raised her hand again, but by then Devin had acted. Running down the platform past her, he fired a shot. It missed. The woman in black screamed.

Another shot rang out.

Maddie dropped the hot pistol. The gunman fell to the platform, and a swarm of train attendants and private servants surrounded him. Next to her, so close that his calm voice made Maddie jump, the Prince of Wales leaned out of the window of his carriage and said to Devin, "What, is it over already?"

"Yes, sir, quite finished."

"Good, good! Let's get on to the baths, then, shall we?"

He withdrew his head, but then Ponsonby emerged, cast a comprehensive glance around, and said, "Well done again, Grant. Will you stay to attend the lady?"

366

"Yes, please, Fritz."

"Right. See you at the Stephanie, then."

Only then did Devin look at Maddie, and only then did she realize that she had not moved a muscle since she fired that shot. He came to her and put his arms gently around her. Then the reaction struck her.

"Oh, Devin!"

She clutched him fiercely and began to sob into his shoulder while he whispered soothing noises into his ear. After a moment they began to penetrate and sorted themselves into "It's all right, my brave darling. . . . We're safe. . . . You've done it. . . . I love you."

"What?"

She pulled back an inch to look at him. He laughed and impelled her gently toward the bench where her empty valise still waited. Maddie tried not to look in the other direction, where someone had thrown a blanket over the motionless figure on the platform. A policeman had been called and was questioning the platform attendant and taking notes when a man in a bowler hat came up to him and said something that made him put away his pencil and go into the waiting room with the stranger. The other onlookers drifted away, leaving the figure under the blanket alone there.

"Who was he?" Maddie asked, outwardly as composed again as the prince, although her heart still beat wildly inside her.

"His name was Frank Hartwell. I think he was Florence Wingate's brother."

"He looked like—"

"I know. That's why I—how I made that mistake in Paris. At a distance, I couldn't tell them apart, as you couldn't, that night on the bridge."

Maddie's mind whirled. She could scarcely sort it all out, and for a few moments Teddy seemed to become Frank Hartwell, as Frank Hartwell had been Teddy in her mind for so long, and the last shred of love and loyalty to poor dead Teddy that she had clung to seemed to drop away, and he died truly at last.

Silent tears rolled down her cheeks, and Devin, misunderstanding what she mourned for, held her and said, "It's over now, darling. There's no more danger."

The train started up again just then, and Devin stood, pulling Maddie up with him and drawing her into the shadow of the ticket office.

When she looked up at him questioningly, he explained, "There is a trainload of no doubt very perturbed passengers about to go past. Since they have been kept inside during all this I expect they are agog with curiosity—especially Daisy and her mother and Laurence Fox. I particularly have no desire to show myself to Laurie, who will never forgive me for denying him the opportunity to photograph all the excitement. Let's get a cab back to Baden—if you're ready?"

"Yes, I think so. Oh—I have a cab already, if he's waited for me."

They emerged from the street side of the station to find Maddie's cab still parked on the other side, the driver fast asleep on his perch.

"I can't believe he's slept through all this!" Maddie

said and laughed, beginning to feel normal again. Devin banged his fist against the side of the cab, waking the driver, who jumped in his seat, clutched at his hat, which had been resting over his eyes, and looked down.

"Gnädige Fräulein!" He saw Devin's arm then, resting on Maddie's waist, and broke into a broad grin. "You have found your gentleman . . . *schön, wunderschön!* So, we go back to Baden now, yes?"

"Yes, thank you," Maddie said, smiling back. Devin opened the door for her, and they were on their way almost before he had closed it behind himself. Maddie suddenly remembered the valise she had left on the platform and laughed. Well, someone would find it and make use of it. She turned to Devin to tell him the joke, but the look in his eyes stopped her.

"I take it the driver is a friend of yours?"

"We have become well acquainted this morning, yes."

"Then I hope we can rely on his discretion."

He took her in his arms then, and neither of them gave a thought to the driver or the rest of the world as their kiss deepened, sweeping them away to a world inhabited only by themselves. When they broke apart at last, Maddie sighed in contentment and, tucking her feet up under her on the seat, leaned contentedly against Devin's shoulder.

"What will happen to the Wingates?" she said at last.

"Oliver will have had them apprehended by now. I don't think Geoffrey had any part in all this—he was just a sort of convenience for Florence, who needed a traveling companion much as her brother needed what I believe you Americans call a fall guy."

Maddie shook her head. "It's still so hard to comprehend."

"I expect Frank Hartwell is going to turn out to be a fascinating case. That apparently is his real name—or at least, the American consulate has confirmed that Florence's maiden name was Hartwell. He was certainly sure of himself, to use his own identity, yet still keep himself so well out of anyone's reach. I doubt that even now I can pin the murder of Michel Lamont on him."

"Do you know—Geoffrey even told me about Frank, once, but I'd forgotten all about it until just this moment."

"What did he say?"

"Only that he was the black sheep of the family. And that he went to the races."

"Which is doubtless how he met your husband. I think we will find out that Hartwell saw the usefulness of having him around and made sure he stayed there. Your husband may have thought it would be a novel kind of amusement to join in Hartwell's intrigues, changing places with him to confound everyone. I doubt he ever realized what a dangerous game he was playing."

"But *why* did they play it? That's what I'll never understand."

He smiled and drew her a little closer. "Your Oliver has an elaborate theory about that. I'm sure he will explain it in detail when we get back to Baden."

"The sooner, the better."

He looked at her questioningly, and she explained, "So that we can begin forgetting it. Devin, I had no idea until today how much I have been living in the past, and now I want nothing more than to put all that in the past."

He considered that for a moment, while he removed her hat and stroked her hair gently. "And what, Mrs. Malcolm, do you plan to do about the future?"

"To start with, I shall go back to calling myself Miss Osborne."

"Oh, no, don't do that."

She moved her head to look up at him. "And why not?"

She had moved just enough to make it easy for him to bend his head and kiss her again.

"Because I think Mrs. Grant would sound much better—that is, if I won't be a continual reminder to you of all that you'd rather forget."

She smiled. "I can't remember anything about you that I'd ever want to forget—if the memories we are going to make after today don't overwhelm all the others."

He touched her lips again and whispered, "Let's see that they do."

Overhead the cabdriver began to whistle a little tune that his uncle, the cobbler, had taught him when he was a child, and that he always whistled on special occasions. But his passengers did not even hear it.

B

ŕ